SLEEPING DOGS

SLEEPING DOGS

THOMAS MOGFORD

B L O O M S B U R Y
LONDON · NEW DELHI · NEW YORK · SYDNEY

Bloomsbury Publishing
An imprint of Bloomsbury Publishing Plc

50 Bedford Square
London
WC1B 3DP
UK

1385 Broadway
New York
NY 10018
USA

www.bloomsbury.com

First published in Great Britain 2015

Lines from *The Odyssey* by Homer, trans. Robert Fagles, are reproduced by kind
permission of Penguin Random House.

British Library Cataloguing-in-Publication Data
A catalogue record for this book is available from the British Library.

ISBN: TPB: 978-1-4088-4661-2
PB: 978-1-4088-4663-6
ePub: 978-1-4088-4662-9

2 4 6 8 10 9 7 5 3 1

Typeset by Integra Software Services Pvt. Ltd.
Printed and bound in Great Britain by CPI Group (UK) Ltd, Croydon CR0 4YY

For Ali

Before you embark on a journey of revenge,
dig two graves

Confucius

The young woman slams the door and leans back against it for just a moment, allowing her breathing to regulate, waiting for her hands to stop shaking. Then she snaps the security chain into place and checks her watch. Twenty minutes until the last bus leaves for Corfu Town. As long as she catches it, she can still make the ferry. She wrenches open the wardrobe and pulls out handfuls of clothes, stuffing them into her old holdall. Skidding across the lino into the cramped bathroom, she grabs the flat-blade screwdriver from the shelf, levers off the bath panel and removes the plastic bag containing a roll of soft euro notes and her passport. Then she hears a sound, and her stomach keels as a fresh surge of adrenalin hits.

She gets noiselessly to her feet, switches off the bathroom fan and listens. Her apartment lies at the end of the strip; in the drowsy afternoon silence she can almost hear the collective snore of the hungover Kavos siesta. She edges forward to the apartment's only window: through the torn mosquito netting, she can just make out the awning of the sports bar below, 'Scorers' printed on its front, stained with yellow sand blown up from the beach. In the waste ground alongside, a lemon tree has stubbornly taken root, its branches laden with sweet-smelling fruit, a legacy of the days when Kavos was little more than a sleepy fishing village. The young woman sees a cicada at the top, pulsing away, and despite herself, she smiles. She likes cicadas: small creatures, big noise.

But then time seems to slow. She watches the front door bulge before she even hears the sound of the kick. The door smashes against the wall, knocking down the only thing she brought from home, a framed photograph of her little brother.

A man appears in the doorway. Wearing a black balaclava. The young woman opens her mouth to scream, but the intruder is already upon her, a latex-covered hand pressed against her lips. She tries to bite his fingers, but he just kicks the door closed and pushes her towards the bathroom. And that is when she really starts to fight.

She hears his focused breathing as he struggles to contain her, changing grip, viciously twisting her hennaed hair by its dark roots. Then, slowly, she finds herself begin to move with him, limbs flailing as he drags her inside.

She recognises the rush of the bath taps as he shoves her against the mould-stained wall. A glass bottle is pressed into her mouth, and she feels the sharp pain of her teeth cutting into her bottom lip, the burn of cheap alcohol in her throat. She just has time to cough out a mist of droplets before the man is dragging her forward again, plunging her face down into the tepid water.

The pounding of the running water deafens her ears. Her ribs feel like they will explode. She thrashes her arms above her head, tearing at his eyes, ears, nose, but finding only the coarse wool of his balaclava. As her strength starts to ebb, she pictures her brother, his determined smile as he visited the hospital in Saranda, month after month, week after week, refusing to give up even when they all knew it was hopeless.

She lets her arms drop, feeling the man push down harder, believing the battle is won. Then, with one careful hand, she explores the bathroom floor. Finds the scattered contents of her wash bag. The soft give of a toothpaste tube. The metallic chill of an aerosol deodorant, and allows herself to hope...

With one last burst of will, she wraps her fingers around the can, hoists it above her shoulder and presses down hard on the nozzle.

At first she thinks she has missed, but then the pressure on the back of her head eases. She hears his groan of pain as she bursts from the water. She tells herself to scream, but her lungs demand one breath, then another, and she inhales greedily as she stumbles back against the wall.

The man is on his knees now, lowing like a bull as he claws at his eyes through the balaclava. Water spills over the bath, and the young woman slips and slides as she clambers to her feet, seeing the bottle of bootleg Russian vodka carefully placed in *the sink. It should have been so easy, she thinks. Just one more dead whore in Kavos.*

'Te qifsha,' she swears in Albanian, kicking the man in his rigid stomach. 'Ha mut!' she adds, and this time kicks him so hard that the cork heel of her shoe breaks. He clutches at his sides, winded, the knees of his grey tracksuit darkening with water.

The young woman picks up the bottle by its neck. But just as she is about to smash it over his head, the man reaches out blindly and grabs her foot.

Lashing out with the other leg, she breaks free of his grip, knocking her eye against the door frame as she stumbles into the next room. But he has blocked the exit with her bed. She looks back at the bathroom, blood blurring her vision, alerted not by a noise now but the absence of it. The taps have been turned off. The man is on his feet. Through the balaclava, she sees his weeping, angry black eyes. Clasped in his fist is the screwdriver.

Calypso turns again to the window, bag in hand. Then she jumps.

PART ONE

Gibraltar

Chapter One

Spike Sanguinetti stared out of the office window at the eastern face of the Rock. He'd felt the wind getting up behind him as he walked to the clinic, and he checked automatically now to see if the cable car was still running. Surprisingly, it was – wavering and creaking along its guy line, heading into the pall of cloud that hung like a halo around O'Hara's Battery. The tourists would be unsettled after such a journey, Spike thought with a wry smile, easy prey for the apes who would be poised at the top like a band of pickpockets in an arrivals hall, ready to relieve them of their sandwiches and cameras.

'Mr Sanguinetti?'

Spike looked back at Kitty Gonzalez. Or Dr Gonzalez, as he should probably call her, according to the framed diploma hanging on the wall above her yucca plant. A PhD in Clinical Psychology from Malaga University. A doctor in Spain, at any rate.

'Your GP was kind enough to pass on your notes,' she said in her soft Andalusian accent, parting the jaws of her laptop. Thirty seconds later, satisfied that she had mastered the salient points of her new patient's medical history, she looked up. 'How long have you had trouble sleeping?'

'Not long,' he lied. 'It comes and goes.'

'And the panic attacks?'

Spike shifted uncomfortably in his remarkably comfortable armchair. 'I wouldn't call them panic attacks, exactly.'

'So what would you call them?' Dr Gonzalez didn't smile back.

'I've just been under a bit of pressure recently.' That was an understatement, he thought, picturing the letters from unpaid creditors piling up on his desk at Galliano & Sanguinetti, the barely restrained fury of his clients' emails. 'I wondered if perhaps there was something I could take,' he added hopefully.

But Dr Gonzalez didn't seem to have heard, just made an illegible note with her slim, gold Dunhill pen. Business must be good, Spike thought as he watched her straighten her black-rimmed spectacles, wondering if the glass was prescription, or just a feint employed to look older and more experienced. To distract from her Hispanic good looks.

'What kind of work do you do, Spike?' she asked, conceding him a carefully neutral smile. 'You don't mind if I call you "Spike"?'

'Not at all, Kitty,' he replied, provoking the tiniest suggestion of a bristle. 'I'm a lawyer.'

'Must be busy. Stressful.'

'It can be.' He shrugged. 'My partner has been on extended sick leave.' He considered telling her about the severity of Peter Galliano's injuries, and how he still felt partly to blame for them, but the temptation soon passed.

'When was the last time you took a break?'

He shrugged again, then regretted it as he saw her scrawl another observation in her notebook. 'A holiday might be a good idea,' she said, looking back to her computer screen. 'You saw a therapist in London, I believe?' The question came out of nowhere, naturally, and suddenly he felt uneasy. 'That was twenty years ago,' he said, rubbing his greying temples.

'Why did you seek help, Spike?'

An irritating turn of phrase, he'd always thought, wondering once again why he'd agreed to do this. 'My mother had just committed suicide.'

He'd intended to shock her, to kill the conversation, but she just looked back at him, saying nothing, trying to force him to fill the silence. He almost laughed. It was a technique he liked to use with clients himself.

'Is something funny?'

'No,' he replied truthfully, 'I'm just relieved that we got the "tell me about your mother" bit out of the way.'

Kitty pushed back her chair and walked over to the sideboard, and Spike found his eyes following her as she filled two heavy crystal glasses with mineral water. Pulling his gaze away, he turned again to the window. The banner cloud on the Rock had finally swallowed the sun, and he caught sight of his own reflection in the hazy glass, face dark and angular, pale blue eyes suspicious and jaded. Then a tumbler of water appeared beside him, and Kitty brushed a hand down the back of her grey pencil skirt and retook her seat. 'Do you do that often?' she asked.

'What?'

'Deflect difficult conversations. Shut them down.'

Spike frowned.

'Must be tough for the people who care about you.' She pressed on: 'Who *are* the important people in your life, Spike?'

Spike thought at once of Zahra – holding her shattered body in an empty house on the Italian Riviera. 'There was someone,' he said. 'A girl from Morocco.' He drank some water. 'I met her on a case. Three years ago.'

'What's her name?'

'Zahra al-Mahmoud.' He felt his throat tighten, and carefully set down his glass. 'We had something for a while. But she moved to Malta.' He paused, wondering if he could leave it at that, then decided he should at least try and get his money's worth. 'She died last year.'

'I see.'

The cable car *had* stopped running. The tourists would have to catch a cab back to the Old Town. A red-letter day for taxi drivers and apes...

'You felt responsible?' Kitty pulled him back. 'People often do.'

'I *was* responsible.' He spoke more sharply than he'd meant to. 'She was killed because of me.'

'But it wasn't you who killed her.'

Yet it was because of him that she had died, he thought. How could he ever hope to explain it? Or what had happened to Charlie? The psychologist hadn't mentioned the boy yet, though he couldn't imagine she'd missed the intense press coverage surrounding the kidnapping of a small child on the Rock, nor the murder of his young mother. And Spike's involvement in both. Maybe she was waiting for him to tell her – some kind of psychologist's ruse.

He got to his feet, feeling the familiar anxiety coiling in his chest. Kitty looked at him, then at the clock on the wall. 'We still have some time.'

'Use it to catch up on your paperwork.'

He sensed her eyes watching him as he grappled with the door handle. 'It won't stop, you know,' she said gently. 'These things have to be dealt with, Spike. I can't help you if you won't talk to me.'

She'd managed to sum up his problems in a single sentence, he thought as he pulled the door shut behind him, reassured by the certainty that he would never set foot in her office again.

Chapter Two

A thin scream jolted Spike awake, and he sat up in bed, heart knocking against his ribs. Then he heard the quiet desperate sob, and remembered. 'See Mama...Want to see Mama.' As the wail started to crescendo, he sighed and pushed back the covers.

The box-room was dark save for a strip of pale moonlight gleaming through the makeshift blackout blind, five sheets of his father's watercolour pad Blu-tacked to the glass. Stacked against one wall was a line of battered tea chests, each containing Spike's own mother's papers – 'See Mama', he might have wailed himself. Pushed against another was the travel cot he'd spent hours trying to assemble that afternoon. Spike stepped towards it, and the little figure inside fell silent, struggling to his feet in the strange zip-up bag toddlers seemed to use these days instead of bedclothes.

'It's OK,' Spike improvised, watching Charlie staring up at him, tiny fingers gripping the rim of the cot, dark eyes wide and panicked. 'Just try to go back to sleep.' He took a hesitant step backwards and heard the boy's breaths quicken in the darkness. 'I'm right here.'

He closed the door, listened for a moment, then headed back down the corridor. At least his father's light was still off. Small mercies. Back in his own room, he considered the bed, then dismissed the idea, sat down at his desk and pulled his laptop towards him.

Once again, his inbox was clogged with new messages. What was it about the prospect of a week away that made clients panic? Cases that had been on hold for months were suddenly demanding his assiduous attention. His current roster included the usual mix of criminal, contract and tax work that was the lot of the lawyer in Gibraltar, a jurisdiction where the roles of barrister and solicitor were fused. A property conveyance for a new-build flat in Ocean Village, a Russian 'businessman' suing his Gibraltarian accountant for embezzlement, a small-time drug dealer claiming his stash was for personal use … Maybe the best policy was just to tell no one that you were leaving.

'See Mama,' the plaintive call began again.

'Jesus,' Spike said aloud. It was a wonder any parent got anything done. Just one night in his house, and someone else's child was threatening to bring a small Gibraltarian law firm to its knees. 'No good deed goes unpunished,' his partner Peter liked to say with a throaty cackle, and in this case Spike was beginning to fear he might be right. Charlie was an orphan, his grandparents were struggling, and – little by little – Spike had found himself drawn into the child's life. At the start, he'd just been trustee of an inheritance that was yet to materialise, but slowly the professional veneer of their relationship had been chipped away, and he'd graduated to occasional babysitter. Organised trips to the playground, to the Gibraltar Museum, which had at first filled him with apprehension and guilt, but which lately he'd started to enjoy. But this was the first time he'd had Charlie to stay, and his sense of utter incompetence had returned. As the crying moved up an octave, Spike snapped shut his laptop and stepped into the corridor, wondering which tactic to use next. But the box-room door was already ajar; easing it open, he could just make out the shape of a lean, elegant figure perching in the gloom on the edge of one of the tea chests.

'Dad?' Spike said, failing to keep the surprise from his voice.

Clamped to Rufus Sanguinetti's chest was Charlie. The old man had one hand across the boy's back as the other stroked his neck, back and forth, back and forth. 'I know,' he was whispering like a mantra, 'I know …'

Catching his son's eye, Rufus raised a finger in warning. Spike nodded, then retreated downstairs to the kitchen.

Chapter Three

Ancient hob finally lit, Spike crossed his arms and waited for the kettle to boil. At least he could do that.

The bead curtain shook, and he watched as Rufus tightened his dressing gown, then curled his long, loose-jointed legs into a wooden chair at the head of the table. They sat together in silence, sipping their tea. 'We used to call them night terrors,' Rufus said eventually, shrewd eyes contemplating his son over the chipped rim of his mug.

Spike remembered the nightmares after his mother had died. The same dream in which he tried and failed to catch her over and over again. He'd been eighteen then. But as a child?

'Sweet boy,' Rufus said, and for a moment Spike thought his father was talking about him. 'How long's he staying?' he asked.

'Just a night,' Spike replied. 'His grandparents are at St Bernard's.'

'Oh?' Rufus raised his white bushy eyebrows. If they grew any longer, they'd start impeding his vision.

'The grandfather's having tests,' Spike said.

'What for?'

'Vascular dementia.'

Rufus pulled off his half-moons in disgust, pale blue eyes gleaming. 'Poor chap.' Even at seventy-six, with the symptoms of Marfan syndrome increasing every year in variety and intensity, Rufus still regarded the ailments of others with the distance of a brawny teenager. 'Surely the boy must have other relatives?'

'None that have shown any interest.'

The implication hung heavy in the close August air, but Spike wasn't yet ready to acknowledge it, eye roving instead around the kitchen, unchanged since his childhood, falling on the salt cellar leaking onto the heaps of overdue library books, the microwave with its food-smeared porthole, the kitchen knives scattered over the windowsill amid his father's packets of medication. It was a room barely fit for habitation by two grown men, let alone an overactive toddler.

'We could always cancel the holiday,' Rufus said.

'It's just a week, Dad.'

They finished their tea, then Spike helped his father to his feet. Feeling Rufus lean on him that little bit more than he used to, Spike was forced to admit that even Charlie's grandfather, currently undergoing a CAT scan in hospital, cut a more spritely figure. Once Rufus was safely stowed upstairs, Spike checked the box-room again, relieved to find Charlie lying on his side in a C-shape, breathing steadily. Reaching a hand into the cot, he traced a cautious finger along the damp, soft nape of his neck. But then the boy started to stir, so he turned away, pulling the door carefully closed behind him.

It was almost midnight when Spike finally switched off his computer and climbed into bed. Charlie would be awake at six, his grandmother had warned. Spike knew he should be trying to sleep as well, but waited until the church bells outside struck the hour, wondering if he was the only person left on earth who knew that today was Zahra al-Mahmoud's birthday. She would have been thirty-six. Young enough to put everything that had happened behind them. Perhaps even to have those children she'd always wanted.

Spike reached over and switched off the bedside lamp. Zahra would have known what to do about Charlie. Now he would just have to try and work it out for himself. Had he been inclined, he might have said a prayer for her. But he wasn't, so he just lay back and waited for Charlie's cries to tell him that morning had come.

PART TWO

Corfu

Chapter Four

Spike rolled down the passenger window and closed his eyes, savouring the warm salted breeze against his skin as the Fiat Panda raced along the coast road.

'First time in Corfu, Mr Sanguinetti?' the driver called over.

Spike nodded, flicking open his eyelids to see the glinting blue waves of the Mediterranean, flanked by a surprisingly lush land-scape. 'Has it been raining?' he asked.

Lakis flashed him another gap-toothed smile from behind the wheel. From the moment he'd picked Spike and Rufus up at Corfu Airport, he'd exuded a relentless good humour. 'In the north of Corfu,' Lakis replied in his rapid-fire English, 'it is always green. That is why it is so exclusive.' He rubbed a chunky thumb and forefinger together with a wink. 'The Rothschilds have a villa here. You know the Rothschilds, Mr Sanguinetti?' His bright, hazel eyes caught Spike's. 'The Agnellis. Abramovich also. Even the Hoffmanns...'

'As in Sir Leo Hoffmann? Of the media family?'

'Their estate is right next to Peter's house. You'll see,' he added knowingly as they rounded a corner to reveal a hilly vista of olive groves speared by cypress trees.

'It's almost like Tuscany,' Spike said under his breath.

Lakis glanced over again. The sleeves of his vintage Bob Marley T-shirt were carefully rolled up to reveal powerful biceps that Spike suspected might run to fat once he reached his thirties. 'You work with Peter?' Lakis asked.

Spike nodded, and Lakis reached unthinkingly for the tiny five-fingered leaf he wore as a pendant and tucked it beneath his hairy neckline. 'And you, sir?' he called into the back of the car.

'I'm just the father,' boomed a voice, reminding Spike that he'd forgotten once again to adjust the setting on Rufus's new hearing aid. 'Here because my son deems it unwise to leave me un-attended at home.'

Lakis chuckled.

'In any case, son,' Rufus went on, 'the Veneto is the more fitting comparison.'

Lakis gave a vigorous nod. 'Your father is right. The Venetians ruled Corfu for four centuries. They paid us a gold coin for every olive tree planted. That is the reason the island is so green.' He gave another flash of his white teeth. 'The oil was exported for lamps. Three million olive trees for a hundred thousand locals.'

A Vespa drew up behind the car, then overtook on a blind bend, a dark Casanova texting above the handlebar, a laughing girl in a pink bikini riding pillion, neither choosing to compromise their hairstyles with helmets. Palm-thatched bars appeared on one side of the road, a sandy beach on the other, and the scooter pulled to a halt, the couple vaulting the railings to join their friends by the water.

'Is this Kavos?' Spike asked, remembering a reality TV show he'd caught on a particularly severe night of insomnia.

Lakis shook his large head. 'This is Ipsos. Ipsos is for Italians, Kavos is for...how do you say, Brits on tour?' He beetled his tanned brow, as though considering whether this might be the sort of holiday Spike was after. 'Italians and British,' he resumed, eyes back on the road. 'Once they owned Corfu, now they cannot say goodbye.'

'How long were the British in charge?' Spike asked.

'Professor?' Lakis called back.

'Fifty years. Fifty of the best,' Rufus added with Gibraltarian fervour.

'Now Greek always...' Lakis broke off as his eyes followed two barely dressed girls leaving a bar hand-in-hand.

'*Eleftheria i thanatos*,' Rufus murmured.

'You speak Greek?' Lakis asked in surprise.

'He studied Ancient Greek,' Spike said. 'Thinks it's the same language.'

'Freedom or death,' Lakis translated with a nod of approval. 'That is what your father says.'

The road started to climb, and a mountain appeared in the distance, its foothills clothed with olives and cypresses, its upper slopes too sheer to grow anything but scrub. A dome of rock crowned the peak, like the roof of an Orthodox church, a tele-communications tower somewhat undermining the effect.

'Our highest mountain,' Lakis said proudly as he pointed up at it. 'We call it "Pantokrator".' He raised his voice again: 'Professor?'

Rufus shut his eyes to mull the question, and Spike stifled a groan. '"Pan" means "all",' he said slowly, 'as in "pandemonium", when all demons are set loose. And "kratos" is ruler, as in plutocrat, a ruler by wealth. So ... all-powerful?'

'Almighty Mountain,' Lakis said, whistling his respect through the gap between his front teeth. 'Bravo.'

A thin strait of water appeared to the right, a wild and spiny range of mountains on the other side. 'Is that mainland Greece?' Spike asked.

'No, no' – Lakis pulled a face – 'that is Albania. Greece is over there.' He gestured to the right, and Spike nodded uncertainly, thinking that he really ought to get hold of a map. Dirt tracks ran off the main road, offering glimpses of converted fishermen's cottages and sheltered pebbly coves. The week was going to be OK, Spike decided. They would swim, read, drink bad local wine. All the things normal people did on holiday. The things he hadn't done in a long time.

Lakis swerved suddenly to avoid an English-looking couple wheeling a Bugaboo pram along the dusty road. Everything about them, from their shoes to their freckled tans, spoke of wealth and good taste, and Spike was reminded of how Peter Galliano had described his part of Corfu – Kensington-on-Sea. Just then, they came to a smoothly pointed stone wall rising from the verge, bisected by an enormous set of wrought-iron gates.

'Hoffmann Estate,' Lakis said, braking sharply to avoid a white refrigerated lorry parked ahead on the road. They watched as two men in shorts unbolted the rear doors to reveal a frosty hollow of hanging carcasses. The men carried out a gutted pig, its pink back sliced open to keep the soft belly intact. The body was passed to four members of staff, then the rear doors slammed and the van was on its way.

Lakis gave a cheerful wave to the Hoffmann staff as they drove past, but no one seemed to notice. He shrugged, then turned the wheel abruptly down a shady path towards the sea. Through the foliage, Spike caught sight of the pale walls of a low house.

'Galliano Olive Press,' Lakis said, bringing the Fiat to a juddering halt. 'Your home.' He bowed his head. 'And mine.'

Chapter Five

Whistling tunelessly, Lakis unloaded their mismatched luggage, refusing Spike's offers of assistance. The punishing midday sun filtered through the lobed leaves of an ancient fig tree, the skins of its fruit withered and puckered, innards of purple flesh and orange seeds bursting through. 'This way,' Lakis called over, then led them down to the whitewashed main building, rectangular against the rocky shoreline, undulating rows of faded terracotta tiles covering its sloping roof.

Rufus's room was large and airy, bookshelves lining one wall and a rather beautiful framed arrangement of seashells on the other. A pristine pair of white curtains fluttered in the breeze, revealing the terrace below and the turquoise sea beyond. 'Master bedroom,' Lakis said. 'Normally Peter's, but now, with the stairs...'

Rufus nodded absently, already absorbed in a critical examination of his library, so Lakis showed Spike to his more modest room across the landing, pushing open the stiff shutters with an unapologetic shrug towards the view of the rusty Fiat Panda squatting on the slope above.

A few minutes later, Spike was escorting Rufus down the curved oak staircase into a gracious sitting room. Flaking blue shutters were closed against the sun, the walls lined with leather-bound books and architectural engravings of Venetian palazzi. Through open double doors lay the terrace. And waiting at the table beneath a canopy of vines sat Peter Galliano, an ice bucket in front of him and a delighted smile on his face.

'At last,' Peter said, tipping his much-loved panama.

For a moment Spike wondered why Peter didn't get up, then saw the two malacca canes propped against the wall and remembered. But Peter didn't seem to notice, already immersed in the task of pouring chilled champagne into antique, wide-lipped flutes. He passed one to Spike with a grin, then pulled a smaller bottle from the ice bucket and expertly knocked off the cap. '*Tzitzibira*,' he said, pushing the bottle over to Rufus. 'Corfu ginger beer.'

'Legacy of the British?' Rufus asked.

'Precisely.' He raised his glass. 'To a wonderful week in Corfu.'

Spike tried not to stare at his old friend as they drank, but beneath the panama, the extent of Peter's weight loss was extraordinary – his entire head looked smaller. He seemed older too: brown beard flecked with white, eyes deeper-set in their nest of laughter and worry lines. Of the ubiquitous Silk Cut Ultras there was no sign.

'You kept this place quiet,' Spike said with a smile.

Peter waved the compliment away with a waft of one tanned hand. 'It's practically falling down.'

Spike followed his father to the low stone wall that ran along the edge of the terrace, fringed by terracotta pots of cacti and parched herbs. Looking downwards, he saw a pockmarked concrete slope running directly into the sea.

'They used to roll the barrels of olive oil down there,' Peter called over.

'Your Venetian ancestors?' Rufus asked.

'Lord no. They were *far* too grand. But that was before Napoleon stole all our land.' He gave a mischievous wink, and suddenly Spike was reminded of the old Peter. The Peter before the accident. 'The olive press is all that survives.'

Tiny black sea urchins clung to the slope beneath the waterline amid slippery patches of algae. With some relief, Spike saw steps built on either side, providing an easier route into the sea.

'*Le pied dans l'eau*, as the French have it,' Rufus said.

'It is well located,' Peter conceded, 'but I haven't managed a swim yet this year.' He ran a finger around the rim of his champagne flute. 'Maybe before the end of the week.'

Spike placed a firm hand on his partner's shoulder. 'It's good to see you, Peter.'

Peter's dark eyes gleamed glassily. 'Before you know it,' he said, 'it'll be business as usual.' Then he added in a more jovial voice, 'Now, I imagine you'll both be wanting a dip.'

Chapter Six

Later, they watched the sun set from the small round table at the edge of the terrace, its top formed by the millstone used to crush olives in the days when the house had been a working press. Spike took a slow sip of his campari and orange, suffused by the warm glow that came from a lazy afternoon spent in the sea and sun. He hadn't felt this good in a long time. Even Rufus looked healthier, silver hair swept back from his brow, wasted frame draped in one of his newer cotton shirts.

As the light started to fade, Peter finally took off his panama. The raised, jagged scar on his forehead was still a lurid purple, and Spike wondered yet again how he'd managed to survive the hit-and-run in Gibraltar. A month in a medically induced coma didn't seem to have cured him of his nicotine addiction, however, as an electronic cigarette had appeared on the stroke of 5 p.m., and now remained almost permanently between his lips, its LED tip flashing red like a warning signal. He drew hard on it, exhaling puffs of water vapour as he consulted his watch. Then came the rumble of a car from the road above. 'Bang on time,' Peter whispered.

Spike waited for further explanation, but his host just offered one of his enigmatic smiles. They heard voices echo inside the house, and a moment later a petite young woman with her dark hair drawn into a low ponytail walked onto the terrace.

Spike pushed back his chair, feeling his stomach flip as he locked eyes with Jessica Navarro. They both turned to Peter, who threw out his arms in sham apology. 'Don't blame me,' he said, lips twitching in amusement at Spike's discomfort. 'It was your father's idea.'

'Dad?' Spike said to Rufus, who was innocently flicking through a dog-eared paperback. 'We were worried you might get bored, son,' Rufus replied without looking up. 'Holed up here with a couple of codgers.'

Spike shook his head, then turned again to his ex-girlfriend, who was managing her dismay with the ease that might be expected of a newly promoted Detective Sergeant. She looked infuriatingly beautiful, he was forced to concede as he took in her deep suntan, the alluring bikini strap marks on her smooth shoulders. 'I thought you were in Portugal.'

'I was. Until this afternoon.' She spoke in the quiet, curt tone he had come to know well. He'd heard it the first time they broke up, when he'd left Gibraltar to start university in London, and a few times since – one of the disadvantages of living on a Rock the size of Hyde Park.

'Now come along, you two,' Peter chided, passing Jessica a flute of champagne. 'You both need a holiday. To old friends,' he tried, raising his glass.

'I'll drink to that,' came an accented voice, and Spike turned to see a dark-haired stranger emerging from the shadows of the house. The young man wore a thin blue cotton jacket over his rangy frame, and had the type of handsome, fine-boned face that appeared to be irresistible to some women, to the bewilderment of most men. As he strolled over to Jessica, she offered him her glass with a bright smile. 'Thanks, Jess,' he said, and Spike winced as he saw her blush. He was just pondering how the two had met – maybe in some cocktail bar in Faro – when Peter called over, 'Arben works at the Hoffmann Estate. He was kind enough to pick Jessica up from the airport.' And Spike felt himself start to relax.

A moment later, Lakis appeared from the house with another bottle of champagne and knocked knuckles with Arben: 'Thanks, man.' Lakis set down the bottle, then turned back to his friend, shifting uneasily on his feet. But Arben just picked up his flute and took a long gulp of champagne. 'I love this place,' he said to Jessica, stepping towards the terrace wall. 'So close to the water.' His English was better than Lakis's, with a hint of an American accent.

Peter ignored him and turned instead to Jessica. 'So am I forgiven?' he asked meekly.

'Of course,' she said, bending down to kiss one of his bristly cheeks.

Arben raised a mocking eyebrow. 'Forgiven for what?' There was a moment of embarrassed silence, which didn't seem to trouble the young man too much.

Lakis cleared his throat. 'Maybe you could help me with something in the kitchen, Arben.' He held out a hand for Arben's glass with a frown of disapproval. 'Now that you've finished your drink.'

Jessica turned to Spike. 'So you had no idea I was coming?'

'None.'

She conceded a ghost of a smile as Arben reluctantly walked towards the house. 'Thanks for the lift, Arben,' she called out. 'I enjoyed our chat.'

'Any time,' Arben replied, laying a familiar hand on her shoulder. 'It was my pleasure.'

'Old friend of Lakis's,' Peter muttered once he was gone. 'Apparently he writes poetry.'

'Of course he does,' Spike said. But Jessica didn't seem to hear, gazing instead out to sea, eyes glowing.

*

Calypso runs barefoot down the beach, heartbeat drumming in her temple, aware of the occasional drunk teenager still passed out on a deckchair, sunburn searing their neck and legs. When

26

she'd first started working in Kavos, she would try and wake them, risking a slurred volley of English abuse. But soon she learnt better, and now she just weaves by, feeling her heavy bag dig into her bruised shoulder, the sweat sting the cut on her face. She raises a hand to her damaged eye. When she pulls it back she finds it covered in dark blood, slick and new, and for a moment she thinks she might faint. Instead she bends over and vomits into the sand, watching blood patter onto the bile as she remembers the man in the balaclava staring down from the window of her apartment, the challenge in his black eyes. That was when she had started to run, and she hasn't stopped since. Until now.

Wiping a hand across her mouth, she forces herself to stand, legs quivering as she continues down the beach, picking up her pace, glancing over one shoulder before veering into the dune grass.

The undergrowth on either side of the path is flattened, as though wild animals have been resting there, which in a sense they have. She sees squares of torn silver on the wet sand, last night's condoms caught on twigs, knickers discarded in brackish puddles. Then the path rises and she finds herself up on the sandy road.

Her breaths rasp in time with the cicadas. Hearing the distant sound of an engine, she raises her head, but it's not the bus, just a private car, Europop blaring through the open windows.

Calypso crouches down in the dry, sharp grass, and then the road is empty. What if the bus isn't running today? She could hitch. But what if it's his car she flags down? Would she recognise his face? Just his eyes, she thinks, feeling her heart start to race again, those dead black holes in the slit of his balaclava.

The nausea is returning, but she knows that if she lets herself rest she may not have the strength to get up again. Then finally – just as she feels the tears of defeat prick in her eyes – she hears the distant groan of diesel. Never has the turquoise livery of a Corfu *bus been so welcome. She touches her eye. It is still bleeding. What if the driver refuses to let her on?*

But then a rustle comes from the undergrowth behind, the sound of someone pushing through the dune grass. So Calypso grabs her bag and runs onto the road, into the path of the oncoming bus.

Chapter Seven

Spike stared again at Jessica, marvelling at how the addition of just one person could completely change the dynamic of a group. She was wearing the sleeveless green top he'd always liked, her arms a rich brown from the sun – record temperatures in the Algarve, she'd said. She had the kind of beauty that seemed to change from every angle, he decided, but then she sensed his gaze, and he turned back to the Mediterranean, relieved as usual to be able to lose himself in its gentle movement. If conversation faltered, there was always the fleck of a wave, a seagull diving, a fishing boat puttering towards its favoured position to trail out nets…

'Aha!' Peter said, clasping his hands together in excitement. 'Now we're talking.'

Emerging from the kitchen was a stout, beaming woman with short black curls and a tiara of sweat on her brow. Breathing noisily through her mouth, she carried a round tray in both arms, her red apron stained with flour and cooking fat. '*Kali spera*,' she murmured, laying the tray down on the table with a sigh of relief.

'Without Katerina,' Peter said, 'I wouldn't be in the condition you find me now.'

'My honour,' Katerina replied, rubbing both hands on her apron. She nodded to the group. 'You have already met my son, I think. Lakis?'

Rufus rushed to introduce himself, Spike grimacing as he watched his father cock his head to offer her a twinkle of his

Genoese blue eyes. Katerina flushed a little, then turned to Jessica, who received a Greek exclamation of admiration. 'You are a lucky man,' she said to Spike, who opened his mouth to protest, but she'd already moved on. 'Why can't you find a nice woman for Peter?' she scolded as she offloaded bowls, triggering an awkward pause as the company contemplated not for the first time whether Peter Galliano was interested in any woman, however nice.

Oblivious to this silent debate, Katerina tucked the empty tray beneath her broad upper arm and proudly presented her work. 'All of Peter's favourites. Tzatziki, taramasalata, aubergine paste.'

'Did you make them yourself?' Jessica asked, picking up a slice of toasted bread burnished with olive oil and garlic.

'Of course,' Katerina retorted, and Jessica gave a sheepish look, sensing that her stock had already fallen. So Spike changed the subject, gesturing over the water, to where a band of lights flashed at the foot of a shadowy mountain range. 'So that's Albania?'

Peter nodded, mouth full of food. 'The port of Saranda,' he said, swallowing. 'At its narrowest point, the Corfu Channel is just two kilometres wide. Under the Communists, young men would try to swim across.' He tugged fondly at the back of Katerina's black skirt as she bustled past. 'You should tell them about your husband, Katerina.'

Spike sighed, dipping some toast into the white taramasalata, which was smooth and sharp, bearing no relation to the tubs of candyfloss-coloured cream he sometimes bought for his father in Gibraltar.

'Viktor' – Katerina crossed herself discreetly as she bent over the table – 'came from Saranda. A proud man. A good Albanian. But under Hoxha, you know …' She clicked her tongue in distaste. 'Well, it was not a good place.' She laid down a hand-painted dinner plate with a thump. 'Every day Viktor would look out and see Corfu. The yachts, the hotels. He could even hear the music' – she laughed – 'like a party he was not allowed to go to.' She caught Rufus's eye and he nodded sympathetically; Spike swallowed a snort. 'So in 1984, Viktor saved up and bought himself a watermelon.' She waited for the expected chuckle, then continued, enjoying herself now. 'He hollowed out the fruit' – she mimed the action – 'cut holes for his eyes and mouth, then put it over his head and slipped into the sea. All along the coast were Hoxha's snipers, hiding in his military bunkers. They watched the melon floating by and came down to the beach, hoping it would drift in. But beneath the surface, Viktor's legs were working like a ...' She made a paddling motion with her strong hands, black eyes sparkling. '*Kuknos*?'

'Swan,' Peter translated gallantly – he had clearly heard the story more than once.

'Many hours later, he made it to Kouloura Beach, just down the coast from here.' She pointed along the seashore. 'He found me and we fell in love. God granted us Lakis and little Spiros and then ...' She broke off.

'Viktor died,' Peter said gently. 'Ten years ago.'

'Cancer,' Katerina said with a phlegmatic shrug. 'From the smoking.' She threw Peter a glance, but he just took a defiant drag on his electronic cigarette and smiled.

'Was it Spiros we met earlier?' Rufus said loudly. Spike glanced at Jessica but she seemed not to have heard.

'That was Arben, Rufus,' Peter replied. 'Spiros is only thirteen.'

'Ah,' Katerina sighed, 'the beautiful Arben.' She shook her head, looking as though she was going to say something, then thought better of it, eyes drawn instead across the dark Corfu Channel. 'Now Viktor is buried in the family tomb in Saranda.'

'He went *back* to Albania?' Rufus asked.

Katerina didn't seem troubled by the question, just picked up a bottle of retsina and uncorked it with surprising strength. 'After

Hoxha died, they started a ferry between Corfu and Saranda. We had many happy times together visiting Albania. Viktor took us to see Gjirokastra, the ruins of Butrint.' She paused and gave a sad smile. 'But my boys always liked Blue Eye, where the water is ... *kobaltio*?'

'The colour of cobalt,' Peter murmured.

'A wild and beautiful place, this new Albania,' Katerina concluded, all emotion despatched with a shake of the crumbs from her apron. 'Now,' she said, plucking the e-cigarette from Peter's mouth and slotting it into his breast pocket. 'You will eat.'

Chapter Eight

Bellies replete with Katerina's rich, cinnamon-spiced moussaka, they sat in a contented silence, watching the lights of a gin palace squeeze along the tight Corfu Channel. Spike glanced again at Jessica through the candlelight, her tanned face glowing, clear dark eyes gleaming with the powerful pine-resin wine. But then he felt his father's gaze upon him and turned away, cheeks burning.

'I had some interesting news this week,' Peter said. 'An offer for the house.' He lowered his voice theatrically: 'From my *neighbour.*'

The group roused themselves from their high-calorie reverie.

'Sir Leo Hoffmann?' Spike asked.

Peter nodded.

'But surely you wouldn't consider selling this place, Peter?' Jessica said.

Peter rubbed the bridge of his nose with one thick hairy knuckle. 'It's a compelling offer, I have to admit. Surprisingly so, given the amount of work it needs.'

'And the size of the existing Hoffmann estate,' Spike murmured, briefly entertaining the notion of a welcome injection of capital into Galliano & Sanguinetti, LLP.

'You know why this part of Corfu is so unspoilt?' Peter asked, glancing playfully around the table. 'Because Sir Leo likes to keep it that way. Apparently, he bought a villa down the coast a few years ago and razed it to the ground because it impeded the view from his bathroom.'

Jessica gave a look of such distress that Peter laughed. 'Don't worry, Jess. I don't think we're in the eyeline of his Armitage Shanks.'

Rufus chuckled without looking up from the slice of aubergine he'd been tormenting for what felt like hours.

'Have you ever been to the house?' Jessica asked.

Peter drained his retsina. 'Not for years. But' – he gave a dramatic pause – 'we shall all have a chance to admire it tomorrow.'

'Oh?' Rufus said, finally paying attention.

'A party,' Peter explained, drawing a stiff white card from his breast pocket and handing it to Jessica. 'At the Hoffmann villa, no less.'

Jessica read aloud the three words embossed in the centre. 'The ... Phaeacian Games?' She glanced up blankly.

'Good lord.' Rufus gave a chortle. 'The man must fancy himself as King Alcinous.'

Spike refilled glasses, suspecting they might need help to get through one of his father's stories. 'It's a reference to *The Odyssey*, of course,' Rufus went on, seeking a token of recognition from the table. Finding none, he was undeterred. 'On his way home from Troy, Odysseus washed up on Scheria, an island now believed to be Corfu. He was found on the beach by a beautiful princess called Nausicaa. She took him to meet her father, King Alcinous, the leader of the Phaeacians, who threw him a lavish party, commonly referred to as "the Phaeacian Games".'

To Spike's relief, Katerina chose that moment to reappear with a tray of fat figs and plums and bowls of thick Greek yoghurt and honey. 'It is late,' she said to Peter.

With a rueful smile, Peter reached for his canes. 'I believe those are my marching orders.'

As their host pulled himself to his feet under Katerina's watchful eye, Rufus reached over and picked up the invitation. 'Well I never,' he muttered to himself. 'The Phaeacian Games.'

Chapter Nine

Spike felt another drop of sweat slide down his cheek as he wrestled with the elderly shutters. He had half-cajoled, half-carried his father up the stairs to his room, a task rendered even more challenging by the retsina already seeping from his pores. Looking down through the bedroom window, he caught sight of Jessica sitting alone on the terrace, her slender legs crossed, a thoughtful smile on her lips as she stared into the dark water beyond. He was just wondering what she might be thinking when he heard his father's sardonic voice behind him: 'She looked rather well tonight.'

'Who?' Spike said, pulling closed the shutters with a bang. He turned to see his father's thin frame propped against a pillow, book clutched in one clawed hand. But Rufus just laughed and shook his head. 'Goodnight, son.'

Making his way downstairs, Spike heard raised voices in the kitchen and almost spun away on his heel. He'd endured enough small talk for one evening. But then he remembered Jessica sitting alone with an empty glass, and pushed open the kitchen door.

Inside he found Lakis standing by the sink, heavy forearms squeezed into a pair of pink Marigolds. Occupying the wooden stool beside him was Arben.

'Don't talk *shit*,' Lakis was hissing at Arben in English. 'You have no idea what...'

Spike rapped impatiently on the open door, and Lakis swung round. Arben didn't move, just watched his friend's embarrassment with an amused smile.

35

'Sorry,' Spike said. 'I was after another bottle of wine.'

As Lakis struggled to pull off his rubber gloves, Arben finally took pity and stood up.

'I can get it,' Spike said.

'Not a problem,' Arben replied. His dark eyes held Spike's, not quite mocking, but almost.

'Thanks,' Spike said, taking the golden, beaded bottle.

'You won't thank me tomorrow. That stuff is *nasty*.'

'I thought retsina was your national drink.'

'Arben's from Albania,' Lakis called over from the sink.

'You know what Lawrence Durrell called retsina?' Arben said. '*A divine turpentine*.' He held out the corkscrew, point first.

Spike remembered Lakis's mixed heritage as he sliced off a first peeling of lead. 'So are you two related?'

'Just friends,' Lakis said, without imbuing much enthusiasm into the term. 'And colleagues. Arben's on the Hoffmanns' permanent staff.' He plunged his hands back into the steaming water. 'They only ask me to help when it's busy.'

'Then maybe I'll see you both tomorrow,' Spike said.

'You're going to the party?' Arben asked, reappraising Spike's crumpled linen shirt and salt-stained red espadrilles.

Spike nodded.

'It's going to be some bash,' Arben said, studied cool slipping just a little. 'Leo's even flown over an opera singer from Malta.'

'Malta…' Spike repeated as the cork finally burst free, thinking of another hot night like this, drinking prickly-pear liqueur with Zahra at a café in Marsaxlokk Harbour. Daring each other to talk about the future. Their future together.

A knife clattered in the sink, and Spike looked up. 'Only Arben's allowed to call the boss "Leo",' Lakis said. 'Everyone else calls him "Sir".'

Arben smiled his condescending smile. 'Anyone can call him that, Lakis. It *is* his name.'

Lakis said nothing, but the atmosphere crackled all the same. And Spike found himself remembering a J. M. Barrie line his father liked to quote: 'I'm not young enough to know *every-thing*...' 'Thanks,' he said, raising the bottle, keen to get out of there.

But Arben was staring at him now, a curious look on his face. '*Syblu*,' he said.

Spike looked back with a frown.

'You would not be welcome in Albania.'

Lakis threw down a handful of wet silver then turned to his friend. But Arben just gestured at Spike's face. 'It's your eyes,' he said with a sly smile. 'Where I come from, blue eyes are a curse.' Then he added sotto voce, 'When a man with eyes like yours used to come to my mother's house, she would hide the children.'

'Probably no bad thing,' Spike replied, thinking of Charlie. 'Good night.' He nodded at both men, then headed back out to the terrace, strangely unsettled.

Chapter Ten

Low on the shoreline, the port city of Saranda flickered in the night sky. An eerie orange light flared on the mountainside above – wildfires, Katerina had said, Albanian goatherds renewing their pastures.

'Penny for them?'

Spike turned back to Jessica. Her heart-shaped mouth was swollen with heat and wine; he fought a powerful urge to lean in and kiss her. 'Charlie's grandfather's ill,' he said. 'I don't think they're going to be able to take care of him for much longer.'

Jessica didn't answer, just ran a long finger along the pale layers of rock that made up the coastline of this part of Corfu. Her unvarnished nails gleamed in the moonlight. She'd always had lovely hands.

'I think they might ask me to take him,' Spike said.

He half-expected her to laugh, but she just nodded. 'A child is a big responsibility, Spike. A serious commitment.' She shot him a sideways glance. 'Not exactly your strong suit.'

'No.' He supposed he couldn't argue with that. 'Maybe if my dad was in better shape. If I didn't have to work so much…'

'No one would blame you, Spike.'

Charlie's mother might, he thought.

'I mean, it's not like you're ideal father material,' Jessica pressed on mercilessly.

'No,' Spike said, surprised to find himself irritated by her certainty. He thought about Charlie's hard-won laugh, his funny questions. Was it really such a stupid idea? It wasn't as if the boy had any better options.

What sounded like a scream came from the promontory, and Spike and Jessica turned to where the Hoffmann villa lay hidden behind a blanket of pine trees. The noise rang out again, a single note, high-pitched and tremulous. 'Arben said the Hoffmanns are laying on an opera singer,' Spike said. 'For the party.'

'Sounds like she could use the rehearsal time,' Jessica replied. He could tell from her face what was coming next. 'So ... did you see the shrink?'

Spike turned away, feeling a growing sense of resentment at Peter's clumsy attempt at matchmaking. They'd tried to make it work before, but somehow Zahra had always got in the way. Even after she'd died. He stared out at the waves, eyes drawn to where the moon created a pathway of silver leading towards Albania. 'Yup,' he said.

Jessica seemed to be waiting for him to elaborate. 'Was it helpful?' she prompted, and he gave her a look that he hoped succinctly answered her question.

'Worth trying someone else, then? They say a lot depends on the dynamic between ...'

This time he didn't let her finish, 'Look, it's just not for me, Jess, OK?'

She must have sensed the finality in his voice, as she changed the subject. No doubt keeping her powder dry for another day. 'Midnight swim?'

'I don't have my trunks,' Spike said, hearing the dourness in his tone.

'Oh come on.' She winked. 'It's nothing I haven't seen before.'

She stepped out of her skirt, then turned away to pull the green top over her head, giving him a glimpse of smooth tanned shoulder blades underscored by a black bra strap. He looked away, but not before he'd caught sight of her lace-edged knickers as she dived neatly into the water. She emerged grinning, slicking back her dark hair with one hand. 'Lost your nerve, Sanguinetti?' she called up.

He smiled as he pulled off his clothes, checking the fly of his boxer shorts was buttoned before diving – less elegantly – into the sea. He kept his eyes open underwater, watching the swirl of bubbles, enjoying the saline sting as he surfaced opposite her. She held his gaze as he swam over, so he took a chance and wrapped his arms around her, feeling her skin warm and slippery with seawater. As he drew her closer, he heard her breathing quicken, but she averted her lips. 'It has to be serious this time,' she said quietly.

'Of course.'

'I'm not getting involved again unless it's serious.'

He wanted her so badly at that moment he would have said almost anything, but then she leant in and he heard her whisper, 'I'm thirty-four, Spike. Too old to be competing with a ghost.' She drew away, and he could see from her eyes that she wanted him to tell her that she'd read it wrong, that he was over Zahra. But he couldn't. 'Maybe we should just see what happens.'

She shook her head. 'Not good enough.'

'We could just …' he tried again, but she'd already slipped from his grasp, diving back down under the water. When she re-emerged, she was ten feet away, sleek as an otter. 'It's good we sorted this out, Spike,' she called over in a curiously cheerful voice. 'Laid down a few ground rules. Now we can just enjoy the holiday.'

Spike trod water for a few seconds, unsure if that meant he could swim over and kiss her. He suspected not.

'Think about it,' she added, then dived down again, remaining hidden beneath the waves for so long that he felt a small stir of panic before he saw her surface by the steps. Then she drew herself out of the water in a single fluid movement, allowing him one last tantalising glance before she pulled her top over her head and walked back up to the house.

Chapter Eleven

The next morning, Katerina had been busy, and they came down to a breakfast feast – jugs of freshly squeezed orange and grapefruit juice, Greek yoghurt, platters of figs, greengages, plums and, for some reason, strawberries. Spike sat next to Rufus, hiding his blood-shot eyes behind a bent pair of Aviators, watching his father thumb through a sun-faded edition of *The Odyssey* as he absently swatted away the wasps that the burning pots of coffee grains on the sea wall did little to deter. Beyond, on the terrace, Peter Galliano lay on a sunlounger, a threadbare towel draped over his buttocks as Katerina ruthlessly pounded what remained of the muscles in his legs.

A teenaged boy edged out of the kitchen, a braille of acne on his shiny brow. In his hungover state, Spike fought a strange instinct to give him a man-hug, to reassure him that this testing time would pass. '*Ef haristo*,' he offered instead, trying out his only words of Greek as the youth laid down a heavy dish of sliced watermelon. He had the same sad dark eyes as Charlie, Spike thought, then realised with a sting of confusion that he was miss-ing the boy. Did Charlie ever think about him? Probably not, he concluded gloomily, recalling depressing snippets of his conversa-tion with Jessica the night before. 'Are you Lakis's brother?' he asked, and the teenager looked up with a wary nod, then pressed his palms together behind an ear in the universal gesture of sleep.

'Lakis came home late last night,' Katerina called over as she ground the heel of her hand viciously into Peter's spine. 'Lots of work for the Hoffmanns, you know?'

'You must be Spiros then,' Spike said with a smile, but the youth was no longer looking at him, staring instead slack-jawed at Jessica as she emerged onto the terrace in a white bikini. Spike handed her a mug of coffee as she sat down.

'Thanks,' she said, quickly sizing Spike up. 'Hope you're feeling better than you look, Sanguinetti.'

She, as usual, radiated health, Spike was irritated to note, automatically reaching up to straighten his sunglasses.

Katerina clapped her hands together. 'Every day, stronger,' she said with satisfaction as she gathered her oils, following up with a 'Peter!' as she saw him slip his e-cigarette out of the pocket of his white robe.

'Sorry, Ma'am.'

Katerina headed for the kitchen, giving Spike a wink that made him question for a moment the nature of her relationship with Peter. 'Lakis will drive you to the party,' she called back. 'Eleven thirty a.m. Don't be late.'

Jessica seemed wholly absorbed in her coffee and yesterday's papers, so Spike dared to check his BlackBerry. Eighteen new emails. Christ. He rose reluctantly to his feet.

'Anything interesting?' Peter asked.

Spike shook his head and mustered a bright smile. 'Nothing that can't wait.'

But back in his room, he spent another frantic hour trying to keep the flailing firm of Galliano & Sanguinetti afloat.

Chapter Twelve

The Hoffmann villa was covered in the same whitewash as the Olive Press, but there any similarity ended. The building was three times as high and many more wide, its vast oak-framed door apparently designed to admit giants as well as mortals. Lakis dropped them in the turning circle, and they crunched across freshly raked gravel past a line of executive cars, following the distant strains of music. Peter led from the front like a crippled Doge, the others trailing behind like a delegation from some ailing city-state. Eventually he steered them onto a path running down the side of the villa, flanked by a tangle of prickly pears and fragrant jasmine.

'The original house was a monastery,' Peter said, gesturing at a crucifix etched high in the stonework as he paused to catch his breath. 'Almost unrecognisable now.'

Spike made a stab at an interested nod, his eye caught by a plump green lizard slinking through the undergrowth.

The path curved around to a sun-terrace, and the music grew louder – Elgar was Spike's first guess, but he settled on Grieg. The space was larger than a tennis court, formed of pale, perfectly flat flagstones sweeping towards a stunning panorama of Albania. A soft breeze was directed up from the sea, as if the winds themselves had been exhorted to ventilate the Hoffmanns and their descendants.

At one end of the terrace rose a stage, occupied by an over-dressed chamber orchestra discreetly tuning up. A Venetian wellhead adorned the centre, stones cut concentrically around it, water cascading down from a marble tray to create a sound almost as melodic as the professionals. Shielding the terrace from the level below was a line of box hedging, two alcoves indented within to allow the occupants a proper appreciation of the view. Behind, an open-sided shelter of weathered teak rested against the facade of the old monastery, with a long table laid up beneath, white cloth clipped in place to safeguard its precious cargo of Wedgwood and crystal. At the near end sat a lone man in a dove-coloured linen suit, grizzled head bent over a book, oblivious to the group's approach.

Peter gave a brisk click of the cane. 'Sir Leo?' he called out, in a voice usually reserved for the most lucrative of clients.

The man glanced up in irritation. He had a high, freckled brow, his hair the curious dessert-wine colour that redheads take on in old age.

'Mr Galliano?' Sir Leo Hoffmann said with a frown as he stood up. 'What on *earth* are you doing coming down the side way? I made arrangements for you to be met and brought down in the lift.' He gave a vague wave of the hand, and a moment later a chair had been pulled out, and Peter was seated comfortably, sipping from a glass of iced water and lemon. The musicians gazed on thirstily as Leo dubbed Peter on the shoulder. 'It's been too long, my friend.'

'Best part of a decade, I should imagine,' Peter replied, raising his sticks with a self-conscious grin. 'I think the years have been kinder to you, Sir Leo.'

As the canapés and goblets of champagne started to circulate, Rufus picked up his host's book. 'You ought to be reading the Fagles,' he said sternly.

Leo turned in surprise, green eyes roaming over Rufus's spare frame, taking in the once-white socks stuffed into leather sandals, the houndstooth jacket that forty years' use in Gibraltar had taught him to wear without breaking sweat. Appraisal concluded, he laughed, a deep satisfying sound. 'I happen to prefer the prose. It's more accurate.'

Rufus gave a stubborn shake of the head. 'If you're going to read nonsense, it may as well be poetic nonsense.'

It was then that Spike saw Leo's book was an English translation of *The Odyssey*. Leo tapped Rufus on one spidery arm. 'You'd better sit down and tell me why,' he said, pulling out a chair.

At that moment, an aged brunette wafted onto the terrace, flanked by a brace of immaculately suited Greeks. Peter struggled to his feet, hardwired gallantry superseding any discomfort. 'Lady Lucinda,' he breathed, planting a moist kiss on his hostess's hand. Her Greek walkers expertly melted away to admire the view, and Jessica threw Spike an amused glance as they sipped their champagne, which naturally was exquisite, cold and dry. They barely noticed as a tall girl appeared beside them, her long blonde hair worked into intricate braids.

'*Meh leneh* India Hoffmann,' the girl said in a quiet but resonant public-school voice.

It hadn't occurred to Spike that, with their dark complexions, he and Jessica might be mistaken for Greek. His surprise must have been obvious as India flushed with embarrassment. Watching the girl shift on one heel, unsure what to say next, Spike took pity and introduced himself and Jessica in English.

'So you're...' She seemed to be trying to place Spike's lilting accent.

'Gibraltarian,' Jessica said. 'From Gibraltar,' she added, unsure what they might be dealing with.

India's face brightened. 'I went there once. On a yacht.'

'Oh,' Jessica said, and the conversation stalled again. The girl must be in her early twenties – old enough to have acquired some social skills, Spike thought uncharitably. India's gaucheness was compounded by her cocktail-party eyes, exploiting her height – nearly six foot in heels – to glance over Jessica's head, presumably for someone more exciting to talk to. Eventually her gaze settled, and Spike followed it to the stage where a group of Hoffmann staff was struggling with a microphone stand.

India refocused. 'God,' she said, looking back with an anxious smile, 'I'm rubbish at these things.'

Spike felt Jessica relax: a little evidence of human weakness went a long way for her. Not a trait shared by many of her colleagues in the Royal Gibraltar Police, he suspected. He looked again at India. Her eyes were the same startling green as her grandfather's, but her pale oval face spoke of generations of English roses gathered to the Hoffmann family bosom. Following her butterfly gaze, Spike saw a young man arrive on the terrace. Even from this distance, he was obviously India's twin. The delicately pretty features had been replicated, but he'd fought back with a crew-cut haircut and a Chinese tattoo on his upper arm of which Spike doubted his grandfather approved. Hoffmann Jr. glanced at his sister's choice of drinking companions, then veered towards a tray of champagne flutes.

'My brother,' India said unnecessarily. 'Alfie.'

Choosing his moment, one of Lady Lucinda's urbane Greeks approached Jessica, patting his wiry grey hair into place. 'I understand we share a profession,' he said. 'Spiros Constandinos, Chief of the Corfu Police.' Seeking permission to take Jessica's hand, he guided her away towards the topiary.

India seemed lost again for something to say, so Spike plucked two glasses from a passing tray and handed her one with a smile. She took a long, grateful gulp. 'So are you in the police force too?'

'Lawyer.'

'Ah,' she said. 'You must own the Olive Press.'

'That's my business partner.' He gestured at Peter, who was patiently nodding as Lady Lucinda described something that required wild motions of her bangle-clad arms. 'We used to work for a big firm in Gibraltar. Then we started Galliano & Sanguinetti.'

The name suddenly sounded horribly parochial on a terrace which Peter had suggested was more usually populated by former world leaders and Hollywood royalty.

But India was watching her twin again, now half-heartedly chatting up the prettiest waitress as he drained a second glass of champagne.

Spike rallied for another try, promising himself it would be the last. 'Is everyone in Corfu called Spiros?'

India turned. 'Half the male population. It's in honour of Saint Spiridon, the patron saint of Corfu. His body is embalmed in a church in Corfu Town.' She lowered her voice with a smile. 'They say that if you kiss his feet it's good luck.'

Spike gave an involuntary shudder. 'It would have to be.' He'd always been faintly repelled by the Orthodox obsession with relics — scraps of desiccated corpses and cloth. Probably best to change the subject. 'Have you been out here long?'

'Just two weeks.' She touched her beaded braids and pulled a face. 'They're silly, I know. But I'm starting school in a few months, so ...'

She looked a bit old for an undergraduate. 'In England?'

'Boston.' She shrugged. 'My father wants me to do an MBA.'

'A Master's has its uses, I suppose.'

'Only if you're interested in making money.' She screwed up her face, and Spike found himself liking her a little more. But then the atmosphere changed, and he turned to see an imposing, well-built man striding over. Spike recognised Zachary Hoffmann immediately. It would have been difficult not to, given how his picture had dominated the British newspapers over the last decade, most of which he seemed to have owned at one time or another. He was stockier than his father, Sir Leo, but they shared the same colouring. His nose was crooked – a Cambridge boxing blue, Spike seemed to recall, a pastime squeezed in between membership of some of the less salubrious University drinking clubs. But he carried himself with the self-regard of a

man who'd already made more money than anyone in the previous five generations of his family. And he was scarcely older
than Spike.

Seeing her father approach, India took out her phone, muttered
an excuse and walked away.

'Was it something you said?' came Zachary Hoffmann's opening jab.

'It usually is.'

The media tycoon introduced himself as Zach, offering Spike a
thick hand as though it were a weapon to be admired. 'Good
holiday?' he asked, barely concealing his lack of interest in the
answer, focusing instead on the epic task of splitting a pistachio
between his thick thumbnails.

'Just arrived,' Spike said, finishing his last inch of champagne
with some regret. 'You?'

'Corfu's like a second home for us,' Zach replied, sucking a
moist green nut from his fist. 'Family's been coming here since
before I was born.' His keen eyes made an analytical sweep of the
terrace. Like father like daughter, Spike thought. Part of him
wanted to grab the man by his Huntsman lapels and say, 'Listen,
I don't want to talk to you either,' but instead he made himself
enquire as to how the Hoffmanns had come to be in Corfu.

'My mother used to summer here as a child,' Zach said in his
weary drawl. 'Introduced the old man to the island and he fell in
love with it. When he saw the monastery, he made an offer even
the Orthodox Church couldn't refuse.' He cracked open another
nut and swallowed it. 'I think he liked it because it was so close
to Albania.' Was that a glimmer of a fond smile, or was Spike
imagining it? 'The Reds still had it then, of course, but sometimes in the evenings I'd find him peering across at the ruins with
a telescope.'

'Butrint?'

Zach looked surprised that Spike had known the name. Spike
was a little surprised himself.

'Archaeology's more Dad's thing. We just used to come here and party.' He eyed Spike, seeking a gleam of knowing recognition, but Spike refused him more than a polite nod, turning instead to watch a new arrival strolling into the crowd, a well-dressed man with a handsome, Indian-looking face. He had the good taste to head straight for Jessica, Spike noted, taking an instant dislike to the man as he watched him steady a champagne flute that Alfie Hoffmann had left teetering on the terrace wall. Seeing Jessica flash the newcomer her most winning smile, Spike was about to suggest to Zach that they join them, when he heard the chink of metal on glass.

'So it begins,' Zach said, rolling his eyes.

Chapter Thirteen

'My friends,' Sir Leo Hoffmann began, 'it has been pointed out to me in no uncertain terms' – he glanced at Rufus with what appeared to be affection – 'that it is an act of monstrous hubris to host a party entitled "The Phaeacian Games".' Leo waited for a ripple of appreciative amusement, but the audience failed to oblige, not least because the sun had now climbed above Mount Pantokrator. Any fool not yet wearing shades reached into a pocket or designer clutch bag to slip them on.

'As many of you will no doubt know,' Leo resumed with misplaced optimism, 'the Phaeacian Games were held by King Alcinous to honour the arrival of Odysseus. A gesture of hospitality traditional to Ancient Greece, and still thriving in Corfu today, which is renowned for its *filoxenía*, or kindness to strangers.' He glanced from guest to guest, and Spike did the same, his eye settling again on the new arrival, a Bollywood star, he assumed, taking in the sharp cheekbones and glossy, jet-black hair. Or the captain of a subcontinental cricket team. He looked about Zach's age, and the two were standing side by side like equals, glancing somewhat disparagingly at the Chief of Police and an obese man Spike had now learnt was the Mayor of Corfu Town.

'The reason for my choice of title for the party will be made clear after lunch,' Sir Leo continued. Thank God, thought Spike – there were only so many tapenade tuiles a man could eat. 'In the meantime, just as Odysseus was entertained by a blind bard named Demodocus' – he nodded vaguely at the wings – 'so I offer you Carla Testa-Ferrata, who has cleared her busy schedule to fly in from Malta and delight us as we eat. Ladies and gentlemen, the great prima donna of our times.'

A heavily made-up woman squeezed into a sequinned evening gown glided onto the terrace. '*Brava*!' Rufus cried, his enthusiastic claps triggering an unsure smattering of applause, the sound instantly swept away by the rising breeze. The diva turned to her exhausted musicians, mustered a heroic smile, then launched into an aria from Monteverdi's *Return of Ulysses*.

In the middle of one long, tremulous note, Spike heard Zach lean over to his friend and say, 'Well, at least it's not The Tales of fucking Hoffmann.'

Spike turned away, watching his father sway at the front of the crowd, eyes closed, lost in reminiscence, oblivious even to the slow deliberate scrape of Alfie Hoffmann drawing out his chair over the flagstones.

Chapter Fourteen

A fillet of monkfish wrapped in bacon was teased onto Spike's plate as Carla Testa-Ferrata wound things up, sheer professionalism overcoming her appalled astonishment that the entire Hoffmann family was willing to talk over her performance. However much Sir Leo was paying her, Spike thought, it wasn't enough. Only Rufus had remained silent throughout, and Spike had watched him dab his eyes as the singer struck a particularly melancholy note from an opera called *Nausicaa*. His mother had loved that aria, humming along as their old twelve-inch crackled and spun.

'How old are you?'

Spike turned to find Zach appraising him with the disarming Hoffmann stare. 'Thirty-eight ... No, thirty-nine.'

'Well, which is it?' Zach said aggressively.

Spike stared back at him, vaguely intrigued by the man's need to provoke but unwilling to play along. Beneath the green eyes, Spike saw grey shadows, crease-marks pinched into the crooked bridge of his nose. Having failed to elicit the desired reaction, Zach asked instead where Spike had studied law.

'London.'

'Inns of Court?' For the first time, Zach looked interested, and Spike felt Peter slide a glance their way: to secure a member of the Hoffmann dynasty as a client would be a coup for any Gibraltarian firm. Spike nodded, half-heartedly spearing another chunk of the pork-soaked fish. He didn't know if it was the heat or the company, but his appetite seemed to have disappeared.

'Maybe you met my wife there,' Zach said. 'You're about the same age. Apparently.' He gave another mocking grin. 'Hélène de Savois?'

An abrupt jolt of memory. A coltish brunette, almost as pleased with the scale of her intellect as with the tiny particle in her surname, denoting descent from Marie Antoinette or some more minor member of the decapitated classes. She'd thrown herself at Spike at a house party, and he didn't recall resisting, though he'd always sensed she'd had bigger plans than netting a Gibraltarian mongrel on a government scholarship. 'Maybe,' he said, avoiding her husband's hard eyes.

'She's flying out on Thursday. You around?'

'Till next Monday.'

'We should meet up,' Zach said, mercifully without sounding like he meant it. His gaze fell on his son, who was toying with his iPhone across the table. He leant over to issue a quiet reprimand, and the phone was swiftly pocketed, Alfie consoling himself with a rebellious cigarette, eyes on his father's face like a toddler testing for boundaries.

Watching the youth smoke, Spike fought a compelling urge to join him. Instead he tried to relax into the chamber music, to savour the excellent white burgundy. But opposite, Rufus and Leo were still sparring over *The Odyssey*. 'Love and vengeance,' Rufus bellowed. 'It's as simple as that.'

Spike closed his eyes and tuned instead into his right, where India was talking passionately to the Mayor of Corfu Town about women's rights in Nigeria. Or was it Niger? Somewhere on his other side, he heard Lady Lucinda laughing at another of Peter's well-rehearsed bons mots – a harsh, jarring bray. A gloved hand discreetly refilled his glass. He pushed away his half-finished plate and gulped down the white wine, suddenly thirsty. Hélène de Savois … He hadn't thought about her in years. Would she even recognise him? After all that had happened, he barely recognised himself.

He looked again at the twins, analysing their fine bone structure, their white-blond hair. Could Hélène really be their mother? He seemed to recall an earlier ill-judged marriage to a skittish London shoe designer. Or had he imagined that? He felt a familiar clammy sweat on his back, and recognised the twisting coil in his chest with a dread. He tried to focus on something else, and Charlie floated into his mind, but then he remembered the night terrors, his terrified calls in the darkness for his murdered mother. How can I be responsible for a child? Spike wondered. For anyone?

A mix of sun cream and sweat was making his eyes sting, so he slipped on his sunglasses. 'Going to get some air,' he said abruptly to Zach, feeling curious stares fall upon him from around the table as he pushed back his chair.

Alfie Hoffmann glanced up as he passed. 'Bog-roll in the bin, pal,' he said in a surprisingly deep voice. 'No country should get to stay in the EU if their plumbing can't handle some shitty Andrex.'

But Spike had already walked past him to the path at the side of the house.

Chapter Fifteen

At the bottom of the creeper-clad flight of steps, Spike caught his first glimpse of the massive Hoffmann swimming pool, shimmering in the sun. A fleet of teak sunloungers surrounded it, a monogrammed beach towel neatly folded at the foot of each. The glass doored bar fridge was stocked with an international confederation of beers and soft drinks. Running alongside the pool, he saw a channel of water sliced into the flagstones – some kind of ornamental rill, he supposed. A selection of Mediterranean fish was swimming along it – rainbow wrasse, sea bream, cardinalfish – each looking slightly puzzled by its incarceration. At the near end, a seahorse dangled below the surface, and Spike focused on its strange, fantastical shape, willing his breathing to calm, his heartbeat to ease. As long as he could get away from other people, he knew the anxiety would fade. He didn't need some Spanish psychologist to tell him that.

He sat down heavily on a sunlounger and put his head between his knees, feeling the relentless Greek sun beat down on the back of his neck, squeezing his eyes closed as he tried to lose himself in the blood-red patterns dancing across his eyelids.

Then he felt the brush of a hand on his shoulder and smelled the citrus note of a scent he'd once known well. 'Zahra?'

He reached out and grabbed her wrist, eyes struggling in the sun. Slowly, a tall slim shape came into focus, and he made out a pale oval face and white-blonde braids. 'Sorry.' He dropped India Hoffmann's hand. 'I thought you were someone else for a moment.'

India took a hasty step back, rubbing her forearm. He could see the concern on her face, mixed with something else. She opened her bag and took out a soft pack of cigarettes. 'Do you smoke?' she asked, lighting one and holding it out to him with a small smile.

'Sometimes,' he said as he took it.

She sat down on the adjacent sunlounger and lit another Marlboro Light. They smoked in silence, then she touched his arm and he looked up. Watching them from the terrace above was Jessica, framed against the sun. She raised her glass to them and turned away.

'She's very beautiful,' India said.

'She is.'

India didn't seem to be asking for further elaboration but Spike offered it anyway. 'It's complicated.'

She gave a knowing smile. 'People always say you can't choose who you love. But I think that's a lie.' She took a last drag of her cigarette then ground it into the stone with her heel. 'At the start there's a moment when you can choose. Ignore the thunderbolt before it turns into something…'

'Complicated?'

She snapped closed her bag and stood up. 'You look better now.'

He *felt* better.

'We should get back.'

He followed her obediently up to the terrace, bracing himself for another hour of inconsequential chitchat, feeling a sudden ill will towards Peter for bringing them here. For subjecting him to this.

Jessica sought his eye as he retook his seat but he avoided it, rescued by another chink of silver tine on crystal.

Sir Leo was back on his feet. 'Just like Odysseus,' he said, 'we have been royally entertained by a bard and partaken in the finest food and conversation.' He waited for a member of staff to refill his glass. 'In ancient days, a libation would be made during a feast to appease the gods.' He sloshed a dash of red wine onto the ground, then urged the table to do the same. 'To Poseidon!'

With shy smiles and whispered amusement, the guests rose to their feet and poured out the top inch of their glasses. Watching the claret splash off the flagstones, bleeding into the hem of the white tablecloth, Spike sensed the silent judgment of the staff, and felt a sudden creep of shame.

'And now,' Sir Leo said, his voice quaking slightly. 'If I could ask you all to follow me.'

Chapter Sixteen

Peter sought Spike's arm as Jessica walked in icy silence on his other side. 'He's ex-Special Forces, I'm told,' Peter said in a conspiratorial whisper.

'Who?' Spike asked irritably.

'The Sri Lankan. Rajesh. Apparently Zach's bought a TV station in Colombia. Upset a few choice souls. Rajesh is his protection officer.'

Just then, a buzzard took off from a pine tree, spreading its frayed wings, its plaintive call just audible above the gentle wash of the Mediterranean. 'Augury,' Rufus cried, and Sir Leo beamed back, 'The gods must be with us.' Spike shook his head. They should just get it over with and move in together.

'Lady Lucinda seems very taken with him,' Peter added. 'Despite his humble beginnings in Bradford.'

'Probably recruited by MI6 for the War on Terror,' Jessica said, her first attempt at conversation since seeing Spike with India.

Spike glanced over his shoulder and saw Rajesh strolling confidently beside Zach. 'Suspect this may be a slightly more lucrative gig,' he muttered as he took in the man's Tod's loafers and elegant Patek Philippe watch. He offered Jessica an olive branch of a smile, from which she naturally turned away.

Sir Leo stopped at the top of a steep set of steps cut into the cliff. 'This way,' he called, and Peter gave a quiet groan.

But the steps led down to an easier path, and the land started to open up, a sheer drop to the sea on one side, and on the other, pegged against the hillside, a white tent. What elaborate finale to the Phaeacian Games awaited inside, Spike wondered sourly. Gladiator fights? Cirque du Soleil acrobats?

Leo placed a liver-spotted hand on the canvas curtain then turned to his guests. 'Corfu,' he said, and Spike could hear the emotion in his voice, 'has many things to offer us. Glorious beaches. Welcoming locals. A verdant and beautiful landscape. But one thing it has never enjoyed is an archaeological site of any note.'

Spike watched the Mayor exchange an expectant glance with the Chief of Police.

'It's an issue which has baffled archaeologists for centuries. Especially as some of the most important Greco-Roman ruins in the world lie just over the water in Albania.' Leo smiled: he had his audience now and was making the most of it. 'What's more, Corfu is referenced in one of the cornerstones of world literature, *The Odyssey*. Other Bronze Age sites mentioned by Homer have been identified, not least the discovery of Troy by Heinrich Schliemann.' His clipped pronunciation gave a first hint of the Hoffmann family's own lowly provenance. 'So where are the remains of the great Phaeacian civilisation which so delighted Odysseus?' Sir Leo slid a paperback from his jacket pocket. 'On Rufus Sanguinetti's advice, I read from Professor Fagles's verse translation of *The Odyssey*.' He cleared his throat. 'Here, Homer is describing the entrance to King Alcinous's palace. *And dogs of gold and silver were stationed either side, forged by the god of fire with all his cunning craft to keep watch on generous King Alcinous' palace, his immortal guard-dogs, ageless, all their days.*'

Sir Leo paused to let the lines of epic poetry sink in, then pulled back the curtain, revealing an archway of carved stone blocks leading into the hillside. Alongside, a crude dark column protruded from the slope. Alfie gave a derisive snort: anticlimax clearly appealed to him.

But the rest of the group gathered around for a closer look and saw that it wasn't a column at all, but part of a statue lying on its side. The pointed ears were rigid and alert, the head three times life-size. Through the corroded surface, Spike could make out a fanged muzzle, wide enough to stick a hand into. Something about the curl of the lips suggested the hand might not make it out again.

'*Doxa to Theo*,' the Mayor of Corfu murmured.

'My thoughts exactly,' Sir Leo said. '*Thanks be to God*. A bronze guard dog, cast in a sitting position, which in ancient times would have been covered in silver plate.' He jabbed a finger at his book. 'Just as the poem says. Now, before we move inside, might I ask you to step back, and look above you?'

The guests followed Sir Leo back along the promontory. 'Careful,' he said, pointing to the edge of the cliff with a smile. Then he gestured upwards, his stance against the brilliant sky the wild salute of a prophet. Following his gaze, they saw the towering east wing of the Hoffmann villa above, the old monastery steeple subsumed into two floors of extravagant extension, Mount Pantokrator presiding over it, lone buzzard still circling on a thermal.

'The Ionian Islands have long been blighted by earthquakes,' Sir Leo said. 'The locals used to believe they were cursed by Poseidon, who wasn't only the god of the sea, but was also known as "*Gaieochos*", "Earthshaker". And up there,' he said, 'I think we may see a little of the Earthshaker's work.'

From this vantage point, it looked as though a giant chunk had fallen away from the peak of Mount Pantokrator.

'A landslide on this scale would have been sufficient to destroy a Bronze Age city,' Sir Leo said. 'Maybe even an entire civilisation. Archaeologists such as Wilhelm Dörpfeld have scoured Corfu for landmarks mentioned in *The Odyssey* – the freshwater stream, for example, where Nausicaa washes her clothes before meeting Odysseus. But wouldn't such a natural disaster have altered those features for ever?' His sharp green eyes darted around the group. 'Perhaps the reason that Corfu's treasures have never been found is because the topography of the island has changed beyond recognition.' Lady Lucinda wrapped a sun-weathered arm around her husband's lean waist, and he smiled benevolently down at her. 'Come,' he said. 'See for yourselves.'

From within the archway came the gentle flicker of oil lamps on ancient stone.

Chapter Seventeen

The amber glow was reflected off a flat, rocky ceiling a foot above Spike's head. Tree roots dangled like desiccated worms, interspersed by fat, glistening stalactites. Spike raised a hand to the surface. It felt damp and friable, dark swirls visible within – fossilised wood, he assumed. A deep rumble came from above, provoking uneasy glances from the group as Zach lit another oil lamp, illuminating a wall constructed of large, irregular blocks.

'These stones are what first alerted me,' Sir Leo said in hushed tones. 'We were sinking a water pipe into the sea for the rill, when the builders told me they'd found some kind of structure hidden in the hillside. I'd just revisited Butrint, and seen from the Temple of Asclepius that the older walls were made of similar polygonal stones to these. Then an expert from London confirmed them as Mycenaean.' He shook his head as though he still couldn't quite believe it. 'That was when we started to dig.'

'If you're right,' Rufus said, 'then where we are standing is older than Tutankhamen's tomb.' He shook his head. 'An extraordinary privilege.'

Spike searched the shadows for Jessica and found her steadying Peter's arm, his face pale and waxy in the light of the oil lamp.

'What's through there, Leo?' Rufus asked, pointing towards another canvas curtain.

'Zachary?' Sir Leo gestured to his firstborn and Zach dutifully hunched through the next archway. A moment later, they heard the click of a lighter and saw the glow of more lamps. Sensing the hold that father had over son, Spike found himself almost forgiving the man his supercilious manner.

Another creak caused further gasps of concern. 'It's just an HGV on the coast road,' Leo chuckled, waving his guests on, 'over forty feet above us.'

But the group didn't seem that reassured as they moved into the second, smaller cavern. Spike stooped, breathing in the close, fetid air, struck by a sudden wave of claustrophobia.

'We believe that may be another of King Alcinous's guard dogs,' Leo said, pointing at a form obscured by lichen-covered masonry, 'but the structure is still unstable.' Spike could just make out a fat clawed paw sticking out of the ground, four times the size of a man's fist. Lying next to it, he saw the sharp prongs of what looked like an archaeological tool. 'This was probably Nausicaa's bedchamber in the southern wing of the palace,' Sir Leo continued. 'The ceilings were palisaded, of course, which is what would have saved them from the landslide...'

'What's over there?' Jessica asked. Spike heard a curious tone in her voice, and the group turned en masse to the other side of the cavern, where a long silhouette lay on the ground beside the far wall. There was a strange hush as Zach scraped the flint to light the last oil lamp. Once, twice, three times... Spike felt a sudden chill sweep the chamber. The wick finally took and a glow spread up the stones. And staring back at them, motionless, lay a figure.

At first Spike assumed it must be a worker, sleeping off a late night, or some unfortunate homeless man who'd sneaked inside for shelter. But, as the oil lamp gained strength, he saw that the figure's eyes were fixed, teeth clenched, one ashen cheek encrusted with something so dark it could only be blood.

There was a moment's silence, then the screaming began, rapid and shrill – Lady Lucinda, bejewelled hands covering her face.

India ran over to comfort her grandmother, but stopped as she saw the body, face rigid with shock. Alfie Hoffmann pushed forward through the crowd, drawing his sister away to shield her from the sight. Spike heard Peter give a groan of pain, and saw that he had been knocked to the ground in the confusion, Jessica kneeling by his side. Behind them, the Mayor started scrabbling with the canvas curtain, desperate to get out.

Then he heard a calm, authoritative voice. 'Everybody just take it easy.' Something in the clarity and volume made Spike assume that the person taking control must be Zach, but it was his protection officer, Rajesh, who had stepped forward. 'We're OK,' he said, a hint of warmth in his Yorkshire accent suggesting that one day this would make a great story for them all to tell. 'The gentleman behind us seems to have had some kind of accident. So we need to get everybody out of here as calmly and efficiently as possible to allow Mr Constandinos and his team' – the Chief of Police edged belatedly forward – 'to do their jobs.'

Spike saw Rajesh's dark, almond eyes flick between faces, gauging reactions. 'Does anyone know CPR?'

'I'm a detective in the Gibraltar Police,' Jessica said quietly.

If Rajesh was surprised he gave no sign of it, just watched as Jessica crouched down to test for a carotid pulse that no one expected she would find. Then she stood up with a discreet shake of the head. No one else would have noticed, but Spike saw her sway a little on her feet, and he grabbed her elbow to steady her. 'OK?' he whispered, seeing Rajesh glance over. She nodded back, but there was something in her face that told him she was not.

'Mr Constandinos,' Rajesh said. 'If you could man the curtains to give us clear access to the exit, that would be enormously helpful.'

As the chamber started to empty, Spike finally made out the face of the dead man. It was one he had seen at the Olive Press just the previous evening.

Sir Leo recognised it at the same time. 'My God,' he whispered, reaching out a hand to support himself on the damp stone wall. 'Arben,' he said, face crumpling. 'My poor, sweet Arben.'

Chapter Eighteen

They stood inside the iron gates of the Hoffmann house as dusk fell, waiting for Lakis to arrive. Peter was leaning heavily on his sticks, his larynx moving back and forth as though he was having trouble swallowing. Jessica put an arm around his broad shoulders, and Spike looked at his father, wondering if he should do the same. But Rufus's eyes were glittering more brightly than he'd seen in a long time, giving Spike a flash of insight into the tedium of a retired schoolmaster's life in Gibraltar.

A moment later, Rajesh emerged from the path down the side of the house. 'Is your driver on his way?' he asked, directing his question at Jessica, who appeared to have been deemed a person of consequence. His sleek black hair was wet with sweat, Spike saw, but his face was composed.

Jessica glanced at Peter. He opened his mouth to speak but no words came.

'Are you all right, Mr Galliano?' Rajesh said.

'Peter is fine,' Rufus said firmly. 'I can assure you that he's been through worse,' he added, and Spike felt a sudden surge of affection for his father.

'Bit of a shock for everyone, I expect,' Rajesh said with a sympathetic smile. He turned again to Jessica. 'I wanted to thank you. It's always a relief to find a cool head in this kind of situation. Like yours, Miss Navarro.'

'Detective Sergeant Navarro,' Spike said.

Rajesh gave a bow of apology – 'Of course' – but couldn't help throwing Jessica a mischievous grin. 'But I expect you don't get to see much action on the Rock, right?'

Jessica gave a stiff nod, but from the way that she narrowed her eyes, Spike knew that the man was dead to her. There was an uncomfortable silence, then the gates of the Hoffmann Estate started to open and the Fiat Panda appeared, Lakis beaming from behind the wheel, oblivious to the events of the day. To the fact that his old friend was dead.

'Just one more thing,' Rajesh said as Lakis pulled up. 'The Chief of Police has asked me to reiterate his request for discretion.' He lowered his voice: 'Until you've given your official statements, I must ask you not to say a word to anyone.'

*

Calypso waits nervously on the edge of one of the fixed plastic seats. The ferry to Brindisi has just left; the only remaining people must be on her boat.

Two old women sit opposite. Their black dresses and sparse grey hair tell her that they are widows for whom survival has long trumped appearance; the bulky canvas bags at their feet that they have been visiting their sons in Corfu Town. Calypso knows that inside will lie heavy canisters of olive oil, bags of flour and sugar – gifts from dutiful daughters-in-law. They sit in silence and pay her no heed. The past has taught them not to stare, even at a terrified girl with a bruised face and a nasty gash above one eye.

The family beside her are not so discreet. The man has a thin blond beard and Northern European skin. His son looks as though he may have some kind of medical condition – a grown man with the face of a child. The father must be kind, Calypso thinks as she watches them laugh together, though she wishes he wasn't, especially when he approaches. 'Do you need any assistance, Miss?' he asks. She wants to fall at his knees and beg him for help, but instead she just whispers back in English without looking up, 'I'm fine,' causing a momentary flicker of interest from the old women, which fades as quickly as it came.

Calypso stares down at her feet, at the cheap flip-flops that already rub painfully between her toes, bought this afternoon from a tourist shop in Corfu Town. She thinks of the bored expression of the bus driver when he reluctantly stopped for her on the road. A man who has picked up enough barefoot women outside Kavos not to worry if one has a little blood on her face. Not as long as she has money for the ticket.

Suddenly she senses someone coming into the waiting room. The icy fear starts to return, but it's just a Greek security guard, black flak-jacket further broadening his worked-out chest. Though he carries a weapon in the holster at his hip, she has seen enough of men to know that the vain ones are rarely dangerous. It's the anonymous types, the ones you wouldn't look twice at, that you need to beware.

A queue starts to form behind the men she passed smoking outside as she arrived. Albanians, of course – only her countrymen would wear leather jackets on an afternoon in the height of a Corfu summer.

Head down, Calypso joins the queue and reaches for her passport, running a finger over the double-headed golden eagle on the front, its purple cover a cheap imitation of the EU document still denied her people. She flips to the last page and stares at the photograph, her long dark hair unrecognisable now, eyes so large that her brother used to joke that she looked like a princess from a Disney cartoon.

The Customs and Immigration officer puckers her lip-glossed mouth, comparing the image of the smiling brunette with that of the redhead trying to look like she's not afraid to meet her stare. The officer is about to hand back the passport, then hesitates, and Calypso feels the panic tighten again in her chest. If they won't let

67

her through, if she is forced to stay in Corfu Town, the man will find her, she knows he will.

'Tell me,' the officer says quietly, and Calypso shuts her eyes, 'are you OK?'

She feels warm tears catch in her lashes, caught off guard by the woman's unexpected kindness, the gentleness of her tone, but all she says is 'I just want to go home', and holds out a hand. The official gives back her passport and waves her through, turning to watch as she picks up her bag and moves into Departures.

Through closed glass doors Calypso sees the ferry being readied by the jetty, 'Finikas Lines' on its hull, the same vessel that brought her here at the start of the summer. At the start of every summer. The Greek security guard blocks the exit, fiddling with his walkie-talkie, waiting for some kind of clearance to let them through. She looks at the digital clock above his head. The boat leaves in ten minutes. They should be boarding by now. Sixty seconds crawl past, then finally the security door slides open and she joins the other passengers on the long walk to the ferry.

One of the old ladies is struggling with her bags. Calypso offers to help but the woman shakes her head, just presses on stubbornly, as she has always done, back hunched.

A man in a camouflage baseball cap – a self-imposed uniform, Calypso knows, but one that makes him feel important – is checking tickets. She steps past him to the lower deck, three rows of tattered seats, metal ashtrays still in the armrests, each crammed with sweet wrappers. As ever, the Albanians cluster at the front, as they do on every bus, boat or train. Calypso still doesn't know why. Maybe it's because Enver Hoxha banned private cars for forty years and they want to know how it might feel to drive.

She chooses a window seat midway down the cabin. The ferry lies so low in the water that she can see only the black hem of the old woman's dress as she edges closer. At last she boards and the jetty is empty. Then the engines rumble and a reek of oil creeps through the lower deck. Calypso sits back. She feels as though she *has been holding her breath for three hours. She dabs the tender skin above her eye and this time no fresh blood stains the tissue. Perhaps it will be OK.*

The man in the army hat is untying the ropes. He's almost finished when he stops and turns. What is he doing? Calypso wants to get out of her seat and help him. Hurry, she thinks, please hurry. She peers desperately through the misty window then pulls back as she sees someone walking down the jetty.

A man's legs come into view, clad in grey tracksuit trousers. As he hands over his ticket, Calypso huddles down in her seat, and closes her eyes.

Chapter Nineteen

Spike lay back on his pillow, listening to the thrum of the cicadas, staring at the bars of white-gold sunshine projecting onto the ceiling through the shutters. The events of yesterday already felt like a bad dream. No one had spoken much over supper, when bland phrases like 'terrible accident' and 'awful shock' had been awkwardly exchanged. Jessica had been particularly quiet: Spike knew now what a shock it must have been for her to discover that it was Arben lying dead in the chamber – the handsome chancer who just twenty-four hours earlier had been flirting with her as he drove her away from the airport. Then, as they'd all retired to bed, Jessica had hung back and whispered something to Spike that had guaranteed him a night of insomnia. That as she'd checked Arben's body for a pulse, she'd discovered a puncture wound in his back. The implication was clear: this was no accidental death.

Spike picked up his mobile and checked the time, trying to remember what it was that had roused him. Six fifty a.m. And Corfu was an hour ahead of Gibraltar. No wonder he felt so exhausted. It was then that he heard it again, a low, hoarse wail from just outside his window.

He rolled out of bed and pushed open the shutters, eyes protesting at the light, brutal even at this early hour. On the slope above, he saw Katerina wrapped in a voluminous white dressing gown, curly hair wild, beating her fists against the roof of a police car. The engine fired, then he saw Peter heave into view, trying to lead the screaming woman away, struggling to maintain balance without his canes.

Spike pulled on his trunks, almost tripping as he ran outside, seeing a cloud of dust as the police car drove away at speed up the slope towards the coast road.

'Katerina?' he called out.

She spun round, jaw jutting with the useless defiance of a beaten boxer. 'They've taken him,' she whispered, instinctively holding out her arms. 'They've arrested Lakis.'

He smelt her face cream, felt the warmth of her tears as she pulled him close, her grip desperate and unrelenting. Looking down, he saw a purple smear running along the concrete beneath his feet, the guts of an overripe fig crushed under the tyres of the departing car.

Chapter Twenty

This time, no home-made delicacies nor hand-pressed juices adorned the table, just a jug of tap water warming in the sun and five thumb-smeared tumblers. Katerina sat in silence, head lowered. She'd changed into a black dress, but without her make-up, her effervescent energy, her face looked sallow and old. 'The state of this place,' she murmured, pink-rimmed eyes falling on the remains of breakfast fizzing with wasps on the sideboard.

Peter Galliano eased himself down next to her. He'd bruised his hip in the melee after Arben's body was found, it had emerged, and looked more diminished than ever. The pair seemed to have aged a decade overnight.

'Katerina,' Peter said softly, taking her hand between both of his. 'You have to tell us exactly what the police said.'

She took a gulp from the generous glass of brandy that Rufus had offered. 'They've arrested Lakis on suspicion of murder. They think he killed Arben.' She shook her head in disbelief. 'I didn't even know Arben was dead.'

Peter gave an apologetic nod. They'd all obeyed the Chief of Police's injunction to keep quiet about what had happened at the Hoffmann Estate.

'Lakis was his friend, Peter. His best friend.'

'The police probably just want to question him, Katerina,' Peter replied, giving her hand a reassuring squeeze. And once again, Spike admired his old friend's superior pastoral skills, his innate ability to put a frightened client at ease. 'Once they've established a time of death, Lakis will provide an alibi and that'll be the end of it.'

Though Katerina looked up at him with hope in her eyes, Spike couldn't help but notice that Jessica didn't seem especially convinced.

'It's because his father was Albanian,' Katerina said bitterly. 'That is how it is in Corfu.' She finished her brandy, her face so pale now that Spike could see the black hairs on her upper lip.

Peter looked as though he was going to say something, but decided against it, reaching instead for his e-cigarette, self-imposed disciplines evaporating in the face of a crisis, as they always did. Spike hoped there weren't any real fags knocking about the villa today.

'You'll help him, won't you, Peter?' Katerina said. 'You'll help my boy?'

Peter drew hard on the device, its tip burning red. 'I have no rights of audience in Corfu, Katerina.'

She gazed around the group in confusion.

'Peter means he can't speak in a Greek courtroom,' Spike said softly. 'He can appear in court in England or other British Overseas Territories. But not here.'

'But the state lawyers …' Katerina buried her head in her hands.

Peter threw Spike a meaningful glance, which he answered with a sharp shake of the head. But then Katerina started to sob, and Peter played his trump card and patted his stick. Recognising when he was beaten, Spike rose reluctantly to his feet.

Chapter Twenty-One

Spike consulted Peter's dual-language map as Jessica sped the Fiat along the coast road. His inability to drive rarely troubled him, but judging by Katerina's face as he'd climbed into the passenger seat, it had obviously bothered her. 'You couldn't be in safer hands,' Peter had offered as reassurance, but her expression of doubt had remained.

Spike gave up and threw the map onto the back seat. 'Just follow the signs to Corfu Town.'

'Very helpful, Spike,' Jessica said with a pitying shake of her head. 'Map reading. Another life skill you've failed to master.'

Spike thought back to Lakis's cheerful patter as they'd made this same journey in reverse just forty-eight hours earlier. His small kindnesses to Rufus, the 'Professor'. And Peter's whispered warning: 'If the Corfu police get the boy to confess, Spike, then that's it.' Time was against them, he was suggesting. Clearly sharing his opinion, Jessica dropped down a gear and overtook another Vespa.

'It was good of you to take the case,' she said, throwing him a sideways glance.

Spike pulled a face. 'It's not as though Peter left me much choice.'

'Katerina and Lakis must be important to him,' Jessica said. 'Usually it's him trying to dissuade you from taking on pro bono work.'

Spike pictured Peter splayed on a sunlounger as Katerina tried to massage some life into his shrunken legs. The way he allowed her to boss him around, to care for him. It was hard to square that with the man Peter used to be – brash, confident, larger than life. Dominating every room and conversation, with a huge appetite for everything, especially success. 'Things change,' was all he replied, pulling open the glove compartment to reveal a three-pack of condoms and a half-empty box of white-tipped Marlboro Lights, loose filter papers and crumbs of tobacco within.

Jessica glanced over. 'So what do you think?'

He closed the compartment, hoping she hadn't noticed the contents. 'God knows. I only just met Lakis. And we still don't know for certain that it was murder.'

'I may not be a pathologist, Spike,' Jessica said, pressing her lips together, 'but it looked like a stab wound to me.'

The road opened up into a dual carriageway as they reached the outskirts of Kerkyra, Corfu Town, the capital which gave the island its name. Open-air showrooms selling replica urns and statues lined the road, interspersed with travel agencies, bakeries, Persian rug stores, video rental shacks. Graffiti marked the concrete – football slogans and complaints about the financial crisis from the little that Spike could decipher. He reluctantly reached back for the map. 'I *think* that's the New Venetian Fortress,' he said, pointing out of the window at an enormous stone bastion guarding the north coast of the town. 'So the police station is on …' He looked down again. 'Alexandras Avenue?'

Jessica immediately turned the wheel and they entered a tree-lined, Parisian-style boulevard of crumbling townhouses.

One gracious, lemon-yellow building stood out from the rest. Its railings were ten feet high, a large blue and white Greek flag hanging limply from the colonial balcony. A tall policeman guarded the gate, arms crossed, eyes concealed by mirror shades. Parked behind him was a line of unmarked black Mercedes, the nearest with a detachable beacon light on the roof. It didn't look like any police station Spike had ever seen.

Jessica parked the car and they both got out. 'Is this police headquarters?' Spike asked.

The guard must have sensed the doubt in his voice as he lowered his sunglasses. 'It used to be a nunnery,' he said, winking at Jessica. 'Then a school. Then Nazi central office.'

'I need to talk to the duty sergeant,' Spike said, and the guard stood aside to let them pass, throwing an appreciative glance at Jessica's slim-fit white jeans as she passed.

A middle-aged man sat in the booth outside the portico.

'I'm here to see Lakis Demollari,' Spike said.

The man shook his head then turned a page of his newspaper, so Spike pulled out his Supreme Court of Gibraltar card. 'I'm his lawyer.'

The sergeant examined the card, then pushed it back. 'The prisoner has already been allocated a lawyer by the state. He saw him one hour ago.'

'I'm assisting the state lawyer,' Spike said, feeling his temper rise, but Jessica eased him aside and placed another card on the desk. Spike assumed it would be her Royal Gibraltar Police ID, but then he looked more closely. '*Colonel Spiros Constandinos*,' the card read in both English and Greek. '*Chief of Corfu Police*.'

'Mr Constandinos is a close personal friend,' Jessica said briskly. 'I'm sure you understand.'

Chapter Twenty-Two

The state lawyer's office was on the same street as the Municipal Theatre, an air-raid shelter of a building with arrow-slit windows puncturing the concrete facade. The front door was unlocked, so Spike pushed it open and walked into a draughty hallway paved in cracked marble. A wooden noticeboard gave details in both Greek and English of the professions housed within. Gynaecologist, orthodontist, psychiatrist... Then, on the third floor, '*Aristotelis Don. Theofilatos, Lawyer*'.

The one-man Schindler elevator was out of order. Passing a fuse box on the stairs with the panel hanging off, Spike remembered Katerina's concerns about the competence of Greek state lawyers, and prepared himself for a disappointing meeting. He found the correct door just past the dentist's surgery, rang the bell and waited. After what felt like an inconceivably long pause, he heard the faint sound of footsteps on the other side.

The door opened to reveal a small man with an impressive head of groomed, steel-grey hair. His well-cut navy suit was pinstriped, his red silk tie perfectly twisted into a Windsor knot. '*Yassas?*' he said.

'I'm here in connection with one of your clients, Dr Theofilatos. Lakis Demollari?' Spike immediately felt the man taking his measure. The genial smile remained in place but the quick dark eyes were subtly reading what they saw. 'You are a friend?' he asked in a crisp, accented English.

Spike pulled out a business card. As the Greek lawyer took it, Spike saw that his hand was deeply wrinkled, and realised that he must be much older than he appeared.

Aristotelis Theofilatos returned the card, and Spike waited for the inevitable rebuttal. But then his handsome face opened up, and he laughed. 'In a case such as this, I may need all the help I can get.' He stood aside, one hand on the door. 'Please, Mr Sanguinetti.'

The office comprised a suite of four elegant rooms. The mahogany reception desk was empty. 'My son and secretary are on holiday,' Aristotelis offered in explanation as he glided over the parquet in his leather-soled shoes. 'In summer, the natives are replaced by the tourists.'

'Not you, though,' Spike said.

Aristotelis turned. 'This is the first August I have been here for twenty years.' He ushered Spike into his own office. It was dominated by antique wood – furniture, panelling, floor – the grain illuminated by the sun pouring in through the floor-to-ceiling sash windows. Both were open, the busy street sounds of Corfu Town filtering up.

'You'll forgive me if I verify your credentials,' Aristotelis said, turning to a state-of-the-art Apple computer on the desk. Perhaps catching Spike's surprise, he added, 'My son has worked with me for ten years. I teach him the Law, he teaches me about the future.'

Spike looked politely away, eyes drawn to a polished sideboard laden with tasteful knick-knacks – ostrich egg, mother-of-pearl letter opener, what he assumed was a replica figurine of one of Degas's dancers – and walls decorated with lithographs of an ornate, stone-clad opera house. 'That was the original theatre in Corfu,' Aristotelis said without looking up. 'Inspired by La Scala in Milan.' He sighed. 'But Corfu Town was bombed by the Italians, then the Luftwaffe, and now we are left with a very modern idea of beauty.' Hearing Aristotelis's fingertips skitter over the keyboard, Spike wondered how much the man's son had really had to teach him. 'Excellent,' Aristotelis said, sitting back and gesturing at a leather-bound armchair on the other side of his desk. 'Now, let us talk.'

Spike sat down and explained that he had offered to assist Lakis – and his mother – in any way he could. Aristotelis must have picked up on his reticence as he nodded sympathetically. 'Not much of a holiday for you, Mr Sanguinetti.'

'There'll be others.'

'You do not look like the type to lie on a beach.'

Dr Kitty Gonzalez might agree, Spike thought. 'I'm working on that,' he replied, eager to get down to business. 'I expect there must be significant jurisdictional issues?'

Aristotelis gave the question a moment's careful consideration. 'We may say that you are acting as Counsellor to the defence lawyer. We see this quite a lot in Corfu.' There was a sparkle in his eyes now. 'Usually when the son of a rich British tourist gets himself into a little trouble.'

'I don't expect payment.'

'Nor do I,' Aristotelis laughed. 'No one on the catalogue makes any money.'

'The catalogue?'

'The list of state defence lawyers. I haven't put my name on it for decades. But my wife is' – he paused as he selected the appropriate word in English – 'indisposed. We were advised to stay at home for the summer, so…' He straightened the knot of his tie, which had slipped just a fraction.

'I tried to visit Mr Demollari this morning,' Spike said, rapidly drawing the conclusion that Lakis was in extremely capable hands. 'All the duty sergeant would give me was your address.'

'You were lucky to get that.'

Spike began to explain that Jessica was waiting to meet the Chief of Police in order to secure the inside track when Aristotelis reached for a folder at the edge of his desk. 'Miss Navarro may be a little late to influence matters, I'm afraid. The police report has already arrived.' He arched a black eyebrow. 'Shall we say ... unusually fast.' He flipped through pages filled with close Greek typescript until he found what he was looking for: the Pathologist's Report. 'The victim, Mr Arben Avdia, died between six p.m. and midnight on Monday, which ...'

'What was the cause of death?' Spike interrupted.

Aristotelis translated as he read, one finger tracing the relevant paragraph. 'He received a blow to the head, probably from a piece of stone. In a ... sea cave?' He looked up with a puzzled smile.

Spike waved it away. Probably best to save talk of King Alcinous for later.

'But the fatal wound was to his back,' Aristotelis continued, looking back down. 'Made by some kind of tool. His spinal artery was severed.'

'How do the police know about the weapon?'

Aristotelis slid over a photograph and Spike recognised one of the architectural trowels that he had seen at the site. 'Because it was found this morning when they searched our client's room.'

The long, thin blade was encrusted in blood. 'I see,' Spike said, trying to keep the despondency from his voice.

'Quite,' Aristotelis agreed. 'Unfortunately it also seems that Lakis Demollari has no real alibi for the estimated time of death.'

Spike sat back as the import of these two pieces of information hit home. There was no doubt about it: Lakis was in serious trouble. 'May I talk to him?'

Aristotelis hesitated. 'You seem impatient, Mr Sanguinetti. I hope that does not mean you are also reckless.'

Spike said nothing, just picked up the desk phone and held it out. Aristotelis Theofilatos paused for a moment, then made the call.

Chapter Twenty-Three

Spike walked along the tongue of land upon which Corfu Town had been built. Once past the New Venetian Fortress, the buildings started to age and intrigue. Italianate palazzi with intricate balconies overhung the narrow streets, opening up into paved squares lined with ice-cream parlours and over-styled cafés. The pavements thronged with cruise ship passengers and day trippers. Only the Orthodox churches and skinny white cats basking on walls felt authentically Greek.

A series of shady alleys fanned into a wide esplanade, protected by another sea fort, the Old Venetian Fortress according to the map, though it looked no older than its younger counterpart. On its flat, circular stone roof, Spike could make out tiny stick people moving around an enormous wooden crucifix. He passed a bandstand, crammed with bored French schoolchildren ogling a cart selling candyfloss on sticks, then heard a surprising sound: the juicy thwack of willow on leather. Looking up, he saw Jessica Navarro sitting at a table outside a café tucked beneath a long stone colonnade. Beyond her lay an impressively green cricket pitch.

'Nice view,' Spike said as he pulled out a metal chair. 'Very colonial.'

'Apparently the street is modelled on the rue de Rivoli. Courtesy of Napoleon's two-year tenure in Corfu.'

Spike canted his head: Jessica was not known for her love of French architecture. She grinned and pointed towards a thin man in black tie watching them as he surreptitiously sucked on a ciga-rette. 'The waiter's been highly attentive. Until now.'

Spike raised a hand and the man approached.

'Ginger beer, please,' Spike said.

The waiter nodded. 'And for the lady?' he smiled.

'I'll have another Mythos.'

Jessica watched him go, then turned to Spike, eyes hidden behind a pair of last season's Gucci shades. 'So?'

Spike told her about his meeting with Aristotelis. 'The process in Corfu is for the police to gather evidence, then send the file to the Public Prosecutor, who decides whether or not to proceed. According to Mr Theofilatos, it usually takes about five days, but in this case the police seem to be moving at light speed.'

'The Hoffmann factor.'

'Sounds like an airport thriller,' Spike replied, watching the waiter approach with a tray. 'If Lakis is charged,' he resumed once the drinks had been offloaded, 'he'll be transferred to prison, where he could wait for months, even years, before the trial.' He sipped his ginger beer and grimaced. He wouldn't be ordering it again. 'How about you? Did you see the Chief of Police?'

'Eventually.'

'And?'

'He spent a great deal of time explaining to me that it was none of my business. But he did say that they're treating it as murder.' She removed her glasses and polished the large brown lenses on the tail of her cotton shirt. 'And that they think it's connected to the Albanian Mafia.'

'The Mafia?' Spike might have laughed had the look in Jessica's eyes not told him she was serious.

'They discovered over a hundred grams of marijuana in Lakis's room.'

Spike thought about the huge stash found on one of the drug-dealing clients he was defending back in Gibraltar. 'Come on, Jess.'

But she wasn't done yet. 'Apparently Arben comes from a village in Albania that produces marijuana. A lot of marijuana. Three quarters of the marijuana in the entire Mediterranean, to be precise.'

Spike suddenly began to feel a little worried. A cry went up from the cricket pitch, and he turned to watch a fielder waiting for the ball to drop, shielding his eyes from the glare. The man caught it, but then it slipped from his grasp and fell to the ground. There was a widespread groan. 'Did the Chief mention the murder weapon?' Spike asked.

Jessica narrowed her eyes. 'They've sent it to Athens where they'll run DNA tests.' She took a sip of her Mythos. 'Though I don't expect there's any doubt that they'll find the blood is a match to the victim.'

'*Buximu*,' Spike cursed, switching to *yanito*, the dialect of Hebrew, Spanish and Italian spoken by native Gibraltarians. 'What kind of idiot do they think would hide a murder weapon in his room when he could have just thrown it into the sea?'

'The kind of idiot who sits around getting stoned every night?' Jessica said.

Spike kept his counsel. He knew that Jessica had seen enough of the damage inflicted by 'recreational' drug users in her time to have earned the right to a low tolerance threshold for the type. On the pitch, the reprieved batsman stroked another ball towards the boundary.

'If you want my professional opinion,' Jessica said, sliding her glasses back on, 'your client is fucked.'

Spike was still weighing an appropriate response when his phone rang. He picked it up with some relief. 'Aristotelis?' He listened for a moment, then gestured to Jessica, who dug out a biro from her handbag.

Ioulias Andreadi, Spike scribbled on the back of the café napkin. *The Old Hospital.*

Chapter Twenty-Four

Spike waited alone in the interview room, staring out of the locked window onto a small overgrown courtyard. According to Aristotelis Theofilatos, the Old Hospital would soon be housing all of Corfu's emergency services under one roof, but judging by the state of that roof, the move was still some way off. Another victim of the financial crisis, Spike guessed. But the Corfu police had made a pre-emptive move, and rooms that had once been occupied by the ill or dying were now being used as holding cells for criminals. The interview room where Spike sat might have been a nurses' station; he could even see where the holder for the hand-sterilising gel had been unscrewed from the wall, presumably to avoid it being used as a weapon.

The air-conditioning worked, but the door had been left ajar, the stuffy atmosphere of the corridors and wards leaching out the coolness. Spike stood up to close it, then heard a squeak of rubber soles and sat back down.

The policeman appeared first, a vast house of a man with sad eyes and acne-scarred cheeks. Behind him trailed Lakis, hands cuffed at his groin.

The guard barked something in Greek, and Lakis sat down, holding out his arms like a child, wincing as the tiny key was twisted in the lock. The officer issued another terse diktat, then retreated, pulling the door closed behind him.

The room suddenly felt ominously quiet. Spike made a swift assessment of the psychological state of his client. Though Lakis wore the same shorts and reggae T-shirt as when he'd picked Spike up from the airport, his once unquenchable enthusiasm and insouciance had vanished. And looking at the scared young man sitting in front of him, eyes downcast, head bowed, Spike found it hard to believe such traits had ever existed. His face was blanched with fear – or exhaustion – and covered in wiry dark stubble. Denied its palliative dose of styling wax, it was clear that his black hair was thinning.

'Is there anything you need, Lakis?' Spike asked. 'Are they treating you well?'

Lakis massaged the red weals around his wrists. 'Twenty minutes,' he said.

'Sorry?'

Lakis raised his voice. 'The guard said we have twenty minutes.'

Spike nodded. 'Did Aristotelis explain why I'm here?'

'To help me,' Lakis said simply, looking up for the first time.

'Absolutely,' Spike replied, keeping his tone confident. 'Peter would have been here as well, but in his condition…'

Lakis cut him off. 'I understand.'

In the absence of his usual kit – the ancient Dictaphone which he used to record his client interviews – Spike had to make do with a notebook bought in haste from a tourist shop. The only one not emblazoned with an image of a beach or traditional caique sailboat had been a fuchsia pink. The cheerful colour leaked depressingly through the first page.

'Tell me about Monday night, Lakis.'

Lakis rubbed his brow as he prepared himself to answer a question he had undoubtedly heard many times before. 'Never ask a client if they're guilty,' Peter always advised. 'Let the accused come up with their own defence, then show them how to strengthen it.' In the early days of their partnership, Spike had made his ethical scruples clear, but his mentor had just laughed and countered with another of his favourite maxims: 'Why don't we just let the law take care of itself?'

'I drove Arben to the Hoffmann Estate at nine p.m.,' Lakis began. 'Most of the staff were working that night because of the party.' He gave a bitter smile. 'I was on laundry duty.'

'And Arben?'

'He went down to sweep the pool terrace.' Lakis held Spike's eye. 'Arben might have talked like a philosopher but he was an excellent cleaner all the same.'

'Did you see him later that night?'

'No.'

'And what time did you leave the laundry?'

'Midnight.'

'Are you sure?'

'I had to get up early to serve you breakfast, didn't I?' Lakis snapped. 'I needed to get some sleep.'

Spike made a note on his pad, giving his client a moment to collect himself. 'Did anyone see you leave?'

'I've already told this to my Greek lawyer.'

'Are you aware that the police found the murder weapon in your room?' Spike deliberately left the edge in his tone.

'Yes...' Lakis's voice was no more than a whisper now.

'Then perhaps you could manage to tell me again.'

'No one saw me leave. Everyone was either gone – or asleep.' He paused, as if weighing up whether to say any more. Then he added quietly, 'But someone did see me at the staff exit.'

Spike looked up.

'I'd parked the car in the field above the road, as usual, so the Fiat didn't *offend*' – his lip curled – 'Lady Lucinda. But as I was going through the gate, I saw a girl sitting in the yard.'

'Who was she?'

Lakis shrugged.

'You didn't know her?'

'I just assumed she was there to help with the party. The Hoffmanns often need extra staff for big events.'

'Did you talk to her?'

'Of course; I drove her home.'

Spike felt his spirits lift. Things were looking up. 'Did you tell Aristotelis about the girl?'

'He was only interested in what happened before midnight.'

Spike nodded. Aristotelis hadn't said that Lakis didn't have an alibi, he realised – just that he didn't have a good one. 'So what was she doing by the staff exit?'

'She told me she was waiting for a cab. I said I'd be up on the road if she wanted a lift.'

'Doing what?'

'Having a smoke.'

Spike frowned. 'Weed?'

'It helps me sleep,' Lakis said defensively. '*Mama* doesn't like it, so I never smoke at home.'

'So you were having a smoke.' Spike tried again. 'OK. And then?'

'The girl followed me up. Said her cab hadn't arrived.'

Spike took out the photocopied file Aristotelis had given to him and started riffling through it. 'Where did you take her?'

'Kavos.'

Spike tried to remember where Kavos was. 'That's a bit of a trek, isn't it?' he said, taking a punt.

Lakis nodded. 'Forty-five minutes each way. But' – a trace of his cheeky smile – 'she was pretty.'

Spike didn't smile back. 'Did she tell you her name?'

Lakis looked scared again. Though his stubble made him seem older, Katerina had said he'd only turned twenty-one last May. 'I asked her but she didn't answer.' He chewed his lower lip. 'She didn't say much at all.'

Spike pulled a copy of the Hoffmann staff list from the file and held it out. 'Is the girl listed here?'

Lakis didn't even bother looking at it. 'No.'

'I thought you said you didn't know her name.'

'I didn't…I don't. But look.' Lakis snatched the paper from Spike's hand and started reading. 'Stamatina Kalyvas.' He jabbed at another name. 'Olympia Nikolaidis.' He thrust the sheet back. 'I know *all* these people. I grew up with them. She's not a member of staff.'

'What about the additional people hired for the party?'

Lakis gave a weary shake of his head. 'The police showed me pictures. Hers wasn't there.'

Spike sat back. 'So what did she look like, Lakis?'

'Big eyes. Nice…' Lakis touched his chest, then looked away. 'Bright red hair.'

'Dyed?'

He thought for a moment, then nodded.

'Where did you drop her?'

'At the end of the strip. She said she lived above a sports bar.'

'Which one?'

Lakis rubbed his eyes. 'I can't remember, Mr Sanguinetti. There are a lot of bars in Kavos.'

'So you didn't see her go in?'

'No.'

'And you don't know her name?'

'I told you!' Spike watched as the boy struggled to get a hold of himself. After a moment he continued, 'But I don't think she was Greek.'

'Albanian?'

Lakis hesitated. 'Maybe.'

'There are thousands of Albanians in Corfu. Don't you recognise the accent?'

Lakis slammed his hands down on the desk. 'I was born here, Mr Sanguinetti. I'm a Greek national, OK?'

Spike laid down his pen. It was time to broach the issue which had been bothering him. 'Why were you arguing with Arben the night he died?'

Lakis didn't look up. 'I don't know what you mean.'

'I was there, Lakis.' He crossed his arms, losing patience. 'Or don't you remember that either?'

'It was nothing.'

'Was it about drugs?' Spike asked, leaning in.

Silence.

'Arben's family are pretty interesting, aren't they?'

'We never talked about his family.'

'The police say he was involved in smuggling drugs into Corfu. Did you know that?'

Lakis laughed in disbelief.

'They think that you were selling the drugs on. Odds are, they're going to say that you fell out over money.'

'And that I killed him because of that?' Lakis lowered his head into his hands, his posture screaming the conviction that everyone was out to get him, even his own brief. When he looked back up, his eyes were hard and contemptuous. 'You don't know shit about me, mister,' he said, and Spike caught a sourness to his breath, the reek of an empty stomach. 'Enough of the bullshit, OK?'

Spike didn't respond, just waited, holding his client's eye.

'Rich people like you and your father and your hot girlfriend come to Corfu for a holiday. For the figs and the Greek yoghurt and honey.' He smirked. 'For the fucking retsina. Then people like me and *Mama* and Arben clean up your shit. Literally. There are thousands of us – waiters, tennis coaches, masseurs, chefs. We pretend we enjoy it, you pretend we enjoy it, and for four months we run around like crazy and make enough money to live for the rest of the year. It works, just about. Until something goes wrong. Or someone gets hurt. And then people like you find someone like me to blame.' Lakis paused, desperation straining his voice. 'But I'm no different to you. When you go back to your life in Spain, or England, or wherever the fuck you're from, I'll continue my studies at the Ionian Academy. I wash your plates, I iron your shirts, but one day I'll be just like you. Then maybe I'll pay someone to look after me.' He grinned. 'Arben was the same. Leo Hoffmann met him in Butrint and …'

'Butrint?'

Lakis broke off. 'He was working at the ruins as a guide. Leo liked how he talked and offered him a job in Corfu.' Lakis blinked, trying to gather together the threads of his monologue, but his anger had faded now, burnt itself out. 'Arben was going to continue his studies when his visa came through.' His voice grew small: 'Sir Leo had offered to pay for him to train as an archaeologist.'

Suddenly the door opened and the enormous guard reappeared. '*Grígora*,' he ordered, and Lakis got to his feet. 'I didn't kill him, Mr Sanguinetti,' he said as he reached the door. This time, when he turned, Spike thought he saw truth in his eyes. 'He was my friend.'

'Then help me, Lakis. I can't help you if you won't talk to me.' Something twisted in Spike's bowels. Where had he heard that before?

'That night, when we argued,' Lakis said as he held out his wrists. 'It *was* about drugs. But not like you think.' He risked a glance at the guard, but the Greek giant's face was impassive, uncomprehending. 'Arben didn't like me smoking. I told him that dope didn't hurt anyone, and he said I didn't know what I was talking about.'

Lakis winced as the cuffs clicked closed. 'Arben hated drugs,' he called from the doorway. 'That's why he wanted to leave Albania.'

The door closed, and then all Spike could hear was the tread of soles on hospital linoleum as the guard led Lakis back to his cell.

Chapter Twenty-Five

Jessica was waiting for him in the car outside the Old Hospital, driver's door open for ventilation. A handsome Greek policeman straddling a motorcycle had pulled up alongside. When he saw Spike approach, and registered the look on his face, he gave Jessica a regretful smile, then knocked down his visor and revved away.

'Making friends?' Spike asked, trying to keep his voice light.

'Jealous, Spike?' Jessica said tartly, and he realised that she was still annoyed with him about his tête-à-tête with India Hoffmann. She tossed him a newspaper as he got into the car. 'Seems our man has made the local news. Only page eight, but he's there.'

The script was in Greek. Spike passed the paper back. 'How do you know?'

'The nice policeman was kind enough to translate. He's called Spiros, by the way.'

'Naturally. Can we go now?'

Jessica twisted on the engine and they pulled out of the hospital forecourt.

'Did the article mention the Hoffmanns?'

'Apparently not,' Jessica said. 'But the word "Albanian" seems to come up a lot.' They rounded a corner. 'According to Spiros, that's the prison,' she went on, pointing at a huge dull building constructed from grey concrete. Razor wire lined the battlements, broken only by platforms on which armed guards sat staring down at the road through dark glasses. 'Maximum security. Not just for Corfiots – some of the worst criminals in Greece are locked up inside.' The double portcullis gate seemed to confirm what Jessica had learnt. 'Not a pleasant place to serve out a life sentence.'

'I get it,' Spike said, then softened his tone when he saw Jessica's face. 'It's not like I don't understand what's at stake here, Jess.'

They drove on in silence. Eventually she defrosted enough to ask him what had happened in the interview with Lakis. She listened, then sighed. 'It's not exactly a watertight alibi.'

Spike had to agree. 'But don't you think it's odd that the Chief of Police didn't tell you about the girl?'

'He was under no obligation to tell me anything.' Jessica shook her head. 'I'm sure he's being pressurised to get a conviction as quickly and quietly as possible.' She looked as though she might know how that felt.

'If you'd just killed a man in cold blood, would you be offering a pretty girl a lift home?'

Jessica said nothing, just shifted the gear into fifth.

'And what would Lakis have done with the murder weapon?' Spike went on, realising he'd already made up his mind. 'Where was the blood? The police should at least be looking for the girl. Making some effort to follow it up.'

Jessica conceded a nod, and he pressed on. 'I'm just asking you to consider why the police are rushing this. You have to agree that the fact the Hoffmanns are involved must have something to do with it.'

She laughed. 'You know you sound like every grubby defence lawyer I've ever met. Spinning convenient conspiracy theories. Clutching at straws. Anything to get your client off.'

Spike smiled back. 'I wouldn't have to if the police did their job.'

That killed the mood again, so Spike took the opportunity to call Aristotelis and tell him about the interview. Something in the

Greek lawyer's muted tone made Spike suspect that he might be with his wife, so he cut the conversation short and arranged a meeting for the following day. 'Can you turn in here?' he said to Jessica as he hung up.

'But the Olive Press is ...'

'I know, Jess. Just back up, will you?'

She threw him a furious look, then reversed into a gap between some rickety fencing. Above the road rose an olive grove, black nets laid out beneath the low branches to catch the fruit.

'Here's perfect.'

'I'm not a bloody cab, Spike,' Jessica called after him through the window.

He tried a charming grin, then scrambled up the bare patch of earth. Either the olive trees had died here – most of them looked ancient, dark ovals scoring their trunks – or this part of the field had been left deliberately fallow. Tyre grooves scored the dried earth as Spike knelt to pick up a cigarette butt, one of many littering the ground. Pressing it to his nose, he caught the herbal sweetness of cannabis.

'What are you doing, Poirot?' Jessica asked as she joined him on her hunkers.

'Just trying to work out how much to trust Lakis.'

'You want me to bag that?' She was laughing at him again. 'Get it checked for DNA?'

Spike rose to the full extent of his six-foot-three frame. Beyond the trees, he could just make out the top of the wall that marked the perimeter of the Hoffmann Estate. 'I think I'll take a more direct approach,' he called back as he strode towards the car.

Chapter Twenty-Six

A chrome intercom was set discreetly into the cool stone gate-post. Jessica held down the button and waited, watching a CCTV camera turn above, zeroing in on the car. Then an internal mechanism clicked and the gates began to open.

Jessica parked at the edge of the turning circle as the guardian of the house appeared, an Englishman named Mike, his nationality a source of local irritation, Katerina had hinted – why not just employ a Corfiot? Mike's thick beard covered half of his face; despite living permanently beneath the Greek sun, his skin remained stubbornly pale. He peered disparagingly at the Fiat, then shook Spike's hand, his clasp as weak and damp as might have been expected. 'Are you here to pick up your father?'

Spike stifled his surprise. 'That's right.'

Despite its size, the front door was perfectly proportioned, opening with the slightest touch of Mike's fingertip. Spike realised he hadn't made it into the Hoffmann house during the Phaeacian Games as the festivities had been conducted entirely outside. The ground floor was an open-plan space so huge that it might have been a warehouse had the furniture not been so artfully arranged. Rooms within a room appeared to be the motif: three massive sofas and a perspex coffee table carved out a sitting room; a wall lined with beautifully crafted bookshelves created a library ambience, complemented by off-white easy chairs and a giant chessboard. A well-stocked drinks trolley stood beside an unusable chaise longue formed of twisted olive roots, while an ottoman containing board games and quizzes – Jenga, backgammon, Trivial Pursuit – looked perfect for the rainy day. Dotted around were what appeared to be original Greek artefacts – priceless amphorae, androgynous statues with their noses missing for centuries.

'Your father's down by the pool,' Mike said, his accent hinting at a rural English childhood, West Country, Spike guessed – 'down' had been 'doane'.

'Got it. Oh, Mike?'

The guardian turned.

'The day of the party. Do you remember a girl with dyed red hair?'

Mike stroked his beard, releasing tiny flakes of skin that spun and danced in the sunlight.

'One of the extra staff?' Spike pressed. 'Possibly an Albanian?'

Mike shook his head, causing Jessica to step hurriedly back. 'I think I'd have remembered someone like that.' He frowned. 'Why?'

'No reason. We can make our own way down.' A bright, dismissive smile. 'Thanks for your help, Mike.'

The man hovered, unsure whether to leave the custodians of a 1999 Fiat Panda unattended in the Hoffmann house. Then he left beneath a mosaic chequered with missing pieces.

Jessica's stern expression dissolved into laughter. Spike put a finger to his lips, then pushed her through a set of sliding doors. Within, part-obscured by an urn threaded with mimosa branches, they found a woman sitting straight-backed at a leather-topped desk, her long fingers dancing over a keyboard. Despite not having seen her for nearly two decades, Spike recognised her profile immediately.

Hélène de Savois finished typing her sentence before standing up. 'How do you do?' she asked formally, her French accent even more pronounced than Spike remembered – an affectation, he'd always thought, but perhaps she spent a lot of time in Paris these days, away from her husband.

Hélène's sunglasses were wedged up on her glossy, caramel-brown hair, her forehead smooth and lightly freckled, stretched so taut that even Spike could tell she'd had a little help. But the clever grey eyes were the same as he remembered. Spike stared into them, searching for a glimmer of recognition, but none came. 'This is Jessica,' he said. 'And I'm Spike.'

Hélène offered a thin smile, then withdrew her hand, slim body already straining back towards the laptop. Spike glanced at the screen and recognised the bullet-pointed format of a legal brief.

'We'll leave you to it,' Jessica said, edging Spike towards the door.

As they emerged onto the sun-terrace, Spike risked another look at Zachary Hoffmann's second wife and was surprised to find her staring back at him. But then she leant over and pushed the door shut. Jessica mimed a shiver, and Spike smiled, unsure if he was relieved or troubled that a woman he had once kissed had felt the need to deny their acquaintance.

Outside, one end of the dining table was being laid up. Spike tried to question a member of staff, but she just shrugged in response, unable to speak English. Out in the Corfu Channel, the afternoon sun had brought out the water-skiers, motorboats dragging rubber tyres stuffed with sunburnt children shrieking in English. From below came raised voices. Jessica nodded at Spike, and they headed together down the steps.

Chapter Twenty-Seven

A ping-pong table had been erected in the glaring sun by the pool. As Spike and Jessica approached, they saw a game in progress, Rajesh and Alfie clipping the ball low over the net, each heavily topspun shot requiring a sprint to receive, bare feet slapping hard against the hot wet paving stones. Watching the two bare chested men was Zach, sitting in a rattan chair, a faded Harvard Business School baseball cap shading his iPad, the glimmering Corfu Channel laid out in front of him as if for his personal pleasure.

Rajesh stooped low to retrieve a cross-shot from Alfie, somehow angling his return for a winner.

'Fuck!' Alfie cried, throwing down his bat in fury and something else.

'21–9,' Rajesh said, waggling a finger. 'Punition.'

Alfie shook his head, then turned his back to the table, his ribs heaving, hands clenching his biceps, obscuring the mystical message of his Chinese tattoo – or an order for chicken chow mein, Spike rather hoped. Alfie's pale skin was streaked with sunscreen, but as he leant forward, Spike saw raised purple welts covering his shoulders and upper back.

Rajesh took a moment to aim, then smashed the ball at the target, relishing the high-pitched snap as it collided with the zip-lock of Alfie's spine.

'Christ!' Alfie stifled a scream of pain as a new welt began to form.

'Just twelve more to go, Alfie,' Rajesh said, stooping to pick up the ball, his torso ridged and powerful, as though each muscle had been individually identified and trained.

Spike looked back and saw Zach still watching from his chair, a smile playing on his freckle-rimmed lips. Then he noticed Spike and Jessica, and stood up.

'Raj,' he said quietly, and Rajesh turned. A long bruise ran down Rajesh's flank, and Spike wondered darkly to which Hoffmann family tradition it could be attributed.

'We call it Red Spot,' Zach said, 'for obvious reasons.' He placed his iPad on the seat of his chair, and Spike saw a complex series of graphs zigzagging over the screen.

Hands were shaken, Rajesh kissing Jessica on both cheeks, from which she pulled away as soon as courtesy would allow, Spike was pleased to note.

'What a mad day that was,' Rajesh said.

'A tragic day,' Jessica corrected, and Rajesh's confident smile fell just a little.

'You're here for your dad, right?' Zach said.

Spike nodded. He was still trying to work out what his father was doing at the Hoffmann Estate as Zach jerked his head towards the pool house. 'He and my old man have been at it all afternoon. Hammer and tongs.' He wedged two stubby fingers between his lips and whistled, but the silhouettes in the pool house gave no indication of having heard. 'You'd better tell them yourself,' he said, tapping a small, slightly cauliflowered ear.

Spike started to walk away, then turned. 'I saw Lakis today.'

Zach gave a baffled shrug, so Spike helped him out. 'One of your employees?'

Zach responded with the unembarrassed smile of a billionaire who couldn't possibly be expected to know the name of every person who worked for him.

'He's also the man accused of murdering Arben Avdia. Presumably you remember him?'

Zach pulled off his sunglasses. 'You're not *defending* him, I hope?'

'Just assisting with the case.'

His unreadable green eyes slid across to Rajesh.

'The thing is,' Spike went on, 'it seems that Lakis has an alibi.' He glanced from father to son to protection officer. 'A girl saw him leaving the estate. A redhead?'

Zach crossed his sandy-haired arms like a bouncer considering whether to expel an annoying drunk. His chest was heavy and completely hairless, Spike saw. He found himself wondering if it had been waxed, then forced the thought from his head with a shudder.

'I'm a bit confused here, Spike. What's your point?'

Jessica chimed in, her voice soft and unchallenging – playing good cop, Spike assumed. 'Lakis gave the girl a lift home.' She cocked her head coyly. 'But we can't seem to find her name on the staff list.'

'You definitely don't remember a girl with red hair at the house on the day of the party?' Spike reiterated to Zach.

Zach shook his head and gestured at Rajesh.

'The only ginge here is the Hoff,' Rajesh said, slapping Zach playfully on the back. From the look on Zach's face, Spike suspected he might be pushing the employer–employee relationship to its limits. A wise dog doesn't nip its master.

'What about you, Alfie?' Spike called over.

The young man turned from the table, twirling his bat in one hand in a vain attempt to regain some dignity. 'A mysterious redhead?' he called back in his throaty voice. 'Alas, no one that interesting has visited the house all year.'

'Sorry not to be able to help,' Zach said, slamming closed the conversation as he waved them towards the pool house.

'Oh well,' Spike replied, challenging him with a smile. 'I suppose we'll just have to keep digging.' Then he felt Jessica's arm steer him on again across the terrace.

Chapter Twenty-Eight

They heard the punishment resume behind them as they walked past Lady Lucinda snoring facedown on a sunlounger, the clasp of her bikini undone. India was bobbing in the middle of the pool on a dolphin lilo, reading a copy of *Prospero's Cell*. She raised a slender arm, then turned back to her book, white braids spreading into the water behind her like a coral fan.

'Sea levels?' Spike heard Rufus boom as they approached. 'What utter tosh.'

The two old men were sitting in the shade, half-drunk glasses of ginger beer in front of them. 'Hello, son,' Rufus called out, as though he'd been expecting him. As Spike helped Jessica over the rill of live fish, Sir Leo got to his feet and drew her in for an enthusiastic kiss on each cheek. Then he turned to Spike. 'You'll join us for a drink, of course?'

'I'd love one,' Jessica said, and Spike crouched down to draw two dark green cans of Mythos from the glass-fronted fridge, ignoring his father's disapproving glare.

'Rufus has been taking me to task,' Sir Leo said. He pointed at a map on the table, pinned down by unlit scented candles to defend against the gusts of wind blowing in from the sea. 'As soon as I suggest another location referenced by Homer' – he held his arms out in disbelief – 'your father shoots me down.'

'Just because you get lucky with one find, that doesn't mean everything else is going to fall into place.' Rufus cleared his throat, and Spike grimly prepared himself for their lesson. '*You will find the scene of the wanderings of Odysseus when you find the cobbler who sewed up the bag of the winds,*' Rufus quoted. 'Do you know who said that?'

Sir Leo shook his head.

'Eratosthenes. In the third century BC. *BC*, Leo! They knew it was cobblers even then.'

Sir Leo's long freckled face didn't smile, and Spike wondered if Rufus had pushed him too far. But then he confided affectionately, 'The boat that carried Odysseus home to Ithaca was turned to stone by Poseidon.'

'Cobb-*lers!*' Rufus shouted.

Sir Leo ignored him. 'So there must be a rock formation to account for the myth,' he pressed on, a hint of sharpness in his tone. 'It could be the lighthouse island off Kassiopi.' He tapped the map. 'Or maybe sea levels have risen to conceal it.'

'But didn't you say that Poseidon's earthquake would have changed the geographical features of Corfu beyond recognition?'

The question was from Jessica. Sir Leo looked slightly surprised that a woman felt equipped to participate, but was delighted nonetheless to have found a potential acolyte. 'Any rock formations at sea would have remained unaffected,' he replied, ignoring the heavy splash as the ping-pong players bombed into the pool, provoking a faint cry of protest from India.

'Sea levels,' Rufus chuckled. 'You're an imaginative man, Leo, I'll give you that. But my taxi driver posited a different theory. He said that the real reason there are so few archaeological sites in Corfu is that the locals cover them up as soon as they find them.' He lowered his voice to a stage whisper: 'To avoid building regulations.'

Spike smiled as he watched his father jousting with his new friend. He hadn't seen him this animated in years. But then the smile faded: he had a job to do and time was short. 'Has the site been reopened, Sir Leo? Or are the police still down there?'

Sir Leo fixed him with his penetrating green eyes, and suddenly Spike could see how this amiable, erudite old man might terrorise a boardroom. 'Arben was extremely dear to me,' he said softly. 'He had a bright, enquiring mind which could have achieved great things.' Leo turned towards the sea, and Albania. 'He was one of the few people I could talk to about the site. Who could appreciate its importance. I'm certain he would have wanted us to continue with the excavation.'

There was a pause, which Rufus loyally filled. 'Leo plans to pay for everything himself. The house will become a museum. He's hoping to turn Peter's place into a study centre for visiting students.'

'I see,' Spike said.

'In conjunction with the Greek government,' Sir Leo added tersely. 'But I'll have final say over the aesthetics.' Spike didn't doubt that for a moment. 'I'm told you're acting for Lakis Demollari,' he said to Spike, almost casually.

Spike suddenly felt like a sixth-former awaiting the inevitable dressing-down from his housemaster. But the old man surprised him. 'I'm pleased to hear it,' he said with a sad shake of the head. 'I fear the poor chap may need all the help he can get.'

'So you don't think he's guilty?' Jessica asked with customary directness.

Sir Leo turned his gaze on her. 'I'm of an age, my dear, where little surprises me. But Arben and Lakis were like brothers.' He darted a fond glance at Rufus. 'Not in the Cain and Abel mould, Rufus. Brothers who loved each other.'

Another pause. 'Apparently a girl was here the night Arben died,' Spike said. 'We're hopeful she might provide Lakis with an alibi, but no one else seems to have seen her. We think she could be Albanian. A redhead?'

Sir Leo's linen shirt hung unbuttoned over his grey-haired chest. A gust of wind billowed it suddenly, and he shivered and pulled it closed with one hand. 'I wish I could help, but...'

'It might be important,' Spike interrupted.

'... but I don't remember seeing anyone like that,' he continued firmly.

Rufus stood up. 'Come on, you two. Peter will be wondering where we've got to.' He patted Sir Leo's shoulder in farewell, but the old man didn't seem to notice, eyes drawn again to the sea.

As they started up the steps, Spike heard a distant clicking, and turned to see India Hoffmann, damp braids swishing, tiny red sarong wrapped around her waist. 'Wait,' she called breathlessly.

Rufus and Jessica turned in surprise. 'I heard you're representing Lakis,' India said, eyes invisible behind her sunglasses. 'Did he do it?'

'He hasn't been charged,' Spike said carefully.

'But...' She was interrupted as Zach appeared, the collar of his pink polo shirt flipped up. 'You forgot your map, Mr Sanguinetti,' he said, slipping a possessive arm around his daughter's thin shoulders. Her height seemed to diminish in his presence.

'How kind,' Rufus said.

'Come on, Spider,' Zach murmured, giving India a squeeze. 'Your stepmum wants at least *five* minutes with you. Goodbye,' he added, leaving no one in any doubt that the visit was over.

But Spike felt India's intense gaze upon him as he followed Rufus and Jessica back up the leafy path towards the car.

*

Calypso feels numb as she moves through the familiar streets of Saranda. But her eyes are drawn constantly behind, checking to see if the stranger has followed. Throughout the crossing, she could sense him watching her. She tried to reassure herself that this was normal, that men always stared. But after they disembarked, he gave her a knowing smile as they moved through customs, narrowing his cold eyes, and she had such a vivid flashback of the man in the balaclava that it sent her running from the port into the arms of the city she knows so well.

Saranda. 'The Forty', in Albanian. Named for the Christian martyrs drowned one by one by the Romans. A city of the dead.

She starts to recognise faces from her childhood. The same old woman on the street corner selling her plastic litre bottles of honey, of pickled mussels, a pair of bathroom scales at her feet to reassure doubting customers. The man with the backseat of his elderly Mercedes folded down, car boot overflowing with bright oranges. The same unfinished buildings, steel girders flaking with decay, signs screwed to the concrete saying Shitet – 'For Sale' – *mobile phone numbers optimistically daubed below. The bearded madman with the snapped teeth, one of the few locals to partake in the crop produced so abundantly on the other side of the mountains. She hopes his brother-in-law still lets him sleep on his floor in winter.*

Suddenly she finds herself doubting her decision to come home. What if her attacker is already in Albania? Waiting for her? What if he comes in the night, kills her father and mother as well? Something brushes against her leg. She drops her holdall, but it's just a stray dog, pink tongue lolling, raised spine of hair along the top of its back a sign of aggression, she worries, until she realises it's just a quirk of its mongrel pedigree. The dog sniffs at her bare ankle, perhaps catching a scent of Kerkyra, the Promised Land, then continues along the dusty pavement. Three times a year, the Albanian police drive out at night armed with their ancient Kalashnikovs. Hunting the stray dogs, then slinging their heavy bloodied bodies onto the dump outside town. Her brother watched them once through the shuttered window of their fifth-floor flat. He cried as he heard the men whoop, the dogs scream. Yet the creatures always return, with the same coats, the same muzzles, like canine ghosts. Calypso starts to feel dizzy. Finding herself next to the café on the corner of her street, she drops into a seat outside.

The same old men are playing chess – one Soviet habit that never dies. Education, she thinks. The one thing people romanticise from the old regime. The ruthless teacher who would thrash the children's knuckles with a chain if they forgot their homework, the tables and Russian poems learnt by rote. Now the children's fingers remain untouched, but they know nothing, understand nothing. Or so her father says.

Other than the wife of the owner, Calypso is the only woman at the café. The chess players sneak glances at her as she sips her Turkish coffee; she recognises them, but with her new hair, the fake D&G baseball cap pulled low over her eyes, the same cannot be said for them. A tourist, they might think – except that tourists don't come to this part of Saranda.

She looks across at the entrance to her apartment block. The top floor has been unfinished for so long that the residents now train vines along the girders. Come October they will harvest the grapes to make raki. A pile of rubble lies opposite – no one is responsible for moving it. Nor for erasing the graffiti on the wall above: 'Fuck the Serb'. From down on the beach comes a distant call to prayer, so soft that she can barely hear it. She remembers the official request to turn it down last year. The Saudis paid for the mosque, but the locals, inured to religion after forty years of state-imposed atheism, choose to ignore the unspoken trade-off, the quiet invitation to fundamentalism.

The front door to the apartment block opens, and a man steps outside, glancing up at the perfect blue sky as though suspicious that it may change colour at any point. Her father's grey leather jacket and Lee Cooper jeans are unchanged. Calypso lowers her head as he passes the café, and he walks by oblivious, back stooped with the hunch that seemed to appear on the day that Vladimir died. For Calypso, Vlad's death was simple – the loss of her brother, her best friend. But to her father it meant something more. The loss of an heir. Women cannot inherit in Albania, so whatever meagre savings her parents have accrued will now pass to a distant cousin.

Watching her father, her Papi, walk past, Calypso realises that she is not yet ready to go home. She needs somewhere to cool her head. To let the bruises on her face heal. To grow out her ridiculous red hair.

And that is when she thinks of Blue Eye.

Chapter Twenty-Nine

No amount of persuasion could prevent Katerina from serving them supper that night. Assisting her was Spiros, who seemed even more withdrawn than usual beneath the weight of his mother's constant criticism. The boy took his punishment with an air of silent resignation, as though somehow trying to atone for his brother's sins.

'I implore you,' Peter said as a platter of Greek pastries appeared that no one wanted. 'Go to bed, Katerina.'

Katerina lifted her apron to wipe her brow, then drew her son close, eyes filling with tears, so that for a moment they resembled a Renaissance allegory of suffering.

'Breakfast is...'

'We know,' Peter said gently. 'Now please. Get some rest.'

She looked as though she was going to say something more, but then she undid her apron and let Spiros lead her up to their quarters above the house.

'Tell me about the witness statements,' Peter said as soon as mother and child were out of earshot.

Spike drew the bottle of retsina from the ice bucket, hearing Rufus's tut of disapproval. One more censorious mutter and Spike was going to have a word with him. In the meantime, he satisfied himself with a mock toast in his father's direction, which appeared to have the desired effect.

'Every member of the Hoffmann staff has an alibi,' Jessica said. 'As do the family. According to the Chief of Police, most of them were watching a film together in the home cinema at the time of the murder. *My Family and Other Animals*, apparently. With the exception of Zach and Alfie, who were playing high-stakes back-gammon in the sitting room.' She pulled a face. 'Another Hoffmann tradition.'

Peter turned to Spike. 'And Lakis?'

Spike explained about the elusive redhead. Peter looked uncon-vinced, combing the fingers of one hand through his brown beard, as he always did when worried. 'Even if the girl exists,' he said, 'and can be persuaded to come forward, the time of their meeting is still a problem.'

Jessica gave Spike an 'I-told-you-so' glance.

'But I still don't think Lakis is lying,' Spike said. 'Why make up such a strange story? Why *admit* he was smoking dope ...'

'Because he knew the police would find his stash,' Jessica said.

Spike ignored her. 'Why invent this mysterious Albanian girl no one else seems to remember ...'

'Especially if she couldn't provide him with an airtight alibi.'

Hearing his father's laconic voice, Spike looked up in surprise. He hadn't expected to garner support from that end of the table. Like an old salmon taking a fly, Rufus plucked at one of the baklavas on the central plate. 'Most odd,' he added as he tore off a flaky corner. 'I agree, son.'

There was a long silence.

'OK, Spike,' Jessica said, standing up with a sigh.

'OK what?'

'I'll drive you.'

'Drive me where?'

'You know where.'

'Tonight?'

'Why not?' She conjured a bright smile, but Spike knew she could think of many reasons why it wasn't a good idea, so he appreciated the gesture even more.

'Can't it wait?' Peter said with a frown. 'Tomorrow's a big day. You need to prepare your defence with Aristotelis, talk to the Public Prosecutor...'

But Spike was already on his feet. Ten minutes later, he found Jessica by the Fiat, hands busily tying back her dark hair. 'Right then,' she said with a grin. 'Let's go to Kavos.'

Chapter Thirty

The hotels were the first sign. For miles they'd passed nothing but seaweed-heaped beaches and bamboo scrubland, but then the hotels and B&Bs began to appear, cheap unpainted cubes set back from the dusty road. The front gates were open, the bargain-basement pools floodlit, but the bedrooms were empty, no doubt strewn with dirty beach towels, half-empty bottles of aftersun and vodka, redolent of cheap aftershave and Lambert & Butler. The guests were elsewhere.

They drove on. Two youths flashed like deer before Jessica's headlamps, the light catching on the green bottles in their hands. One of them shouted something, but the Fiat had already rumbled past, pressing on through the darkness towards the deep dull throb that grew in strength with every minute.

Spike opened the glove compartment and took out Lakis's soft pack of Marlboro Lights.

'Trying to fit in?' Jessica asked, but Spike just rolled down the passenger window and lit up, feeling the welcome blast of nicotine hit the back of his throat.

More revellers appeared on the road, girls this time, holding hands, legs gleaming beneath their micro-skirts, strappy tops revealing chubby shoulders that even in the glare of the headlights looked painfully sunburnt. Jessica slowed to avoid one girl as she bent down to remove a stone from her shoe; she banged on the car window with her fist and bellowed something abusive in a surprising Home Counties accent.

A few yards on, a police car was parked by the verge. Spike assumed it was a roadblock, but the two uniformed men inside ignored the Fiat as Jessica drove carefully by. As they passed the 'Silverstone' go-kart track, then a Lidl supermarket, the music grew louder, and two police motorbikes appeared, officers side by side like gatekeepers. Beyond them, the road was clogged with people, arms raised, bouncing up and down to the music that was pumping from the bars on either side.

'Lakis said the girl lives at the far end of the strip,' Spike shouted.

Jessica glanced at the dashboard clock. It was already gone midnight. She braked, performed a rapid U-turn and parked in the forecourt of 'Barry Sheene's' moped rentals.

'Thankfully the car is pre-trashed,' she said as a more aggressive group of lads sauntered by. There was something endearingly old-fashioned in the way each gender stuck together like a tribe, Spike thought. Perhaps there were heavily tattooed chaperones moving in secret between them.

As they continued on foot up the road, Spike wondered how Lakis could have driven the girl all the way home through these crowds. Maybe he knew a back route – or she did.

A football chant started up, and Jessica moved closer to Spike's side. As they passed the policemen, Spike took her hand. For a moment it felt like she was going to push it away, but she didn't.

Chapter Thirty-One

'Flamingo Bar', 'The Face', 'Sizzlers', 'Porky's Fast Food' ... One youth, wearing nothing but boxer shorts and a cobweb of cheap tattoos, stopped in front of Spike, held out his thick arms and roared like a gorilla. Spike felt Jessica pull at his hand, and they moved aside and left the boy to beat his chest alone.

'Lakis said it was a sports bar,' Spike said.

'What?' Jessica raised her voice.

The noise from 'Sex Club' was deafening, the open doors revealing flashing coloured lights reflecting off a cauldron of waist-high foam. Spike and Jessica watched a teenager stage-dive off the bar into the suds. They didn't see him come up again.

'We should be looking for a sports bar,' Spike shouted.

Every few yards they passed a twenty-four-hour medical centre, waiting rooms already at capacity with bloodied and vomiting partygoers. The tattoo and piercing parlours were almost as prolific, and they watched as a middle-aged woman emerged from one and struck a pose to two girls, who whooped in admiration as they examined the dolphin now inked at the top of one of their mother's sunburnt breasts.

'Argie Bargie's', 'Snobs', 'KFC – Kavos Fried Chicken' ...

Spike felt something and turned sharply to find a girl with short dark hair and an even shorter dress pinching his buttock. 'Greek God, Greek God,' she and her friends chanted in a Newcastle accent. His molester was quite pretty, he thought, and was about to smile when Jessica yanked his arm and they were on the move again.

The throb of music deepened as a series of more hardcore clubs appeared. They'd walked for nearly a mile but the strip seemed to go on for ever. No wonder the town was hidden at the bottom of the island, Spike thought. On the map, Corfu looked like a miniature Italy, ankle bent back, poised to kick something, a football perhaps, or a beer bottle. Kavos festered at its toe like a verruca.

At last the clubs started to dwindle, and Spike saw two sports bars facing each other. Both looked large enough to have rooms above.

Jessica pointed to her left. Spike nodded. And in they went.

Chapter Thirty-Two

The television sets in 'Back of the Net' had evidently been installed before the plasma revolution: five heavy boxes mounted on the walls by iron brackets. Not only was the football match they were showing appropriate to their vintage, but it also helped to explain why the bar was almost empty.

'Two halves of Mythos,' Spike nodded to the barman, immediately feeling the unwelcome attention of a skinhead with stretched earlobes who was swaying on the stool beside them. Australian, Spike assumed.

As Spike paid up, the drunk slurred something incomprehensible at Jessica, who pointedly turned her back.

'I'm looking for someone who lives here,' Spike said in a low voice. The barman frowned without taking his eyes away from the screen, where a still hirsute Ryan Giggs was wheeling away after another jinking goal.

'A young woman,' Spike said, and the skinhead glanced over again. 'With red hair.'

The barman shrugged. With his straggling goatee there was something of the Hell's Angel manqué about him. 'Just Phil and Nicky above 'ere,' he said in a cockney accent.

'Nicky?'

'Fat bloke from Essex,' the barman said. 'Runs the bungee rocket on the beach.'

The skinhead laughed. The wooden plugs in his earlobes had holes the size of penny pieces. 'Fockin' pansy,' he muttered, shaking his head at the screen, where a fresh-faced David Beckham was risking a high five with the mighty Cantona. Not Australian after all, but Liverpudlian. The drunk turned again to Jessica and the barman glanced over nervously. 'First time in Kavos, babe?' he asked.

Jessica sipped her beer, no doubt working out whether to reply or ignore would be the more dangerous tactic. 'Yes,' she said in the end, and the skinhead scraped his stool closer. 'Ditch the spic,' he said, jerking a thumb in Spike's direction, 'and I'll show you the town.'

Jessica gave him a chilly smile. 'I'm all right, thanks,' she said, turning away again.

Spike was going to let it go, but then the man ran a callused finger down the smooth brown skin of Jessica's neck, and he carefully set down his glass and stood up.

'Spike,' Jessica warned, but now the skinhead was on his feet, squaring up to Spike, not as tall but with broader shoulders beneath his singlet. He cleared his throat, hacking up a gob of spit from the depths of his oesophagus, then presented the bolus to Spike, pale against his chapped lips. But before he had time to launch it, Spike had grabbed him by the ear and yanked him off his stool. He howled with pain as Spike applied pressure to the piercing, his nicotine-stained fingers clawing at Spike's hands.

'Spike!' Jessica was shouting now, but he was already dragging the man towards the exit as he emitted a mass of threats and insults. Other drinkers watched on, vaguely interested, while the barman stepped out from behind the beer taps and folded his flabby arms.

'You cont,' the skinhead spat, 'fockin' shank ya...'

When they reached the door of the bar, Spike released the man's ear and kicked him in the small of the back. He stumbled, then collided with a police motorbike conveniently parked on the road outside.

'Oi!' came a shout, then '*Malaka*,' in Greek.

Two policemen appeared and pulled the skinhead to his feet. He swung a fist, but within moments they had him in a double-nelson, marching him towards whichever shack they were using as tonight's drunk tank.

Spike turned and walked back into the bar to a round of desultory applause. 'One less fuckin' Scouser,' one fan muttered as they all sat back down to their pints, nuts and telly.

Jessica was still standing by the bar. 'I could handle it, Spike,' she said with a flash of her dark eyes. 'What do you think I do when you're not there?'

Spike was pondering this as two fresh half-pints magically appeared. He took out his wallet but the barman waved it away. 'Joe's been stinking the place up since ten this morning. It's on the house.' Then he leant in. 'There's a redhead lives across the way. Above "Scorers". Pretty girl. Nice…' But before he'd even had the chance to smirk and touch his chest, Spike had grabbed Jessica's hand and was leading her out of the pub.

Chapter Thirty-Three

Despite its name, 'Scorers' was a more sedate affair. Wooden decking extended beneath its yellow-stained awning; Spike felt the surprising crunch of sand beneath his feet and caught sight of the beach behind. Through open windows, he saw that the big screen was showing a game of cricket, but the players wore a garish orange and turquoise rather than white, the contest taking place in some distant league and time zone. The middle-aged clientele was all male, one eye on the game, the other on the bottle-blonde waitress, whose denim hot pants had the hem turned up another inch the better to show off her tanned thighs. The thickset Greek behind the bar looked able and willing to enforce a 'look but don't touch' policy. Spike was about to go in when he heard Jessica call his name.

'There's a side door,' she said in a low voice. 'Looks like it leads to rooms above.'

He followed her around the building. A lemon tree had seeded itself in a patch of waste ground, its branches almost comically freighted with ripe, fragrant fruit – perhaps it had tapped into the Kavos sewer system. They stopped in front of a frosted-glass door which opened into a cramped staircase. 'Come on,' Jessica said, pushing Spike ahead.

Upstairs they found a small first-floor landing. Spike flicked on the lights, a single bare bulb swinging from the low ceiling. One door had been left ajar, revealing a storeroom filled with stacked plastic chairs, trussed-up parasols and a vat of what smelled like chicken-fat – Spike hoped the owner wasn't waiting for the end of the season before tipping it into the sea. The other door was shut. Jessica traced the outline of a mark midway up the white MDF, and she and Spike exchanged an ominous glance. It looked a lot like a footprint.

Jessica knocked. No response, so she tried the handle. Locked, but something rattled in the latch. She shoved it with her shoulder and it shunted slightly. 'Can you lift it into the frame?' she whispered to Spike, who obediently knelt down and slipped his fingers beneath the door, hauling upwards. When Jessica applied her shoulder again, the latch clicked.

'Did they teach you that at the police academy?' Spike asked, but Jessica didn't smile back, just pointed at the security chain which was hanging limply like a silver worm, nub still nestling in its catch.

Before Spike could say something about breaking and entering that would no doubt irritate her, Jessica put a finger to her lips and moved inside. A square of mosquito netting gaped in the sea breeze, but the air was close and musty, and they saw damp on the walls, dark mould in their corners. Then Spike noticed the ceramic base of a heavy lamp smashed across the scuffed lino, the rickety table-for-one overturned – all the hallmarks of a struggle – and his spirits sank. Where was the girl?

On top of the unmade bed sheets lay a framed photograph of a teenaged boy in school uniform, his handsome head tilted to one side, a stud in one ear. Spike turned it over. The photographer's sticker on the back was in a language he didn't recognise. Beneath, the floor was littered with clothes and underwear; Jessica opened the wardrobe and jangled a finger along the bare wire hangers inside. 'Looks like she left in a hurry.' Then she turned and caught sight of something on the other side of the room.

'What?' Spike said, following her gaze.

They stepped towards a pool of liquid spilling from under the closed door. Putting her finger back to her lips, Jessica yanked open the handle and pulled down the light cord. They took in the puddle of water in the dip of the tiles. Judging by the concentric stains around it, it had been evaporating slowly over a number of days.

Jessica knelt by the bath, finding toothpaste, painkillers and a pink can of deodorant rusting on the floor. She tried the medicine cabinet: empty. Then her mouth tightened and she pointed at the door jamb.

A slick of dark, dried blood stained the bare pinewood. Brick-red spots speckled the base of the lavatory. Then, with a growing sense of dread, Spike saw that the blood spatters were everywhere – on the bath panel, the underside of the sink, the threshold, where a rusty brown footprint conjoined the rooms.

Crouching down, Jessica pointed at a black comb that had fallen behind the U-bend. She picked it up and extracted a few long hairs from between the plastic teeth. The strands gleamed red in the fluorescent strip light.

She was about to speak when they heard a noise. Spike stood up and switched off the light, and they waited together in the darkness beneath the whirring fan as the door slowly opened.

Chapter Thirty-Four

'Cal?' came a tentative female voice.

They heard the door close as the blonde waitress from the bar downstairs stepped into the flat. 'Cal?' she said again, followed by a 'Fuck me *ragged*!' as she saw Jessica walk out of the bathroom.

'It's OK,' Jessica called out, taking her ID from her pocket. 'I'm with the police.'

The waitress had one hand pressed to her heart as though it was about to arrest. She glanced at the card, then at Spike. 'He's a lawyer,' Jessica said, but it didn't seem to be a revelation that put the woman at ease. 'Is Cal OK?' she asked warily.

Spike was about to answer, but Jessica got there first: 'When did you last see Cal?'

Spike watched the waitress's eyes roll to the left as she counted back the days. Close-up, she was less attractive than she'd first appeared.

'Tuesday,' she replied in her Essex twang. 'She come into the bar to pick up her wages, but she never been back since.' She looked from Jessica to Spike, the doubt clear in her childish blue eyes. 'She in trouble, then?'

'We're just trying to work out where she is,' Jessica said. 'Why don't you sit down?' She glanced around the flat for an intact chair, then gestured apologetically at the bed.

The waitress picked up the photo frame and perched on the bed as primly as her hotpants would allow. 'That's her brother.

He's dead,' she said with an indifference that suggested her own childhood had not been untouched by tragedy.

Jessica sat down beside the girl, and Spike turned away to the window, letting her do her thing, staring down at the stained awning of the bar below.

'Is Cal her real name?' Jessica asked.

The waitress put down the photo. 'It's Calypso. That's all I know.' Her eyes fell on the pool of water leaking out of the bathroom. 'Has something happened to her?'

'That's what we're trying to work out,' Jessica said with a reassuring smile. 'Can I ask you your name?'

'Penny,' the waitress said. 'Listen, I only come up here because I heard you walking about and thought she must be back.'

'Do you and Calypso work together?'

Penny looked again at Spike, then nodded. 'I've got to get back.'

'Does she have a boyfriend? Someone she spends time with?'

'Keeps herself to herself,' Penny said, getting to her feet.

Spike turned from the window. 'Did she ever mention a man called Lakis? A Greek?'

Penny shook her head as she moved towards the door. Spike walked after her and laid a hand on her wrist. She stared at it, then at the business card between his fingers. 'Calypso might be in danger,' Spike said. 'If she comes back, you need to call me.' He took two fifty-euro notes out of his wallet and held them up. Penny hesitated, then took the money, sliding it into the back pocket of her shorts as she left.

They heard the drone of another siren down on the strip. 'We should get out of here,' Jessica said, turning out the lights. Spike nodded, but before he followed her out, he picked up the photo frame, unpeeled the sticker from the back and slipped it into his wallet.

Chapter Thirty-Five

The motion of the car almost sent Spike to sleep as they drove back to the north of the island. Then the front wheel hit a pothole, and he jolted upright in the passenger seat, wiping drool from the corner of his mouth. He looked over at Jessica, who was staring ahead into the dark empty road. 'Well I thought that went *very* well,' she said. 'We go to find Lakis an alibi, then stumble across a crime scene – which we then contaminate.' A sarcastic laugh. 'If Calypso really was with Lakis around the time Arben died, that means he was the last person to see her before *she* disappeared.' She rubbed her dry eyes. 'That was a hell of a lot of blood, Spike. Evidence of forced entry. Of a struggle.' She glanced over. 'We ought to go to the police. Tonight. Before they find a body and come looking for us.'

'I have to talk to Lakis first,' Spike said. 'Just give me until tomorrow.'

She shook her head, and Spike felt his weariness deepen. The dashboard clock read 3.33 a.m., and he remembered with a silent groan that he was due to meet Aristotelis at eight. He wound down the window, forcing himself to rally. 'Think about it,' he said. 'Why would Lakis send us to find Calypso if he'd killed her?'

'He only mentioned her to you when things were starting to get desperate,' Jessica replied. 'Maybe he decided a potential alibi was better than none at all.'

Or maybe Calypso is still alive, Spike thought, and running from whoever killed Arben. He stared out of the open window into the blackness of the Corfu Channel. When he turned back, ten minutes had somehow elapsed, and Jessica was fiddling with the radio, twisting the dial until she found an English-language station – Katy Perry singing 'The One That Got Away'. Jessica let her get through the first verse and chorus before she reached back down. 'Don't want to nod off at the wheel,' she said, firmly flicking the radio off.

*

As the bus struggles along the foot of the mountains, the driver slips in a cassette of polyphonic music – the local folk songs that UNESCO has improbably included on its list of protected cultural heritages. Calypso listens as the voices drone and wail, unaccompanied by instruments. The only other passenger rises from his seat. She hopes he is going to tell the driver to turn it down, but no, he is smiling, requesting an unscheduled stop. A few minutes later, he gets off by a timber yard. Swinging from the doorway, Calypso sees a sheep's skull – the favoured talisman in the south of Albania for keeping the Evil Eye at bay, for distracting fate from cursing the family within.

The gypsy encampment outside town has grown larger, she notes, makeshift homes created from black plastic bags wrapped around wooden stakes. Laughing toddlers with snot-glazed noses chase each other around the bonfires and piles of stolen scrap metal that sustain their parents. A few years ago, the EU paid for an apartment block to be built in Saranda to house the Romani, but within a few months they'd returned to their encampment. As far as Calypso knows, the EU haven't been back since, despite all the blue- and gold-starred flags flying proudly from the buildings. Don't forget us, the people of Saranda are saying: you may not think you want us, but we need you.

The bus starts to climb. Shepherds and goatherds appear on the mountainside, each guarding a small number of livestock, crooks at the ready. There are still grey wolves in the mountains, though Calypso has never seen them. But it's the stray dogs the herdsmen really fear. A pack of three could wipe out a flock in a single night.

The bus slows into a switchback turn, and Calypso sees one shepherd squatting in the shade of an igloo-shaped concrete bunker. At least the great dictator's defence system is getting some use. Hoxha built a million bunkers to prepare for invasion from the imperialist West. A million bunkers for three million people, and their curved shapes still blister every hillside. Around them grow clumps of agave cactus, planted by hand, now running wild, their spines intended to entangle parachuting invaders in the war that never came.

On the next building Calypso sees a Stars and Stripes flapping proudly by the EU flag. These days, Albania loves its old foe, America. Especially President Clinton, the hero who led the charge to rescue their Kosovan brothers. Hundreds of young Albanians are even named after Clinton's fellow interventionist – Tonibler, or just Bler for short. Calypso smiles. Hoxha would be turning in his grave – had it not already been dug up, and his position in the Martyrs' Cemetery next to Mother Teresa switched for a more modest plot in suburban Tirana.

A pickup truck is coming the other way. Crammed into the back, tied down by guy ropes, Calypso recognises the long, lush stems of cannabis plants. Even the front cabin is full – the driver can barely see through the windscreen. Late August, Calypso thinks, the start of harvest season. The bus driver looks the other way as the pickup passes. So does Calypso. So does the government of a country which they say attributes nearly half its GDP to the illegal activity of a single village on the other side of the mountains.

Thankfully, the bus ignores the sign marked 'Lazarat' and continues along the spine of the mountain. Calypso remembers the story of the coachload of innocent American tourists who *passed out as they drove past Lazarat on their way to view the ancient stone houses of Gjirokastra. The heady smell is always there, but in harvest season ... it is something else.*

She peers down the mountainside, seeing Saranda below, nestling in its curved bay. On one side run the brackish waters of Lake Butrint and the border with Greece; on the other, the Albanian Riviera, a contradiction in terms, people joke, yet its coastline boasts beaches more beautiful than anything she saw in Corfu. But every time optimistic foreigners come to develop it, they leave with their tails between their legs. She remembers her mother's excitement when she heard that 'Club Med' had arrived. Six months later, the company had abandoned the resort half-built, scared off by the cars burnt out overnight, the angry mobs demanding compensation. In a country where no one can agree who owns the land, it's hard to put down foundations. Unless you want to pay. And keep paying. To three different sets of people.

'Syri i kaltër?' the bus driver calls above the crazy music, checking her destination.

Calypso shouts back 'Po!' – 'Yes!' – then settles down in her seat, watching the landscape soften into lowland forest – sweet chestnuts, poplars, locust trees. They pass the hydroelectric dam, and she strains to catch her first sight of the water – still a bright, freakish turquoise. No one knows for sure what causes the colour, but the locals have a story, as they always do. Of a fierce dragon who terrorised the mountains, stealing the children. The villagers hid fire inside a carcass of meat and left it on a rock. The dragon took the bait, then flew in agony down the mountainside and exploded in the forest. The colour of its blue blood tainted the spring.

Calypso first visited Blue Eye as a child. Then, when the hotel was finished, she asked for a job. She hopes Petra is still in charge. That she will pretend not to notice the bruises on her face and the fear in her eyes. That she will remember who Calypso used to be and take her back.

124

The driver stops beside a track off the main road. Calypso gets out, relieved when the bus finally pulls away and the music drifts into the distance along with the wheeze of the engine. Now all she can hear is the chorus of bullfrogs, males singing to their mates. Each year, while they were setting up for the summer, Petra's husband, Samir, would spear the frogs with a trident, then sever their hind legs and boil them in oil like chicken drumsticks.

She glances over her shoulder and sets off up the path, picking up a few loose stones in case of strays, a habit acquired in Saranda. The frogs fall silent as she passes, and finally she can make out the rumble in the distance, deep and angry, like a dragon's roar. The sound of the Blue Eye Spring.

Chapter Thirty-Six

'I did not think it was relevant then. And I do not think it is relevant now.' Aristotelis Theofilatos was sitting behind his desk in another elegant suit, charcoal grey this time, set off by a mustard Hermès tie. 'Whatever the state of the girl's apartment,' he added.

'Lakis says that Calypso saw him just after midnight,' Spike persevered.

The Greek lawyer shook his head, his usual composure disturbed as he struggled to control his frustration. 'But that still doesn't help us if the pathologist is asserting that Arben was killed *before* that.'

'You must know that time-of-death analyses are rarely accurate, Aristotelis.'

Watching the man raise his hands in a gesture of weary surrender, Spike tried another tack. 'There's a CCTV camera outside the main Hoffmann gate. The girl would have had to walk past it to get to Lakis's car.'

'How can you be sure she was even there?'

'Because Lakis told me she was,' Spike replied stubbornly. 'And I believe him.'

Aristotelis reached over and switched off his computer. 'In our line of work, Spike, one must endeavour to remain' – fastidious as ever, he weighed the words available to him in English – 'objective' was the one he settled on. 'It can be particularly difficult when a client is young. When he is afraid. When his mother has wept in your arms and made you promise to protect her son.' He paused. 'Such things can affect one's judgment.'

Spike thought back to another mother who had vouched tearfully for her son's innocence as he languished in Her Majesty's Prison, Gibraltar. Solomon Hassan... Spike had risked his career to acquit him of murder, and it was only later that he'd found out that his old school friend was guilty. The crime-scene photo of a young woman violently killed on a Moroccan beach flashed through his mind, but he forced it away. This wasn't Tangiers. And Lakis wasn't Solomon.

When he looked up, Aristotelis was observing him closely. Spike hoped his son hadn't shown him how to delve too deep into Google. 'I think we should move to requisition the Hoffmann CCTV footage,' Spike said.

Aristotelis's eye fell on a tiny crease in his tie. He smoothed it out. 'I concur.'

Spike jolted in surprise – this was the first suggestion that Aristotelis had agreed with all morning.

'I'm puzzled that the police have not already done so,' Aristotelis went on, packing up his briefcase. 'Go and talk to Lakis again about the girl. And I will return to Alexandras Avenue and make enquiries about the CCTV.'

They crossed the polished parquet together. 'How is your wife?' Spike asked.

Aristotelis pursed his lips. 'It is not...' For the first time, his English seemed to desert him. 'Encouraging.'

They continued in silence down the stairs and out onto the busy street.

Chapter Thirty-Seven

'I can't believe you *went* there?' Lakis said, looking up at Spike with a small smile. 'To find her. I thought…' His voice trailed off.

'I told you I'd help you, Lakis.'

The young man's whole bearing seemed to have lightened. He was wearing a fresh white T-shirt and a pair of blue scrub trousers, presumably requisitioned from the hospital storeroom. His hair was clean and fluffy and he'd had a much-needed shave. He looked like a young Accident and Emergency registrar reporting for duty.

'What did she say to you?' Lakis asked eagerly. 'Will she back me up? Tell the police that she saw me? That I drove her home?'

Spike stared into his client's open face, searching for signs of deceit, for any indication that he knew that they hadn't spoken to Calypso – and weren't likely to. But he found nothing but a genuine, honest optimism. 'Calypso wasn't there, Lakis,' he said, watching for his reaction.

'What?'

'We found her apartment but the girl was gone. We don't know where she is.'

Lakis's head dropped, hope dissipating.

'But,' Spike said, 'Aristotelis *is* exploring the possibility that you were both caught on the Hoffmanns' security camera leaving the estate.'

Lakis gave a shallow nod, then took a swig from the cold can of Fanta that Spike had brought him, eyeing the door as though he expected the guard to reappear and confiscate it. As he wiped his mouth with the back of his hand, Spike saw that he had a cut on his Adam's apple. He hoped it spoke of nothing more sinister than a blunt razor.

'How's my mother?' Lakis asked.

'Worried.'

Lakis looked away. 'You know,' he said, 'through my window I can see a wall covered in graffiti. Most of it is about the *krisis*, but there's one line that makes me laugh.' He managed his old grin again. 'It says, *My mother doesn't have a cock but she has bigger balls than you.*'

Spike gave a polite smile.

'That is what my mother is like, Mr Sanguinetti. But…' His face darkened. 'Since my father died…Well, she holds on to me. She needs me.' He looked back at Spike. 'You know how mothers are?'

Not really, Spike thought, but nodded anyway.

'How is Spiros?' Lakis asked.

'It's hard to tell. Your brother doesn't say much.'

'He's funny like that. At home, when he's just with us, he won't shut up.' Another infectious grin. 'He does impressions…better than the TV.'

Spike cleared his throat. 'The thing is, Lakis, when we went to Calypso's apartment, it looked as though the door had been kicked in.'

Lakis stared back blankly as he registered Spike's words. Then he started to shake his head. 'But I didn't go to her place. I told you, I *told* you…'

'There was a lot of blood, Lakis. Evidence of a struggle.'

'I never went inside,' Lakis said. 'I dropped her off, I watched her walk away, I don't even know where she lived…'

The door creaked; Spike expected the guard to enter but instead saw Aristotelis Theofilatos. The set of the old man's face told Spike they were in trouble before he even opened his mouth. '*Katastrophee*,' he said in Greek.

'What?' Spike asked, rising to his feet as he saw the guard appear behind the lawyer.

Aristotelis turned to Spike. 'It is very bad news.'

Chapter Thirty-Eight

Lakis stared out of the interview-room window, chewing his lower lip. He'd said nothing as Aristotelis addressed him in Greek, just examined the coarse black hairs on his knuckles with empty eyes. Then Aristotelis laid a paternal hand on his client's shoulder and turned to Spike, who was pacing the room impatiently, imagination shooting off in different directions, wishing he could muster even his father's command of Ancient Greek. 'So?' he said. 'How bad is it?'

The older lawyer shot him a glance, urging him to calm down, and it was only when Spike gave a curt nod and took a seat that he started to talk.

'The forensic laboratory in Athens has sent through the results,' Aristotelis said. 'The blood on the murder weapon has been confirmed as Arben's. Not only did the victim have a rare blood type, but the DNA match was as close to one hundred per cent as is possible.' Aristotelis paused. 'This is perhaps not unexpected, but unfortunately they also found a fingerprint belonging to Lakis on the handle.'

Spike looked over at Lakis's hunched shoulders, the classic posture of defeat. 'What about the CCTV?'

'There is nothing on it. Nothing that will help us.'

'No girl?'

Aristotelis shook his head and turned back to Lakis. He rested his brow on the table as Aristotelis spoke softly to him in Greek.

'What?' Spike said in exasperation. He was starting to feel like a useless monoglot, an encumbrance.

'The Public Prosecutor has confirmed her intention to press charges,' Aristotelis said. 'Lakis will now be transferred to prison. The high-security unit.'

Lakis slowly raised his head. It seemed that Aristotelis had neglected to tell him the last detail. 'High-*security*?'

'I'm afraid so.'

'In a cell with the rapists? The murderers? The Golden Dawn terrorists from Athens?' He glanced from Spike's face to Aristotelis's, then fired out a question in Greek.

Aristotelis nodded. 'The investigating judge will have to prepare his case,' he said in English, voice calm and reassuring. 'So we could be in court by ... the middle of next year?'

Lakis pointed at Spike and laughed. '*We*? Mr Sanguinetti will be at home in Gibraltar next week.' His voice dropped to a whisper. 'I'm a dead man.'

The door creaked as the guard came back in. He slid his huge hands beneath Lakis's arms and steered him towards the door with surprising gentleness.

'Tell my mother,' Lakis called back to Spike. Then he was gone.

Chapter Thirty-Nine

Lakis waited in the reception of the Old Hospital as the interminable forms were signed, the boxes ticked, due process served. He seemed oblivious to it all, staring in bewilderment at the posters on the wall of police motorbikes performing improbable jumps. The silent Titan stood beside him, gripping one shoulder with his thick fingers in case Lakis should make a futile run for it, as Spike supposed prisoners must sometimes do.

In the courtyard below, the prison van was waiting, large enough to transport a local football team, bars grilling the rear window. Glinting from its roof was a sun so offensively bright and pure that it seemed a cruel taunt.

Paperwork completed, Lakis was led through the door, flanked by two policemen as his former guard watched on with something like pity in his eyes. Perhaps he had children of his own at home, Spike thought – a young son with a mischievous smile who might one day make a terrible mistake.

He followed the group outside, and they all paused for a moment at the top of the marble steps, squinting into the sun, watching as the driver of the prison van made his final preparations. Spike looked over at Lakis, seeing him suck in air through the gap between his front teeth, eyes glazed. He placed a hand on Lakis's arm and the young man turned to him. But then one of the policemen gave a stern shake of the head, and Spike let his hand drop.

The van driver made a salute, and the guards took Lakis's handcuffed arms and guided him down the steps. Spike wasn't sure if they would let him ride with them to the prison; if not he would make the short journey on foot. To the left of the van, he saw a line of squad cars, then another vehicle parked by the courtyard exit, engine running. A battered navy blue Mercedes with blacked-out windows.

As the line of four moved down the next step, Spike saw one of the Mercedes's tinted windows roll down. He heard the rear doors of the van pulled open, ready to receive their human cargo, then looked again at Lakis, trying to catch his eye, to give him some kind of silent assurance that everything could still be all right. But Lakis's eye wasn't on the van. He was staring at the Mercedes, a strange look on his face. Spike followed his gaze. The window had inched down further. As he watched, something thin and dark was pushed through the gap.

Spike peered into the sunlight, then suddenly understood. He heard himself shout, 'Get down!', his voice strained and hollow. 'Everyone down!' Then he threw himself towards Lakis, but the police guards, unable to understand English, tackled him, and they fell back together against the chipped marble.

For a moment, Lakis stood alone on the steps. The gunfire came in a single burst. His chest and arms thudded and shook, his confused eyes peering down at Spike as the bullets passed through his torso and ricocheted with a whine off the building behind.

The policemen flattened themselves to the ground as Spike watched Lakis teeter on the steps. Spike managed to wrench his leg free, then launched himself at Lakis as a second spray of bullets volleyed from the car. One caught Lakis in the ribs, the force spinning him round to face Spike. Then his knees buckled and he toppled backwards into Spike's arms. Spike gently laid him down, vaguely aware of a screech of tyres as the Mercedes sped out of the forecourt, unpursued.

A ribbon of blood spilled from the corner of Lakis's mouth. 'I didn't kill Arben,' he whispered, and Spike nodded. His lips began to form another word, and Spike leant in closer, feeling the faintest exhalation in his ear. 'Look after them,' Lakis breathed. 'And pray for me.' Then he closed his eyes. Spike felt for a pulse, fingers slipping on the sodden skin of his client's neck. But there was too much blood, his entire chest was drenched in the stuff, flesh peppered with holes, vital organs sprayed and punctured.

Spike looked over his shoulder and saw the guard watching silently from the Old Hospital entrance, his pockmarked face wet with tears. Clambering to his feet, he felt a pain in his leg that made him slap a hand to the back of his thigh. He recognised the warm slick of blood: Lakis's blood, he assumed, until he tried to take a step forward and fell. And then he was lying on his back in the dusty courtyard, staring up into the impossibly blue sky.

Faces loomed above. Spike heard shouting voices that blended into a soothing blur, a background hum, so soporific that he couldn't help but close his eyes.

Chapter Forty

Spike knew he was probably delirious, but in his dream he saw Charlie, and he was glad. They were at the Gibraltar Museum again, visiting the reconstructed cave where the Neanderthals had been found. But it was the bones that interested the boy. 'Whassat?' he asked, and Spike tried to explain that Gibraltar had been the last refuge of Neanderthal man as the Ice Age spread south, that their remains had been discovered on the Rock years before those in Germany, so 'Neanderthal man' should really have been known as 'Gibraltar woman'. But the boy wasn't listening, staring instead at the smaller skull of a child. 'Whassat?' he kept repeating. 'Let's get some ice cream,' Spike replied, but the boy stood firm, accusing eyes burning from his hot little face.

'Spike?' He heard Dr Kitty Gonzalez's soft Spanish voice. 'You don't mind if I call you "Spike", do you?' He was just opening his mouth to reply, but then Kitty was gone, and Charlie too, and he was walking through the Old Town beside his mother, wondering if her high spirits were genuine, or just because she'd downed a double gin after breakfast. Suddenly she stopped him with a hand pressed against his chest, forefinger to her lips, and they watched together in silence as Rufus crossed the path in front of them, on his way to teach a lesson, unaware of being observed as he walked alone up Cannon Lane. His mother waited until her husband was out of sight, then continued with Spike up the hill, his cheeks blazing with shame. She was dead three months later, and he knew that a part of him was glad.

'Spike?' came another gentle voice. Zahra? No, Jess. 'Everything will be OK,' she said. 'Try and sleep.' And he did.

Chapter Forty-One

When Spike next woke, he was propped against a pillow in the Old Hospital. In the adjacent bed lay an elderly man wearing a month's worth of white stubble, producing a noise that sounded alarmingly like a death rattle. Not the Old Hospital, then, but a new one. Spike turned his head. At the foot of his bed slept Jessica Navarro.

Spike eased himself up, feeling a throbbing pain in his thigh. He must have said something, maybe sworn, as Jessica opened her eyes and leant forward. 'Hi,' she said softly.

Close-up, she looked exhausted, eyes bloodshot, hair unwashed. Very unlike Jess. 'You OK?' he asked, and was relieved to see her smile. 'You're the one who got shot in the leg,' she replied.

He turned and felt a sharp nip in the back of his hand, saw the drip stand affixed to his vein. Then he remembered. 'Lakis...?'

She shook her head and dragged her chair closer.

'Does Katerina know?'

She nodded. 'It's been two days, Spike.' She glanced over her shoulder, checking for eavesdroppers but finding only a row of semi-conscious Greeks. 'Are you sure you want to talk now?'

Spike was starting to feel a little dizzy, but nodded anyway.

'Lakis was shot multiple times,' Jessica said. 'They used a Kalashnikov.'

He wondered vaguely if this was another dream.

'If the two guards hadn't been so busy trying to restrain you, the police say you might all have been killed.'

'Do they know who did it?'

'They think it was the Albanian Mafia,' Jessica said. 'A vendetta.'

Spike could have laughed, but then he remembered the blue Mercedes, Lakis's eyes as he'd held him in his arms. 'The police were right about the drugs, Spike,' Jessica went on. 'About everything. They think the killer probably crossed the mountain border from Albania to Greece on horseback, then picked up the Mercedes in Igoumenitsa and caught the car ferry to Corfu. The car was found torched in the hills above Corfu Town.' She shook her head in disbelief. 'It was a professional hit.'

Spike caught a first glimpse of the broad back of an armed guard standing outside the ward. Jessica saw his face and placed a hand on his arm. 'It's just a precaution. The police here take Albanian vendettas pretty seriously.' She shrugged. 'Lakis killed Arben, so his family took revenge. Any one of Arben's brothers or cousins could have pulled the trigger. The whole family is notorious. The one good thing is that this should mark an end to it.'

'An end?'

'An eye for an eye, Spike.'

'So that's it?' It might have been the medication, but he was having trouble taking it in. 'What about the Albanian police?'

'Apparently this sort of thing goes on all the time in Albania. There's even a set of unofficial laws codifying how vendettas should be performed.'

Spike shifted position, stifling a wince, and Jessica eased back his bed sheet. 'There's some blood on the dressing,' she said calmly. 'I'll get the doctor. Just in case.'

She stepped away but he grabbed her hand. 'How bad is it?'

'Just a graze.' She winked. 'But at least you'll have an impressive scar.'

And then she was gone. When she returned with a nurse, Spike was almost asleep. Some kind of adjustment went on with his drip, then his leg, and he thought he felt Jessica stroke his face. He shut his eyes. This time, there were no dreams.

*

Calypso continues down the path through the woods. On one side, she sees the disused concrete tubs still rotting in the under-growth. In Communist times, the hotel was a collective trout farm. Hoxha diverted the river so that it would cascade through the tanks, where the smolts were fattened up with feed imported from China, the dictator's last ally before he broke from them as well. Too soft, like all the rest. Now the tanks are home only to the adders and bullfrogs, but their presence still reassures Calypso – perhaps nothing else will have changed.

Yet it has. This is August and the place is empty. Usually she would have passed a kissing couple by now, hoping that a few days at the Blue Eye Hotel would freshen the wellspring of love, or at least help consummate it. She would have seen the cars of the young crowd driving up from Saranda for a party at the bar beside the spring. Was that why the bus driver gave her that look, because the hotel has closed down?

She stops outside the restaurant, a circular cabin with a con-ical, blue-painted roof built on decking that extends over the river. The windows sparkle in the sun, but inside, the chairs are stacked on empty tables. She tries the door. Locked.

A dog appears from the shade of an outbuilding. Calypso clenches the stone in her hand, then sees it is Laika, Petra's dog, half Alsatian and plenty of something else. As the dog waddles stiffly over, Calypso wonders if she is injured, then real-ises that six years have elapsed since she was last here. A long time in dog years. A long time for anyone. She puts down her stone and strokes the dog's head, looking into her milky, cataracted eyes. Perhaps Laika remembers her, but then she was always a friendly beast.

'Petra?' Calypso calls out. The dog sweeps her tail back and forth at the sound of her mistress's name, then watches as Calypso walks past the restaurant. Ahead lie the chalets – wooden huts catering for couples and small families. The scenery is such that most guests are prepared to forgive the swarms of mosquitoes

that infest their en-suite bathrooms in summer. Calypso sees the steep hillside rising behind, thick with trees and creepers, the river thundering past. The planks of the chalets gleam with creosote. Shut for renovations, she concludes, trying to ignore the nagging thought that the Petra she knows would never close the hotel in the height of the season.

She crosses the footbridge past the chalets, where the water runs swift and shallow. It is only after it meets the spring that it widens out, becomes slow and glassy. As she steps off the bridge, she hears birds crackle from the tall trees, something large shifting in the undergrowth. A deer, she hopes, rather than a wild boar. Or a dragon. When the hotel is open, the wildlife keeps a respectful distance, but now? She readies the stone in her fist.

But then she sees the spring, and her spirits lift. Its colour in sunlight is the brightest cobalt, bubbles of mysterious white swirling within, breaking the surface, releasing a rainbow of blues and greens as it reflects off the shifting pebbles. As though a wound has been scored deep in the flesh of the earth and its cold blue blood is gushing out. In the 1980s, divers descended down to fifty metres, but still no one knows how deep it goes, nor what creates the colour.

She steps onto the viewing platform and stares out, seeing the surface downstream breaking with gas bubbles and the lazy rises of trout. The bar area is still there, though its decking is bare and the door to the DJ booth hangs open. Beneath the hump of another footbridge, she makes out two figures standing in the water. She shouts, but the roar of the river carries her voice away.

Smiling, she picks up her bag and runs along the path. Standing in the water is Petra. Beside her, bare-chested above a pair of old waders, is her husband, Samir.

'Tjeta,' Calypso calls out in Albanian, and the two of them turn. Samir holds a claw hammer in one hand, Petra, a toolbox. She is wearing shorts – the water from the spring is eight degrees all year round, but she was always tougher than her husband. 'Calypso?' she calls back in amazement.

'It's me, it's me.' She laughs – a sound she barely recognises.

Petra passes the toolbox to Samir, then wades through the water, her legs forming Vs in the smooth surface before the current claims them back. She is shielding her eyes from the sun, so it's hard to read her expression, but Calypso isn't sure it is friendly as she pushes through the reeds to the water's edge. A first mosquito pierces her skin, and she slaps a hand to her thigh, emerging with its soft dark body curled in her fist, a smear of red on her palm.

'You should not have come,' Petra says as she steps out of the river. Her bony knees drip with water, yellow-brown below her shorts. Above she wears a greyed brassiere, revealing folds of skin on her sides and stomach, a consequence of age rather than greed, Calypso knows.

'I wanted to telephone,' Calypso says, trying to keep her voice light, but already she can picture herself hitching back to Saranda, back to the cracked pavements and their sagging loops of electricity wires.

Calypso sees Petra take in the cut above her eye, the bruise on her cheek. But rather than comment, she just reaches down and pulls off one rubber shoe. Behind her, Samir hammers a nail into the bridge. The water gleams around him like sapphires.

'They've forced us to close,' Petra says, pouring out a heelful of river grit.

'The government?'

'What government?' Petra snorts, then turns and points into the mountains. 'Lazarat people,' she adds with a shrug that says everything.

Calypso follows her gaze and sees a dark vehicle snaking slowly along the mountain road towards them. Then Petra shouts something at her husband, and he turns to look, one hand shading his suspicious eyes, the other gripping the hammer.

Petra puts a chilly arm around Calypso's shoulders. 'Stay close,' she says. 'Understand?'

Chapter Forty-Two

Jessica indicated absurdly early for the Olive Press, driving with the vigilance of a nervous geriatric who'd just misplaced her bifocals. The Citroën C1 which had been trapped behind them for most of the way back from the hospital hurtled past on the main road, horn blaring.

'It doesn't hurt that much,' Spike protested as Jessica inched along the old, uneven track. But they both knew he was lying, and he was grateful when she dropped down a gear to negotiate the potholes.

And there they all were, gathered in the shade of the ancient fig tree like a cut-price Greek chorus. Peter, one cane raised in greeting; Rufus, face troubled and drained beneath his now outrageously deep tan. And standing outside the entrance to the staff quarters, Katerina in a calf-length black dress, her surviving son scowling beside her, arms crossed tightly against a T-shirt emblazoned with the Jamaican flag. Lakis would have approved, Spike thought.

Jessica pulled open the passenger door and handed Spike the crutch the hospital had forced upon him on his discharge that morning. He considered resisting, but she looked tired and fierce, traditionally a volatile combination, so he accepted meekly and let her help him out.

'It's like a Florida care home round here,' Peter quipped as he wrapped a bear-like arm around Spike's shoulder. His tone was jocular but Spike could see the strain in his eyes, and guessed what he was thinking – that he was somehow responsible. Spike knew the feeling well.

'You had us worried there for a moment, Sanguinetti,' Peter added quietly.

'It's just a scratch,' Spike said with a wink. Then he turned to his father, who was hanging back, shirt flapping around his pigeon chest, and hobbled over, right leg throbbing after the long journey cramped in the Fiat. He hadn't really expected Rufus to visit him in hospital – his father hated the places, and besides, he'd never been much good at emotion. 'Son,' he said, voice catching just a fraction.

Spike drew Rufus close, inhaling the comforting smell of childhood trapped in his frayed cotton collar. 'When Odysseus finally made it home,' his father whispered, 'he almost lost his kingdom. It was only by looking back on past battles that he found the strength to keep fighting.'

Unsure how to take this particular homily, Spike just patted Rufus's bony shoulder and said, 'Well, that's food for thought, Dad.' Then he remembered Katerina, and looked up to see her watching this modest family reunion. He gave her a wave, which somehow felt wrong, but she half-smiled and walked over. '*Ef haristo*,' she said, her heavy-lidded eyes reminding Spike of a face he wished to forget. Of an event he was already packing away amongst the memories too troubling to revisit. The sort of material that might send him back to Dr Kitty Gonzalez's door.

'You don't need to thank me, Katerina,' he said.

But she reached over and laid a hand on his arm. 'You were with him. At the end.' Then she turned and walked back towards her flat. Spiros remained motionless, staring at Spike in silence, face blotched with acne and anger. Spike wondered how much he blamed him – all of them – for what had happened to Lakis. Then the boy fell in behind his mother, narrow shoulders rigid.

'They're still waiting for the police to release the body,' Peter offered in mitigation. 'It's been … difficult.' A glance behind to check Katerina and her son were at a safe distance, then he continued, 'She wants to keep busy but I've told her we can fend for ourselves. We've been eating at the local taverna.'

Jessica, the only able-bodied member left in the household, was unpacking shopping from the car. As she lugged a load of bags inside, Peter threw an arm around Spike and whispered in his ear, 'I've booked a table for two this evening. On the waterfront.'

'For two?' Spike frowned.

'You and Jessica.'

Spike was about to object, but Peter silenced him with the sort of look not seen since before the hit-and-run. Spike was strangely glad to see it back. 'Jessica never left the hospital, Spike,' he said firmly, and Spike knew he was about to receive the benefit of his friend's wisdom, whether he liked it or not. 'That girl's not going to stick around for ever. We don't get infinite chances at happiness in this life.' Then he turned and walked towards the Olive Press, now using, Spike was pleased to note, just one of his canes.

Upstairs, Spike found his bedroom immaculate, clothes folded in a style he didn't recognise – more of Jessica's work, he assumed gratefully. Dominating the chest of drawers was an enormous bouquet of orchids, leaves spiny, orange blooms fat and fleshy. He plucked out the card. *Thank you for trying. Leo Hoffmann.* The sweet scent of decay was overwhelming.

'Wasn't a *hundred* per cent sure you'd like them,' came Jessica's voice as Spike carried the flowers out to the hallway.

She was standing at the top of the stairs, her hair dark with sweat. 'I wondered if you'd like to have dinner?' he said abruptly, suddenly feeling again like the gangly youth in Reebok Pump trainers who'd dared to ask out the best-looking girl at school. The first of many occasions when she'd said no. But this time her face brightened. 'Tonight?'

She was trying to look nonchalant but he could tell she was pleased. 'Can we go somewhere beforehand?' he asked.

'Of course. Where?'

'Just something I promised to do for Lakis.'

145

Chapter Forty-Three

The church formed one end of a modest piazza, unprepossessing in design and covered in a flaking, off-white stucco. Spike and Jessica crossed the cobbles towards it, avoiding a rowdy group of teenagers flipping skateboards, high on hormones and e-numbers.

'Spiridon was a shepherd from Cyprus,' Jessica paraphrased from the tourist pamphlet she'd found in the Olive Press. 'When his wife died, he joined a monastery and discovered he had a talent for miracles.' Spike was trying to listen, but he was having trouble paying attention, the wound in his thigh pulsating with every step. He'd increased the codeine but the pain was proving stubborn.

'When Cyprus fell to the Saracens, his remains were transported to Corfu. Since then, his main achievement has been keeping the Turks at bay. Apparently he can whip up a south-westerly at a moment's notice.' She skimmed through the rest of the leaflet. 'Other than that, he cures diseases, offers salvation. Helps finds lost sets of car keys.' She smiled up. 'Your standard all-purpose saint.'

Spike was grateful for Jessica's efforts to take his mind off the pain, but was starting to think that a stiff drink might be more effective. 'Just a moment,' she said as they approached the door of the church, drawing a thin navy cardigan out of her bag and slipping it over her slender arms.

The interior was dark and stuffy, a long line of pilgrims snaking across the cracked marble floor towards a panelled doorway to the right of the altar. Crossing herself, Jessica retreated to an oak pew beneath the dimly lit frescoed ceiling as Spike took his place in the queue – at least he wasn't the only person carrying a crutch.

A heavily built and bearded Orthodox priest was acting as doorman, shifting the elderly and infirm through at an impressive rate. Spike watched a young woman with plastic tubing beneath her nose step out of the line to rest for a moment in a pew. The knapsack on her back contained an oxygen cylinder. Reading the quiet determination on her face, he started to feel a little less sorry for himself.

A few minutes later, he had made it inside the crypt. Censers hung like gilded fruit from the vaulted ceiling as another priest in a black stovepipe hat watched over the sarcophagus, chanting a delicate song. The line of worshippers was kneeling in front of it, shuffling along one by one. Whenever they reached the end, they stood up, then lowered their heads to kiss the contents.

Spike rested his crutch in the corner, then knelt down with a grimace, hoping that the wound hadn't opened up. The specialist had insisted that this kind of injury required at least a week's bed rest, but Spike had about as much faith in the medical profession as in the priesthood.

As the doorman drew the velvet curtain across the entrance, marking the end of visiting hours, the old lady kneeling beside Spike lost patience and started kissing the panelled walls. Watching her with distaste, he edged along the cushion, less and less sure as to why he had come. Because a dying man had asked him to, he supposed.

The crypt suddenly felt overwhelmingly hot and small, and he fought an urge to run away, to leave this strange room drenched in cheap incense and eerie incantation. He started to push himself up, feeling the sweat slide between his shoulder blades, but then he saw a tall girl in a headscarf bowing to the casket. Even in profile, he knew at once that it was India Hoffmann. Tears streaked her face in the half-light; as the priest touched her brow, she closed her bright green eyes and turned for the door. He got to his feet, but then the priest gestured benevolently at his bandage and ushered him towards the end of the casket. He was about to point out that he had no business here, that he wasn't a practising Catholic, let alone Orthodox, but then he found himself staring down into the velvet-lined coffin at the 1,700-year-old remains of Corfu's patron saint.

Inside the outer casket, he saw a finer box, wrapped in silver chains, two glass panels at either end. In the smoky gloom, he could just make out a stretched, leathery skull, and at the other end, a pair of faded embroidered slippers. Just as he was observing that St Spiridon had had quite small feet, the priest traced a cross on his brow and eased his head downwards to the smeared glass.

Spike felt his breathing quicken as he murmured the words he'd prepared for Lakis. They sounded as pointless and inadequate as he'd feared. Whatever God Lakis had believed in had proved remarkably indifferent to the boy when he was alive. Somehow, Spike couldn't imagine Him showing much more interest in the afterlife.

The reek of incense was overpowering. Spike felt the thump of his heart and started to worry that he might faint, that his legs would give way, so he lowered his forehead, hitting the panel with a bang. But the glass of the casket was deliciously cold, and he focused his mind on the small badge of skin in contact with it, waiting for the tightening in his chest to ease. Finally he straightened up, nodded his thanks to the priest and pushed past the curtain.

Back in the main body of the church, he held out his hands and was relieved to find that his fingers had steadied. Jessica was still in her pew, head bowed, looking impressively devout.

'Did you see her?' Spike whispered, and she looked up in surprise.

'Who?'

'India.' He cast a glance around the emptied church but the girl was gone. When he looked back, Jessica refused to meet his gaze, occupying herself with the business of leaving.

'She was crying,' Spike said, provoking a glare from an old man noisily slotting coins into a metal box, clutching a fistful of tapers.

'Well, she's obviously gone now,' Jessica replied, the coolness in her voice reminding Spike that even a bullet wound to the leg did not entirely absolve him from his perceived crimes with India Hoffmann. 'So, are we done?'

He gave a small nod, and limped out after her.

Chapter Forty-Four

The taverna was preposterously charming, as though purpose-built for romantic first dates and trembling proposals. The most desirable place for a couple to sit was at one of the rustic wooden tables clustered on the pebbly beach, kissed by the gentle tide of the Mediterranean, and it was one of these that Peter had solicitously secured. Less appealing was the fact that the headland was dominated by the Hoffmann villa. A vast triple-decker superyacht was now anchored beneath the archaeological site, presumably belonging to the family or one of their guests. Spike heard a shriek from behind and glanced back to see a bikini-clad lovely leaping with pinched nose from the swimming platform at the stern.

'There's no escape,' Jessica said as a moustachioed waiter in a mauve waistcoat clipped their checked paper tablecloth in place. 'Apparently Sir Leo wants to complete the Phaeacian Games tomorrow night. We're all invited.'

'Think I'll pass,' Spike muttered dourly. 'Claim injury.' He tapped the tasselled leatherette menu. 'Do you want to look at this?'

Jessica shook her head, so in honour of Katerina they ordered her 'big three' of tzatziki, taramasalata and aubergine paste, throwing in some saganaki, stuffed vine leaves and meatballs for variety's sake. Moments later, a napkin-lined basket of dense white bread appeared, along with the obligatory bowl of peppery olive oil. 'Thank God for the Venetians,' Spike said, dipping in a crust.

The drinks were close behind; Jessica took a gulp of red wine, then placed her glass on the table. They both watched in silence as her long fingers toyed with the base. 'Katerina wants to bury Lakis in the family tomb,' she said, and Spike felt his eyes widen in surprise. 'Once the body is released.'

'In *Albania*?' Spike wasn't sure what to say next, so resolved to concentrate on the wine, hoping the alcohol might work its alchemy with the codeine.

'You don't want to talk about it, do you?' Jessica asked.

He shook his head, relieved at the diversion as the first dishes arrived. Nothing tasted as delicious as Katerina's fare, but the food was still pretty good, and eventually the wine and drugs did kick in, bringing their ersatz sense of wellbeing. The sun was setting, the sea providing its usual soothing rhythm. On the beach, families of well-spoken English holidaymakers were packing up their snorkels and masks, heading up to their well-situated villas, salivating at the prospect of the golden hour when they would close their children's bedroom doors and virtuously crack open the first beer of the day. Spike half-listened as Jessica began a story about a lovelorn colleague from Gibraltar, Inspector Isola, watching her face light up as she reached the funny bits, admiring the way she treated the waiter with courtesy – as she did everyone. Maybe Peter was right. He should take a chance. Try to be happy like everyone else. So he leant over and took her hand. 'What?' she said, breaking off her story with a suspicious smile.

'I just wanted to thank you. For staying with me. At the hospital, I mean.'

He saw her cheeks flush, her dark eyes sparkle expectantly, and felt the familiar twinge of panic. 'You really didn't need to,' he added, removing his hand from hers and placing it back on the table. 'I would have been fine.'

'Of course you would, Spike,' she said in the small tight voice that meant he'd disappointed her yet again. She gave a shiver, pulling her silk shawl tighter around her shoulders. September was drawing near, Spike realised. He cleared his throat. 'Lakis said something to me before he died.'

'He asked you to pray for him,' she replied without looking up. 'You said.'

'After that.' Spike paused. 'He looked into my eyes and swore that he didn't kill Arben. And I believe him.'

'Then who did?' she asked sharply. 'It's not like the Albanian Mafia despatches a professional assassin on a whim. *They* thought Lakis killed Arben. They knew all about him – where he was being held, when he was being transferred.'

Spike made a half-hearted attempt to cut through the saganaki, but the cheese had already turned to vulcanised rubber. If you didn't eat it right away, you missed your chance. 'What about the police?' he asked. 'Have they found Calypso?'

'Aristotelis spoke to the Chief while you were in hospital. They're looking into it, whatever that means.' She pushed away her plate with a sigh. 'Anyway, I thought you didn't want to talk about it.'

So Spike raised a hand and gestured for the bill, trying to ignore the cheers and splashes from the yacht behind.

Chapter Forty-Five

They walked back to the Olive Press in silence. A harem of chickens was pecking around the dried grass above the road, waiting for the farmer to come and close them into their coop, where the cockerel was already waiting like a self-satisfied sultan. The evening air warmed the fig leaves, releasing a musty sweetness spiced by the wild sage they were crushing underfoot.

'How's the leg?' Jessica asked stiffly. It was more than he deserved. He looked down at the strapping beneath his faded blue shorts. There'd been no more blood since he'd last changed it. 'Not too bad,' he replied, testing the mood with a conciliatory smile, which she rightly ignored.

Above the house, they saw a lone figure sitting outside the staff quarters. In her long black dress, with her greying hair unkempt, Katerina already had the look of a tragic Greek widow captured on camera for a coffee-table book. An unlabelled glass bottle sat by her chair leg, a tumbler of cloudy liquid in her hand. 'I won't ask you to join me,' she said. 'I am not good company, you understand.'

Spike and Jessica nodded in silence. Bereavement was a sort of quarantine, Spike remembered. People tended to keep their distance.

'Peter spoke to the police,' Katerina went on, taking a sip from her glass. 'They have released the body.'

'Thank God,' Jessica said.

'Tomorrow we take Lakis to Saranda.' She looked up. 'Perhaps you will come?'

Spike shifted uncomfortably, suddenly missing his crutch, but Jessica answered for them both. 'Of course.' *Really?* Spike thought. Katerina gave a faint nod. 'Lakis would like that.'

'It would be an honour,' Jessica said.

The woman looked back towards the sea, which Spike and Jessica took as their cue to leave. Upstairs, all was quiet, Rufus and Peter having turned in some time ago. Only the constant whisper of the Mediterranean was audible.

'That was good of you,' Spike said.

Jessica shrugged. 'It's the right thing to do.'

In that moment she looked so young and vulnerable that Spike couldn't help but reach out and touch her cheek.

'Don't,' Jessica said, arching away.

But he left his hand there and turned her face back towards him, seeing her eyes full of an anticipated disappointment that shocked him. So before he could think better of it – blow his chance, as he usually did – he leant in and kissed her. Time seemed to compress: he remembered her taste, the urgent sound of her breathing, as though it were yesterday. Then he took her hand and led her towards his room.

*

Calypso lies in her bed in the chalet nearest to the river, grateful for the mosquito netting that shrouds her as she watches the creatures' dark, spindly shapes alighting on the mesh. The roar of the river drowns out their ominous whine, but not the love song of the bullfrogs, who are in a frenzy tonight – perhaps it is to do with some particular moment in their cycle, or the position of the moon. Or perhaps they are just as relieved as she is that the man from Lazarat has finally driven away.

Lazarat. Calypso remembers as a child when the village was nothing. A smattering of farmhouses on the mountainside above Gjirokastra, town of the dictator Hoxha's birth. Known only for its çaj mali, or *mountain tea*, dark green, surprisingly mild and delicious. But then Albania started to change. The metal net that had enclosed the country, sealing it in, was sliced away, and it was then, people said, that a young man from Lazarat travelled to Amsterdam. He brought back a handful of cannabis seeds and planted them in the mountains. And they grew. How they grew. And soon the çaj mali plantations of Lazarat were replaced by field after field of cannabis.

The export trade began, and the mobsters from Tirana took an interest, as they always did when they smelled money. But rather than give in, Lazarat's residents joined together, fortifying their village, determined to protect their profits. A single road still leads in and out. The snow-capped peaks of the Gjerë mountain range make ambush from above almost impossible. Gradually, the farmhouses were replaced by wire-fenced villas defending the swimming pools and private gyms within. Las Vegas, the people of Saranda started to call this strange village in the hills. The government tried to take over, but it seemed that half the weapons stolen from the Kalashnikov factory in the People's Riots of '97 had ended up in Lazarat. Rocket launchers, mortars, machine guns. Incredible stories reached Saranda of grand-mothers hunched in the back of Hummers, spraying bullets. So the police backed off, making vague promises to return with a stronger arsenal.

But everyone knows there is too much money at stake. Four billion euros a year at the last estimate. Nine hundred metric tons of cannabis shielded from the eyes of Corfu by a single mountain.

The idea of an old man from Lazarat driving to Blue Eye in his bullet-proof Bentley, ordering Petra and Samir to close the hotel – to reduce the number of tourists on the roads in harvest season – amazes Calypso. As does the fact that Petra would obey. But perhaps Calypso should be grateful. She has work. Had the hotel been open, her position would already have been filled.

Now there is the coldroom to clean, the latrines to retile. And her accommodation is a hotel chalet with her own bathroom and a double bed.

Yet something is still missing. She has tried not to think of her apartment in Kavos, of the shabby rooms that cost such a huge proportion of her wages, just as she has tried not to think of everything that went so wrong in Corfu. The man in the mask, his strong hands forcing her head down into the tepid water, willing her to die. But left in that apartment is the only possession she truly cares for. And she cannot push that out of her mind.

When they realise she is not coming back, will they throw away her brother's photograph? For the first time since leaving Corfu, Calypso dares to switch on her phone. Checking that she still has credit, she scrolls through her short list of contacts and finds Penny's name. They have never been friends, but she owes Calypso a favour. She dials the number. Outside, the bullfrogs chant and scream in the night.

PART THREE

Albania

Chapter Forty-Six

The funeral party sat in silence, stomachs adjusting to the rhythmic roll of the waves. The lower deck was largely empty, most of the passengers clustered up front, following the captain's course as attentively as though they were steering the boat themselves.

Spike looked out through the misty perspex, watching the rocky, verdant coastline of Corfu unspool, thinking of his father's talk of Odysseus, of the relief the man must have felt finally to be leaving this island, unaware of the perils that still awaited him. He saw Pantokrator rising in the north-east corner, the Hoffmann villa perched on its unspoilt promontory like a priceless gem cradled in an open palm. Alongside, minute by comparison, stood the Olive Press, where Peter and Rufus had waved them off after breakfast, one tall, one short, the odd couple left in their holiday home of old books, ginger beer and supermarket champagne. Just out to sea, Spike made out a tiny island, little more than a rock crowned by a lighthouse, and wondered if it might be the remnants of Sir Leo's petrified ship. Then he banished the idea, determined not to let the omnipresent Hoffmann family follow him even to Albania.

Katerina sat in the central row beside her son, who was focusing on a game on his mobile phone, dressed in too large a suit, Lakis's probably, Spike thought grimly. The wires of his headphones had found their way into his mother's hands, and she was drawing them between her fingers like worry beads.

Jessica touched Spike's arm. His instinct to jolt away was engrained, but he overrode it, squeezing her hand between their knees as she stared down with a secret smile, perhaps remembering last night. It wasn't the first time that he'd woken up next to Jessica, but it was the first since he'd fallen in love with Zahra. Since she'd died. He'd often anticipated how it might feel afterwards – the sense of betraying a dead woman, of disappointing a living one. But it didn't feel like that at all. It felt good.

His phone beeped, offering hearty greetings from 'Eagle Mobile', the local Albanian network. When he looked back up, he saw the purser kneeling in the aisle by Katerina, addressing her with the solemn self-importance of an undertaker, a demeanour somewhat undermined by his military camouflage baseball cap and fighter-pilot shades. The purser had told them earlier that Lakis's body had been loaded into the hold before departure – apparently a fairly common occurrence when an Albanian national died in Corfu, as the ferry was still the only route into Saranda. His earnest condolences had been peppered by pleas for Katerina's discretion, concerned that the other passengers might discover that the ferry was doubling up as a hearse.

Spike watched the man steel himself, then whisper a few words into Katerina's ear. Her eyes widened in disbelief, then she hissed something back at him. The passengers in front turned to look, and the purser hurriedly stood up and walked away.

Spiros said something to his mother, and she drew him close. He permitted the embrace for a moment, then pulled away, dropping his eyes again to the safety of his phone. He was going to be a good-looking young man, Spike could see, but there was a sensitiveness about him Spike knew could harden into something destructive. Whatever happened, he suspected that Katerina had a difficult decade ahead of her.

'What is it?' Jessica asked, trying to catch Katerina's eye.

But Katerina just shook her head. 'There are...' The purser glanced back. 'There are *two* coffins on the ferry,' she whispered. 'He says we must wait for the other to be taken off first.'

Spike stared down at his polished brogues, trying not to think of what lay beneath them. Two dead bodies sliding about in the hold, knocking into each other.

Chapter Forty-Seven

The city of Saranda curved around its amphitheatre-shaped bay. The concrete blur only hazily visible from Corfu now resolved into Soviet-era tower blocks, a low port complex, a few stunted palm trees embedded along the sandy beach.

Jessica had moved into the seat next to Katerina. In anyone else, Spike might have thought it presumptuous, given the short time they had known each other, but he was reminded how much better Jessica was at reading people by the way Katerina had taken her hand and clasped it to her chest. Spiros said nothing, just chewed his lower lip like his dead brother had as he scrutinised the embroidered pattern on the seat-back in front of him.

The harbour comprised a concrete inlet with a customs hut on one side, the road behind shielded by a wire fence. Cars were parked along it, glinting in the morning sun, impatient drivers waiting with folded arms. Spike frowned. Katerina had said that just one person was coming to meet them, Lakis's uncle Idriz, her late husband's brother.

The other passengers were already on their feet, gathering their belongings as the purser moved to the bow, mooring ropes in hand. As the boat docked, Spike made out the waiting party more clearly. And their cars – Hummers, top-of-the-range Mercedes saloons and jeeps. Standing by the fence, he saw a man holding up a metal pole with a photograph glued to a plywood board. Spike craned his head for a better view, hoping he was wrong. But the long, handsome face immortalised in the picture was unmistakable. It was Arben Avdia.

Seeing Katerina cover her mouth in shock, Spike knew he wasn't the only one who'd seen it. 'It's just a coincidence,' Jessica said, but Spiros was already shaking his head, a strange smile on his lips, as though concluding that bad luck was now to be their lot in life. 'The ferry can probably only make a trip like this once a week...'

Yet this was more than just an awkward situation, Spike thought – a tragic homecoming of two friends become enemies. If that really was Arben's funeral party, then there was a strong possibility that the man who'd shot and killed Lakis was waiting on the dock with the rest of his family.

Beneath his chinos, Spike felt his thigh start to throb as he heard Jessica continue in her low calm voice, 'We should probably wait below deck for a few moments, just until the other family have driven the body away.'

'We should wait – for *them*?' Katerina spat.

Spike took another look at the knot of thickset men in black suits watching the ferry swivel against the jetty. 'Yes,' he said. 'We should wait.'

As the other passengers disembarked, Spike heard a scraping and juddering from below, then saw a grey rug laid out on the concrete. A moment later, the purser emerged with the captain, carrying a heavy, varnished coffin with handles so shiny they would not have looked out of place on St Spiridon's casket. As the landing party pressed closer to the wire, the sailors carefully laid their burden down. By now, a few pedestrians had stopped on the road to enjoy the curious spectacle.

Then the second coffin appeared from below deck, less ostentatious than its twin. Spike felt the sweat start to prickle on his back as he saw one of Arben's relatives register it, then point it out to a companion. A small, harassed customs officer scuttled out of his hut and thrust a wad of forms into the captain's hands for signature. Then he unlocked a padlock and a black, freshly waxed hearse reversed through the gate, each window crammed with wreaths and festooned by pictures of Arben's smiling face.

The larger coffin was heaved into the air, leaving Lakis alone for a moment in his cheap wooden box on the harbourfront. Spike heard Katerina emit a choked sob, but his focus was on a member of the funeral party who was forcefully questioning the captain. Beneath the man's heavily gelled hair and long thin side-burns, Spike made out a tall frame and fine features that reminded him of Arben. Then the rear of the hearse slammed shut and the motorcade of gleaming cars pulled away, the sound of their hooting swallowed eventually into the concrete city behind.

The purser summoned Katerina with a crack of the fingers as a beaten-up Mercedes appeared on the road, a metal cross glued to its roof. A squat dark man beckoned it towards the gate, sweating in tight flannel trousers. 'Idriz,' Katerina sighed in relief.

The hearse driver opened the boot and the coffin containing Lakis's body was slid into the back. It was only then that his mourners were permitted to disembark.

Idriz gave a cheery wave as they crossed the concrete harbour. Katerina nodded back, clasping her son's hand.

As they entered the customs building, Spike scanned the road and saw the tall Albanian standing on the street corner, hands thrust into the pockets of his designer suit, watching them from behind his sunglasses.

Chapter Forty-Eight

Idriz was waiting beside another Mercedes, even older and rustier than the hearse. What was it about Albanians and Mercs, Spike wondered as he turned back to their host. The man looked like Lakis fast-forwarded into middle age, then sent back in time, with his grey shoes and kipper tie, his open face and easy grin. Spike liked him immediately.

Sweeping a hand across his coal-black comb-over, Idriz pulled Katerina into his plump arms and whispered something into her ear. It was only when she nodded that he released her with a squeeze and offered a formal hand to his nephew, Spiros.

Spike looked again at the other side of the road, where the man in the dark suit was still watching them. There was something in the intensity of his gaze that filled Spike with a sense of unease. He turned to the sleepy-eyed hearse driver and said quietly, 'I think we should go,' but the driver seemed determined to smoke the very last strands of tobacco in his cigarette, and the Albanian was already striding across the road before he reluctantly flicked away the butt and squeezed his taut belly beneath the wheel.

When Idriz caught sight of the stranger approaching, he frowned and tried to usher Katerina towards his car. Spike was about to step forward but Idriz shook his head. 'Don't,' he whispered.

The hearse driver was just starting his engine as the Albanian stepped onto the pavement, pulling off his silver hip-hop sunglasses. His aggressive eyes found Spiros, then he lifted his hand and slapped the boy hard across the face. Katerina screamed, but Idriz held her back. 'No!' he shouted at Spike as he tried to shove the man away. There was a moment's silence as the Albanian eyeballed Spike. Then Spike felt the grip of Jessica's fingers on his sleeve.

Spiros was staring down at the pavement, angry eyes filled with tears. Nobody moved as they heard the Albanian issue a final threat, then watched him stroll back to his brand-new Cherokee, forcing the traffic on the road to stop to let him cross. The windows of his jeep were as dark as the paintwork, concealing him entirely as he drove away, alloy wheels sparkling in the mid-morning sun.

Idriz vented a slow puff of air through his lips. 'Lazarat people,' he sighed. Then he clapped Spiros heartily on the back and unlocked the door to his car. 'Let's go!' he said with a cheerful grin, somehow mustering the enthusiasm of a newly ordained tour guide.

Chapter Forty-Nine

Idriz followed the hearse through the centre of Saranda. Squeezed into the backseat between Spiros and Jessica, Spike stared out of the window at the city going about its daily business: schoolchildren heading home for lunch, pretty girls trying to camouflage their blotchy skin with cheap, pale make-up; the boys darker, as groomed and styled as Italian footballers, their Balkan swagger at odds with the childish rucksacks they wore on their backs. Vendors occupied street corners selling grilled sunflower seeds, dried whitebait, huge plastic bottles of honey. Corfu Old Town, so close geographically, might have been on the opposite side of the earth. Almost every building was made of concrete, the upper storeys unfinished, grimy striped awnings demarcating flats, doorless ground-floor entrances protected only by part-retracted metal grilles. Most of the shops seemed to sell just a single product – one piled exclusively with washing machines, another with TVs. Just as Spike was starting to think that everything dated from the Communist era, they passed a railed-off segment of what looked like Roman walls – thin stacks of terracotta bricks rising a few feet below street level. He knew that Butrint, with its ruined temples and bathhouse and aqueduct, must lie just a few miles to the south; Saranda had clearly been an ancient settlement as well. Looking down at the cigarette ends and rusting cans, Spike pictured Sir Leo shaking his head in disapproval. The Hoffmanns again, forcing themselves into his thoughts ... He cast a sideways glance at Spiros, watching him stare down blindly into the footwell, one cheek still an angry red from the slap that had welcomed him to his father's home city.

The hearse veered into a road flanked by a steep, pebble-crusted hillside of uninhabited apartment blocks. A kiosk squatted on one corner, and Spike took in the posters screwed to its hoardings, recognising the strange accents – 'ë', 'ç' – from the sticker he'd found on the back of Calypso's photograph. Lakis's assumption that the girl was Albanian appeared to have been correct.

Hanging from the porches of the houses, Spike saw macabre talismans – sheep's skulls, children's dollies, cloves of garlic. Just as he was wondering if this meant they were nearing the cemetery, the hearse stopped outside a new-looking restaurant, the proprietor hedging his bets with EU, Stars and Stripes and Albanian flags flying proudly side-by-side from the first-floor balcony.

Four men in shiny suits were waiting outside. Idriz passed one a roll of cash, and they set about hauling Lakis's coffin out of the back of the hearse.

'OK,' Idriz said in English, clapping his hands together. 'Now we go.'

They followed the coffin on foot up the hill, stopping outside a stall selling flowers, their blooms wonderfully bright, Spike thought, until he realised that they were made of plastic. Idriz picked up five wreaths, dispensing another roll of lek, the Albanian currency. Spike remembered Peter at breakfast employing his enviable powers to persuade Katerina to let him pay for the funeral. Looking at the wads of soft notes changing hands, Spike hoped his friend had taken the time to work out the exchange rate.

Holding their plastic wreaths, they followed the coffin in silence through the cemetery gate. Inside, Spike saw a great sweep of graves and tombs climbing into the hillside. He gazed around in morbid fascination, eyes falling on the happy photographs of the dead embossed into monumental granite headstones, massive crosses and statues – even the pediments of intricate miniature buildings – rising above them. More care seemed to have gone into the architecture of the necropolis than into the city that supplied its denizens. Marble vases had been sculpted into the lids of the tombs, adorned by the same bright artificial flowers that Spike carried. A few were littered with beer cans and bottles; at first Spike assumed this was rubbish, the debris of teenaged Goths, perhaps, but then he saw that the drinks were unopened – grave goods to appease the dead. An ashtray had been sculpted into one sepulchre, a single unlit cigarette resting in its nook, a Bic lighter thoughtfully provided should fire prove to be in short supply in the afterlife. Death in Albania was a serious business.

Then he was staring at a photograph of Lakis's father, Viktor, surrounded by a bas-relief laurel wreath, glazed into the granite of the comparatively modest Demollari family tomb. Viktor's face was lined, but his smile was youthful and good-natured – Lakis's smile. Katerina lowered her head as Spiros stared into the six-foot cavity that awaited his brother, tugging at the unfamiliar black tie noosed around his neck. She placed a hand on his arm, but he shook it off, eyes moving up to Lakis's new headstone, unengraved save for a small image of a crescent moon. Not even Idriz could work that fast.

The pallbearers laid the coffin down, taking a moment to dry sweaty palms on the sides of their trousers. Then they squatted down and heaved up the plywood box, before lowering it into the hole. Spike clasped Jessica's hand. In the absence of a priest, Idriz said a few words, speaking in the soft, French-sounding vowels of Albanian. Katerina was weeping now, her rounded shoulders heaving, but then she raised her head and stepped towards the open grave.

'I speak in English,' she said, struggling to steady her voice, 'because my Albanian is no good. And because my friends from Gibraltar have come to say goodbye to Lakis as well.'

Spiros pushed a tear aggressively from his eye, as though crushing a beetle. Anger was his form of grief, Spike realised. It was something he could relate to.

'Lakis was my eldest son,' Katerina went on. 'I knew him.' She twisted the black material of her skirt between her fingers. 'I loved him. He was a good boy no matter what has been said. And what has happened to him' – she broke off – 'I cannot explain. Something cruel...'

Just then, they heard a shout and turned to see two men striding towards them between the gravestones. Spike immediately recognised the tall stranger from the port. But it was the other man who claimed his attention. In his right hand he held a small black revolver.

Chapter Fifty

The pallbearers backed away, arms in the air, evidently not considering the provision of security to be part of their job description. As the two Albanians drew closer, Idriz pulled his nephew behind him. And with a jolt of confusion, Spike remembered that it was Spiros who had been attacked at the port, saw that it was the boy at whom the gunman was pointing his revolver. Why were they targeting him?

The tall man started shouting, and Spike made out the word 'Kanun' repeated again and again. Then he saw his shorter companion slide back the safety catch on the revolver with a practised thumb.

The other mourners in the graveyard melted away. Spiros's head hung low, tears dropping steadily from his tightly closed eyes. Spike looked down and saw a dark, shameful stain spreading over his thigh.

Idriz was holding out his arms in supplication, talking rapidly in Albanian, desperation straining his voice. He reached out to touch the gunman's suit jacket, but the man placed a hand on Idriz's forehead and shoved him violently back. Idriz fell hard onto the ground, and the gunman shook his head with a disparaging smile as he levelled the revolver at Spiros's temple.

'Idriz!' Katerina shrieked.

Then Jessica stepped forward, shaking Spike's hand from her wrist. What was she *doing*? 'Tell them that he's just a boy, Idriz,' she said quietly.

The Albanians just laughed. 'Tell us yourself, pretty lady,' the tall man replied in heavily accented English.

'OK,' Jessica said with a nod. 'He's just a boy. His name is Spiros Demollari. He likes swimming, Panini stickers. Just a boy.' She managed a smile, then glanced from one man to the other. 'Maybe you have a son. A daughter?'

The gunman gave a slight frown.

'A brother?'

'We know the boy's name,' the tall man barked, 'and he is old enough.' He gave a nod at his companion, but now Idriz was back on his feet, pleading with them again in Albanian. They ignored him, but then something he said seemed to have an effect, as Spike saw the short man hesitate. He leant over to exchange a few terse words with his friend, then the pistol disappeared into his belt. It looked as though they were going to walk away, but then the gunman rolled his tongue and spat into the open tomb onto Lakis's coffin. His companion laughed, waving a warning finger at Idriz before joining the man on the path back to the road.

For a moment, nobody moved. Then Katerina drew her son towards her and held him as he wept silently into her shoulder. Jessica turned to Idriz, who was steadying himself on his brother's headstone, trying to light a cigarette with shaking fingers. 'What did you *say* to them?' she asked.

Idriz finally got the better of his lighter. He took a long drag, then gestured with his cigarette at the restaurant opposite the cemetery. 'Later.'

Spike watched the two Albanians climb into their blacked-out jeep. Then he walked over to Jessica, kissed her full on the lips and called over to Idriz, 'May I have one of those, please?'

Chapter Fifty-One

Only one table in the corner of the restaurant had been laid up, five place settings, one sad-looking plate of food congealing under its cling film in each. Otherwise, the vast space was empty. Hanging from the ceiling was a bizarre installation of Albanian modern art: pink plastic globes attached to varying lengths of cord, like an avant-garde twist on the censers Spike had seen in St Spiridon's chapel.

A few minutes earlier, still dazed, the group had filed into the massive WCs and meticulously washed and dried their hands in honour of the dead. In honour of Lakis, Spike had kept reminding himself, the exuberant young man gunned down beside him in Corfu Town. Then Idriz had pressed a packet of cigarettes into Spike's clean hands and his spirits had briefly lifted, only to fall again when he was instructed to add them to the pile of cartons stacked on a side table. Tradition dictated these would be distributed to the poor – whether the waiters were to be among the lucky recipients, Spike wasn't sure, but they already had their eyes on the soft packs of Marlboro Reds.

Jessica was waiting for them at the table upstairs, staring out of the window at the street below, where another hearse was drawing up. Spike placed a hand on her shoulder, then sat down heavily beside her.

'Don't worry,' Idriz muttered, following her gaze as he peeled back the puckered film from his plate. 'It is not the other boy. They will bury him in the mountains. In Lazarat.'

Lazarat. Just the sound of the word caused Spike's heart to race. So he busied himself with the important job of pouring glasses of water for everyone, including Katerina and Spiros, who were still absent, presumably attending to the boy's trousers. Spike could have used something stronger, but Idriz had given a sorrowful shake of the head and explained that alcohol was forbidden at Albanian funerals. So instead he raised the tumbler to his brow and closed his eyes. When he opened them, he saw Jessica watching him. He gave her what he hoped was a reassuring grin and leant over to pluck a packet of cigarettes from the side table. She didn't look impressed, but he just shrugged. 'I don't think Lakis would mind, do you?'

Jessica changed the subject with a cross of her arms. 'Do people usually bring guns to funerals in Albania?'

Idriz forked up a piece of cold grilled lamb. 'It is *Kanun*,' he said, as though that explained everything.

'*Kanun*?' Spike said, reaching over for Idriz's lighter. 'Was he the tall one or the short one?'

Idriz snorted as he swallowed. 'The big man was Alex. The other, Ismail.' The way he impaled his next morsel suggested he wanted to leave it at that, but Jessica had other ideas. 'And *Kanun*?'

Idriz laid down his fork, sweeping an impatient hand across his pate, checking the complex constitution of his comb-over was still in place. 'The *Kanun* is an ancient set of laws,' he said. 'In Hoxha's time, under the Communists, such things were prohibited. But now it comes back.' He glanced over his shoulder to ascertain whether his sister-in-law was still out of earshot, then lowered his voice. '*Kanun* law regulates *gjakmarrja*. Vendetta.' He sighed. 'When a family takes blood. For revenge.'

'But I thought they'd already done that,' Jessica said. 'Killing Lakis to avenge Arben.'

'It is not enough,' Idriz replied sadly. 'Under the *Kanun*, there is always more blood to take.'

174

'So is that why they came after Spiros?' Jessica asked. 'And Katerina?'

Idriz shook his head. 'In Albania, women are just for babies. In the mountains, they still sew a bullet into a virgin's wedding dress.' He grinned. 'So the husband may shoot her if she misbehaves.'

Seeing Jessica's face, he gave an apologetic shrug. 'It is not what *I* think. This is…' He couldn't find the word, so just waved a hand towards the window. 'In the north. The old ways. And Lazarat people, they bring it back.'

Spike thought again of what had happened in the graveyard, how close they had come to witnessing another murder. 'So what did you say to them?' he asked.

'That Spiros is not yet of age. In the *Kanun*, it is written that you may only kill the male relative if he is over fifteen. Spiros is thirteen.'

'So in two years' time they can come after Spiros again?' Jessica said.

'Maybe.' Idriz helped himself to some more food. He was the only person eating. 'But if he stays in Kerkyra…'

Again, it looked as though he wanted to finish the conversation there, but Jessica pressed him. 'They killed his brother in Kerkyra. In Corfu.'

Idriz burst a cherry tomato between his teeth. 'Vendetta is a big problem here. Many thousands of people have been killed in recent years. Many children' – he gave a heaving sigh – 'they cannot leave the house. No education, because it is not safe to go to school. There are lawyers from government agencies who mediate' – he used the English term with an ease that suggested it was common parlance – 'but…' He shrugged.

'They spat in his grave,' Jessica said.

Idriz dabbed his mouth with a yellow paper napkin. 'They could have done worse.'

Jessica raised her eyebrows in disbelief.

'Sometimes they take the body out of the coffin during the funeral. And burn it with kerosene. In front of the wife, the father. Everyone.'

Spike stubbed out his cigarette half-smoked. The nicotine was starting to turn his empty stomach.

'Lazarat people,' was the only explanation Idriz could provide, before he raised a finger to his lips, seeing Katerina and Spiros walk in. The boy's face was still livid, eyes downcast, hands instinctively covering the drying stain near his crotch.

'We will catch the next boat,' Katerina said, her voice hoarse and low.

Idriz glanced at his watch. 'I will take you.'

Katerina removed the cling film from the remaining plates. Spike made a half-hearted attempt at some browning lettuce, then set down his fork and looked out of the window, watching a pack of stray dogs sidling up the road. A hearse driver kicked out a lazy leg at them, and they retreated, but not far.

Turning back to the table, Spike got to his feet. 'To Lakis Demollari,' he said, lifting his water glass. Katerina hesitated, then raised her tumbler as well, and they all chinked edges. It was the first time that day Spike had seen Spiros look up. His dark eyes reminded Spike of something that made him avert his gaze. The empty sockets of the sheep's skull dangling from the downstairs doorway.

Chapter Fifty-Two

There was still a little time before the ferry left, so they killed it on the beach beside the port, watching overexcited children play on a plastic jumbo aeroplane, clambering over its sun-bleached wings and leaping down screaming onto the yellow sand. Just across the water, Spike could make out Corfu, green and tantalising on the horizon. He thought back to a time when he'd sat on a beach with Zahra in Tangiers, staring out at Europe, the unattainable Shangri-La. As if sensing Zahra in his thoughts, Jessica shifted closer, stretching out her toes in the warm sand. The sun had climbed overhead, and the white jasmine dividing the beach from the road gave off a delicious scent, far sweeter than anything in Corfu. Feeling Jessica look at him, he turned his head and kissed her. When he opened his eyes, he sensed Katerina's approving gaze, then watched her face fall as she saw her son skimming stones alone at the water's edge.

One of the children ran over to retrieve his beach ball, then stopped when he saw Spike, staring into his eyes. Idriz appeared, arms loaded with canned soft drinks. He muttered something at the child, who shouted '*Syblu*' as he ran back to join his friends. It didn't sound like a compliment.

'Your eyes,' Idriz said, distributing cans of 'Fresh' cola. 'They don't like them.'

'So I understand,' Spike said, adding in a stage whisper for Jessica's benefit, 'I have the Evil Eye.'

She nodded as though the revelation didn't come as too much of a surprise.

'It's because of the Turks,' Idriz went on, producing a worrying wheeze as he manoeuvred himself onto the sand next to Katerina. 'They conquered us, and many had blue eyes.'

'The Turks?' Jessica said dubiously.

'Maybe.'

Spike took out his wallet.

'No,' Idriz protested, glaring at Spike as though he'd just slapped him. 'Please…'

But Spike just shook his head and handed over the sticker he'd taken from the back of Calypso's photograph. 'What does it say?'

Idriz pulled out a pair of large blue-rimmed spectacles from his breast pocket and slipped them on. 'It's an address.' He squinted in for a closer look. 'From a shop in Saranda. A photographer worked there for many years. But now it is closed.' He took a slug of his cola and belched. Katerina grimaced, then gave her brother-in-law's ample paunch an affectionate pinch.

So that was it, Spike thought. The only connection they had to Calypso led to another dead end. Not that it really mattered. Corpses didn't need alibis.

Spike picked up the last can and walked across the beach to Spiros. The boy took it without thanks, just tipped half down his throat and screwed the base into the sand. Then he threw out another pebble, which bounced twice before vanishing below the water.

Spike bent down and picked up a broken piece of tile. 'Here,' he said, holding it out with a smile. 'I think the manmade stuff skims better.'

Spiros glanced at him, then tossed out another of his stones. Out in the channel, the Finikas Lines ferry made its slow way towards the harbour.

'Your mother's worried about you,' Spike said. 'I think your brother would have been too.'

'Please, Mr Sanguinetti,' Spiros replied in a quiet but fluent English that Spike had never heard before. 'You could not help Lakis. And you cannot help my mother and me.'

Looking into the boy's dark, accusing eyes, Spike realised that there was nothing more he could say. So he just added his shard of terracotta to the pile of stones, then walked back towards Jessica and the heady scent of jasmine.

Chapter Fifty-Three

They waited together in the Departure area, staring through the glass doors as the same crew prepared the same ferry. Then Spike heard his phone ring. Number unknown. Under normal circumstances he would have let it ring off, but it wasn't as though there was a great deal else to do.

'Is that Somerset J. Sanguinetti?' The uncertain voice was female, with a strong Essex accent.

Spike sighed, wondering how much he was going to be charged for answering a spam call on a Gibraltarian mobile in Albania, but before he could hang up the woman continued, 'You gave me your business card,' and something in her disappointed tone gave him pause. 'Who is this?' he asked, and saw Jessica glance up.

'It's Penny. Cal's friend?' The explanatory follow-up came so quickly it suggested she might be used to men forgetting her name.

Spike was already on his feet. 'Go on,' he said, signalling to Jessica to follow as he walked to the other side of the room.

'You said I should call you if I heard from Calypso.'

'And?' Spike suddenly felt nervous about what she might say next, despite never having met the woman.

'She rang me last night.'

He exhaled in relief. 'Is she OK?'

'Dunno.' Over the line he heard Penny drawing rapidly on a cigarette. 'I think so.'

He was waiting for her to elaborate when Jessica tapped him on the arm. 'Who is it?' Jessica mouthed, and Spike nodded at her and said, 'Penny?'

Jessica's eyes widened.

'Are you still there?' Spike asked.

'Cal told me not to tell anyone she'd been in touch. But I'm a bit short this month, so ...'

Spike interrupted, tone firm and businesslike. 'Will a hundred do?'

He could almost hear her relief at the other end of the line. But then she hesitated. 'How do I know I can trust you? Cal's my friend ...'

'Let's make it two hundred,' Spike said, and Jessica rolled her eyes. 'Where is she, Penny?' he asked.

Another draw on the cigarette. 'Gone home,' Penny replied. 'She asked me to send something to her.'

'What's the address?'

From the corner of his eye, Spike saw the officious man in his military cap wrenching open the doors. The passengers in the waiting room started to form an orderly queue.

'Albania,' Penny said.

'Where in Albania?' Spike asked, trying to keep the impatience from his voice.

Katerina readied the passports, attended by Idriz, who seemed keen to see his family as close as possible to the ferry.

'She said she's staying at the Blue Eye Hotel.'

'Where's that?'

'Look.' It sounded as though she was having second thoughts. 'She just told me to put the name of the hotel and "Saranda" on the envelope and it'd get there. My shift starts at six p.m., so maybe you could come before then with my money and ...' But Spike had already hung up, seeing Katerina near the front of the queue, too weary to notice that half of their group was missing.

'What did she say?' Jessica asked.

Spike smiled. 'That Calypso is alive and well and staying at a hotel in Saranda.'

Jessica stared back at him. 'What do you want to do?'

He saw the flash of excitement in her eyes and made up his mind. 'We could give it a night?'

'And if we don't find her?'

'We go home.'

She nodded, then took his hand and they walked over to Katerina together.

'We're going to stay on,' Jessica said.

The man behind them in the queue muttered something in Albanian. Katerina looked bereft, strangely hurt. She was about to say something, but then the impatient passenger thrust his passport into the air and shouldered past her, and she allowed herself to be carried forward by the crowd. As the glass doors closed behind her, she glanced back, and Spike could see anxiety in her eyes. But then she turned and ushered her son towards the boat that would carry them home to Corfu.

Outside on the street, Idriz hung back, suddenly awkward, unsure of his role. Jessica checked her watch. 'Come on,' she said. 'I need a drink.'

Chapter Fifty-Four

Idriz took them to a café above Saranda Harbour and ordered three cold Tirana beers. He seemed to have relaxed since watching the ferry set sail across the waves towards the safety of Corfu, and was snugly wedged now in a plastic chair, pulling thirstily on the neck of his bottle.

'You have family?' he asked Jessica with another of his big, good-natured grins.

'Not yet,' she said, automatically crossing her arms.

Idriz raised his thick eyebrows meaningfully at Spike. 'Still time, eh?'

Spike tried to muster some annoyance, but couldn't quite manage it, so just shook his head in amusement. But Idriz wasn't finished. 'You have brothers, maybe?'

'A brother and a sister,' Jessica said, not appearing to enjoy this line of questioning.

Idriz clicked his fingers for another round of beers. 'In Albania, you know, if a son is born, the family throws a big party. In the evening, the men fire their Kalashnikovs out of the window.' He pointed a large thumb heavenwards. 'Up into the sky.'

Spike fought back a smile as he watched Jessica's reaction. 'So if it's a daughter,' she said drily, anticipating the punch line, 'there are no Kalashnikovs?'

'No!' Idriz bellowed in glee. 'No party!' He shook with laughter, one hand on Spike's shoulder, and eventually even Jessica couldn't help but join in. 'Is that true?' she asked once the convulsions had died down, but Idriz just winked, so Spike decided it might be time to change the subject. 'Do you know the Blue Eye Hotel?'

'Sure,' Idriz coughed. He jabbed his cigarette towards the mountains, and they all turned to look at the pebbly terraced fields above. 'Don't worry,' he added, reading their expressions with a half-smile, 'Lazarat is on the other side. And they are gone now, these people. Too big for Saranda.' He suddenly appeared a little drunk, though it was only their second round. 'Small village but lots of money. And *power*...'

'How far away is the hotel?' Spike asked.

'Thirty minutes. I could drive you, but...' He pecked delicately on his cigarette.

'What?' Jessica said.

'It's a nice place for a couple to spend the night. Very romantic.' He nudged Spike with a flabby elbow. 'They say the waters at Blue Eye are magical. That they give a man special powers...'

Spike ignored him. 'Is there somewhere we can hire a car?'

Idriz stubbed out his cigarette. 'Of course.'

'I didn't bring my licence,' Jessica murmured, but Idriz gave her a look suggesting that such niceties might be unimportant in Albania. 'It is my cousin's shop. I will take you there myself.'

Spike nodded and pushed back his chair. 'Just got to make a call.' As he waited for the line to connect, he looked back at the table and saw Idriz laughing again with the exuberance that reminded Spike so much of Lakis. Jessica leant in to light his cigarette, and Spike felt a surge of... what was it? Pride? Desire? Maybe a bit of both.

Chapter Fifty-Five

Spike was expecting to leave a message, as his father seldom answered his ancient Nokia, but on the third ring he heard his slightly bemused voice. 'Hullo?'

'Dad?'

'Son?'

Spike never felt comfortable talking on the phone to Rufus. Between them they didn't seem able to work out who should speak when.

'Just a moment.' Rufus was on the move, and Spike realised he always did the same when talking on the phone. Who had picked up the habit from whom?

'You all right?'

'Fine, thanks, Dad.'

'Yes?'

'What?'

At the other end of the line, he could hear Rufus shuffling forward again. 'How was the funeral?'

'We got him into the ground,' Spike said, suspecting it might be better to keep his father in the dark about some of the more unusual aspects of the funeral.

'Not the way I might have phrased it, son,' Rufus sighed, 'but that's the important bit, I suppose. Are you on the boat?'

Spike paused. 'That's just it, Dad. Jess and I decided to stay on for a night.'

'I see.' He sounded upset. 'I'd have loved to visit Butrint.'

Spike suddenly felt guilty, aware that his father might never have another opportunity to see the ruins.

'Maybe I could catch the ferry tomorrow?' Rufus added hopefully. 'Join you for a day.'

'It's work, Dad. We won't be visiting the sites.'

'Cobblers.'

'It's to do with Lakis.'

That silenced him.

'We're looking for someone,' Spike said. 'Someone who might be able to help clear Lakis's name.'

'It's a bit late for that, isn't it?' Spike expected Rufus to retort, but instead he just said, 'Do take care of that arm, won't you?'

'Leg,' Spike corrected, but Rufus didn't seem to have heard. 'Peter *will* be disappointed...'

Spike interrupted. 'Dad?'

'... but I'm sure you know best.'

Spike smiled. His father could load a sentence with more disappointment than a spurned spinster.

'Be careful, son,' Rufus said after a pause. 'Albania used to be known as Illyria. The kingdom of the shipwreck in *Twelfth Night*. "*And what should I do in Illyria?*"' he quoted as if to an audience. '"*My brother he is in Elysium.*"' His voice suddenly sounded a great deal more distant than just a few miles away. 'A strange land where nothing is quite as it...'

Thankfully the line went dead, so Spike returned to the table, finding Idriz mid-anecdote, dyed hair in disarray, pudgy hands gesticulating wildly. A stray dog was watching him with sad, hungry eyes. As Spike approached, it shrank back in fear, then slunk away.

*

The dog is leaning against the hillside. Resting, Calypso assumes, yet something about her stance feels wrong. Surely only horses sleep standing up. 'Laika?' Calypso calls out.

The dog opens one eye. 'Barker', her name means in Russian, but this morning she hasn't made a sound. She manages a feeble wag of the tail, acknowledging Calypso's voice, but still doesn't move, just stands there slumped against the grassy slope. Throwing down her bucket, Calypso runs onto the riverside path.

Once again, she finds Petra and Samir thigh-deep in the blue water. They have replaced most of the slats on the bridge now, apart from a few in the centre which are still slimy and rotten. Calypso wades in, gasping at the chill, icy despite the constant sun. When Petra registers the look on her face, she passes Samir her tools and splashes through the water towards her.

A few minutes later, the three of them are gathered around Laika.

'My poor girl,' Petra whispers as she eases the dog onto her side, 'my sweet angel.' It has never occurred to Calypso that she and Samir may have wanted children. They always seem so self-contained. But now she sees something in Petra's gaze as she stares down at her Alsatian crossbreed, lying on her side in the dust, still trying to wag her tail.

'We must go to the vet,' Petra says.

Samir massages the dog's hide with his powerful fingers. He gives his wife a look – kind, but firm.

'It could be poison,' Petra tries again. 'The herdsmen leave poisoned meat for the eagles.'

Laika's tongue lolls from her mouth, panting in short bursts.

'She is old, Petra,' Samir says in his deep, gentle voice. 'We should let her sleep.'

But Petra buries her face in the dog's bristly coat. And when she lifts her head, her thin lips are firmly pressed together. It is a look of determination Calypso knows well.

'I'll bring the van,' Samir says. Two decades of marriage have taught him that sometimes it is wiser simply to concede.

Samir's hooded eyes always look sad, but now he seems more mournful than ever. He might be handsome if he could only smile,

Calypso thinks as he walks away. To have found Petra – beautiful Petra with her cheekbones and her thin practical body – he must be grateful. Sometimes Calypso wonders if there is anything he wouldn't do for his wife.

The white van reverses, then Samir gets out carrying a dust-sheet. As they roll Laika onto it, the dog whimpers, but Petra strokes her head, singing softly into her velvet ear, and she seems to understand. Then Samir hoists the shroud into his massive arms with a grunt.

Realising this may be the last time that she sees Laika, Calypso reaches into the van and runs a finger along the white strip of fur between her eyes. The dog gazes up at her. Then the rear doors slam shut.

'We'll be back in a couple of hours,' Petra calls through the open window, her face drawn and pale.

Calypso longs to go with them. She is scared to stay here by herself. But she knows that this might be the only thing she can do for these people who have sheltered her without asking questions.

The van pulls away. And then it is just the roar of the river, and Calypso is alone again.

Chapter Fifty-Six

There was only one place to hire a car in Saranda, 'King Zog Rentals', a tiny office behind the port with its meagre fleet parked on the pavement outside. Idriz's influence managed to secure them two days with a Kia Picanto for 7,000 lek. Spike still wasn't clear on the exchange rate, but the 'slitting my own throat' gesture the owner had made seemed encouraging, and the nearby cash point had produced a pleasing wad of notes.

'Does "lek" mean anything?' Jessica asked as the owner flicked through his remittance like a croupier.

'It comes from Alexander the Great,' Idriz said proudly. 'His mother was from Albania.'

Naturally, Spike thought, imagining his father arguing that out with Sir Leo over a couple of ginger beers by the Hoffmann pool. Was that where he was now? Shooting the breeze with his new pals?

Jessica started the small South Korean car as though she'd owned one all her life. 'If the police stop you,' Idriz called through the window, 'give them seventy lek. No more,' he warned, one hand slapping the tinny green roof in farewell.

And then they were on their way, Spike with another tourist map on his knees, Jessica at the wheel. A new car, a different landscape, but the same problem – Lakis Demollari.

They drove along the wide road out of the city. Stray dogs lined the verges, warming themselves in the sun, unperturbed as the buses and articulated lorries thundered an inch from their outstretched muzzles. Every third building seemed to be a *lavazh*, or carwash, which didn't bode well for the condition of Albania's transport network. The doorways were hung with the same sinister trinkets they'd seen everywhere else – rag dolls and animal skulls, garlic and brightly coloured toys.

'Maybe they've heard the man with the blue eyes is in town,' Jessica suggested with a smile.

'Was in town,' Spike said as they passed a gypsy encampment and started climbing into the mountains.

Gradually, the road began to narrow and the turns grew more precarious. Jessica hugged the car to the steep mountain wall, keeping as far away as possible from the massive gorge which had suddenly appeared around one corner. Spike ventured a cautious look into the lush green ravine, then pulled back. He'd never been good with heights, despite growing up on the Rock.

A white van tore around the bend, almost colliding with them. The couple inside nodded their apology, then sped on down the hill towards Saranda.

'Have you found it yet?' Jessica asked, glancing nervously at another of the flower-swagged marble monuments which appeared to commemorate each fatal accident on the mountain road.

'It's hard to get a sense of scale,' Spike bluffed, twisting the map in his hands.

Jessica laughed, and Spike suddenly felt a deep affection for this beautiful woman with her slim brown arms and glinting eyes, who for some reason still liked him after all these years. Watching her with the breeze buffeting through the window, the incredible blue sky above, he felt an unfamiliar sense of wellbeing. But then he saw a black pickup truck speeding towards them, its rear heaped with a cargo of foliage strapped down by a net.

'That,' Jessica said, eyes watching the truck race into the distance through the rear-view mirror, 'was a hell of a lot of weed.'

Spike craned his head as the driver steered around the corner and out of sight. Looking back at the map, he found the village of Lazarat marked close by, just on the other side of the mountain.

The landscape started to change as they zigzagged down the valley. The oak trees and lush green vegetation reminded Spike of medieval English woodland. They drove over a concrete bridge, and Jessica slowed the car. 'Look at the water,' she said in a hushed voice.

Spike sat up to get a better view of the nuclear-green torrent beneath them, so bright it seemed spot-lit from below. There were certain fruits, he thought, so intensely sweet that you would shy away from them if you knew they were synthetic. But if they were natural... Jessica seemed to be thinking along similar lines. 'It's beautiful,' she said as she pulled away, 'I think.'

The forest started to close in. Sprays of water cascaded down the rocky cliff above the road. After a few miles, they reached a tree-lined track that led into a leafy car-park area. Two wooden signs were hammered into the ground, one in Albanian, the other in English: BLUE-EYE HOTEL.

'I take it back,' Jessica said. 'You're a navigational genius.' She turned off the engine, and then all they could hear was the chorus of bullfrogs, and beyond, the distant roar of the river.

Chapter Fifty-Seven

They passed a skipload of concrete vats dumped in the undergrowth by the path. 'Idriz has a strange idea of what constitutes "romantic",' Jessica said, swatting away another mosquito as they walked towards a wooden gazebo at the edge of the river.

Through the window they made out chairs stacked on tables. 'Looks closed,' Jessica said as they skirted around the building. A slatted deck overhung the water; beyond, they saw a cluster of small chalets built against the steeply wooded hillside, a footbridge leading to a shady riverside path on the other side.

'Anybody there?' Jessica called out, then, 'Calypso?', but the rush of the fast-moving water drowned out her voice. She pointed at a line of washing outside one of the chalets. Spike nodded, then tried the back door of the restaurant and was surprised to find it open. When he looked back, Jessica was already halfway to the chalet.

The floorboards inside were wet and smelt of pine detergent. Spike let the door go and it swung closed behind him with a bang. He saw something move at the edge of his vision. 'Calypso,' he said, hearing a sound from behind the bar. 'I'm a friend of Penny's,' he tried, almost tripping over an overturned mop bucket, soapy water seeping into the floorboards.

Behind the bar, he found another door and pushed it open. Inside, the kitchen units gleamed: even the extractor hood had been polished with oil. The fridge was empty, door open, plastic shelving scoured, ultraviolet mosquito lamp buzzing above.

A single sheet of notepaper was secured to the metal splash-back with a magnet. Spike leant in for a closer look, seeing the strange language he now knew was Albanian. Suddenly, he caught a flicker of movement reflected in the stainless steel and turned, raising his arm just in time as a heavy weight swung towards him. The blow was so severe it would have knocked him unconscious – or worse – had he not had time to duck. Instead he felt an agonising pain in his shoulder as he threw his arms over his head, obeying some instinct to protect his face. He heard an ear-splitting clatter, and when he looked down he saw a cast-iron casserole rocking to a halt on the stone floor. The kitchen was empty, the door to the bar swinging.

Spike straightened up, massaging his injured shoulder, feeling a bruise already forming, then started wrenching open drawers. Inside the third, he found a sharp paring knife and ran back into the restaurant. Through the window, he glimpsed a small figure sprinting past in the direction of the car park.

He thought about calling for Jessica, but the noise of the river was too great. Ahead on the path, he saw the figure slow down, then turn and run on.

So he went after her, knife in hand. His progress was laborious: for a moment he'd forgotten his injured leg, but now each step made him flinch, and he half-expected to see the warm stain of blood on the bandage that would mean that the wound had reopened.

Reaching the grassy car park, he stopped to catch his breath. The girl was doing the same, bent over, hands on her narrow hips, red hair fastened in a knot on the top of her head, watching him with frightened eyes, weighing his next move.

'Calypso!' he shouted after her, but she saw the knife in his hand and darted away. He took a moment to curse, then continued down the path. An outdoor bar area appeared as the river widened out, another footbridge beyond. Calypso was standing at the bottom of it, chin raised as though challenging him to follow. Spike shook his head and sighed. He really wasn't cut out for this anymore.

Slipping the knife into the pocket of his jacket, he held up his hands and walked slowly towards her. All this stopping and starting, turning and waiting – it reminded Spike of the Barbary partridge up on the Rock. In nesting season, the females would limp in front of you as though injured, encouraging you to follow, letting you believe you could catch them as they lured you further and further from their nests, only to fly out of reach as soon as the predator had been drawn off course.

'Penny sent me,' Spike called out. 'I'm a friend.'

But Calypso just stared back from the other side of the bridge, her fine-boned face unreadable. He showed her his empty hands, then took a step forward.

'I just want to talk,' he said with a smile that faded as soon as he ascended the bridge, feeling the slats sway precariously beneath his feet. His fingers reached automatically for the slimy ropes that served as hand-rails as Calypso waited on the other side. She wore olive-coloured jogging pants and a crop top. Although one eye was blackened, Spike could still see that she was as pretty as Lakis had described.

She watched him move, glancing down at his brogues, which were spattered now with mud and grit. When he was almost half-way across, she turned away and started running again.

'*Chufla*,' Spike swore in *yanito*, continuing after her as quickly as his bad leg would allow. But when he got to the middle of the bridge, he felt the first slat come away beneath his foot. He grabbed at the rope, but then another came away, and then he was flailing his arms, desperately trying to grip onto wood or hemp to stop himself from plunging into the fast-flowing river. As soon as his fingers found a board, that came away too, and then he really was falling, and he could sense her watching from the bank, triumphant, as he hit the water.

The first shock was the temperature. Then the judder through his legs as they slammed against the gravelly bottom. The river was barely a metre deep, sending a sharp pain reverberating through his thigh. He fell backwards and slipped under, and for a moment the world was green and blue and his ears were filled with the roar of the current rushing over pebbles. He clambered to his feet, gasping and disorientated. Calypso was gone.

'Jessica!' Spike called downstream, then glanced up at the bridge, seeing blue sky shining through the gap in the rotten wooden planks through which he'd fallen. He shook his head at his stupidity as he waded towards the bank, river weed looping around his knees, his breathing quick and shallow from the pain in his leg and shoulder and the chill of the water.

As he hauled himself out, water cascading from his legs, he looked down and saw a jacuzzi jet of bubbles boiling in the corner of the pool, shades of emerald and indigo flitting and dazzling like a kaleidoscope.

He was still pushing through the reeds when he heard a scream cut through the roar of the river, and set off at a lumbering run down the path that led back to the chalets.

Chapter Fifty-Eight

Calypso was crouching on the decking outside the restaurant, one hand clutching her mobile phone. Opposite her stood Jessica.

'Stay back,' Calypso warned in a surprisingly clear English, holding up the handset. 'I will call the police.'

'I'm with the police,' Jessica called back, voice calm and authoritative. 'I want to help you, Calypso.'

The girl's eyes widened in alarm, no doubt grappling with the terrifying question of how Jessica knew her name.

'I know you were at the Hoffmann house the night that Arben Avdia was murdered,' Jessica continued.

'That means nothing to me.'

'He was a young man, Calypso. From Albania, like you.' She took a step forward. 'What are you afraid of? If you talk to me, maybe I can help you.'

Spike stayed close to the river, out of the girl's eyeline.

'A man attacked you, didn't he?' Jessica said. 'At your apartment in Kavos.'

The girl looked up, startled.

'I was there, Calypso. At the bar.' Jessica gave her a reassuring smile. 'I met Penny. She's worried about you. She told me where to find you.' A sympathetic pause. 'She told me about your brother.'

Calypso flinched, and Spike saw some of the fight drain out of her.

Jessica moved closer. 'Who hurt your eye, Calypso?' She tilted her face. 'Was it Lakis?' She used the sort of tone a mother might to soothe a frightened child, and Spike suddenly thought of Charlie – how good she would be with him.

But the girl was shaking her head. 'The man who came for me was not Greek,' she said, putting a hand to her swollen eye, remembering. 'Maybe English.' Her voice cracked. 'He wore a mask. He tried to kill me.'

Spike chose that moment to drop his sodden phone, and Calypso turned, seeing him dripping with water, clutching his bruised shoulder. Jessica glared at him as the girl began to back away, a muscle beneath her eye twitching with fear.

'Wait,' Jessica called out, but now Calypso was pointing at Spike. 'He has a knife, he followed me ...' Her thighs tensed as though she was about to run again. This time Spike knew for certain that he wouldn't be able to catch her. He wasn't sure Jessica could either.

'He's not the man who attacked you,' Jessica said. 'Spike's just a lawyer.'

Thanks very much, thought Spike.

'The man had a mask,' Calypso shouted back, 'I couldn't see his face ...'

'Then look at his eyes,' Jessica said, taking a risk. 'Spike has blue eyes. Look at them.'

Jessica beckoned him closer, and he stepped up onto the decking, his thick dark hair slicked back, feeling like a captive paraded at a slave auction. What if Calypso's attacker's eyes had been blue, he had time to wonder, but then she turned back to Jessica and gave a faint nod.

'We're just trying to find out what happened the night you were at the Hoffmann Estate,' Jessica tried again. 'Two young men are dead. Another's in danger.' She lowered her voice: 'He's only thirteen.'

That seemed to hit home, so Jessica pressed on mercilessly. She was good at that, Spike thought, suddenly feeling a little sorry for the detainees she must interview at New Mole House in Gibraltar. 'The boy's name is Spiros Demollari. Lakis's little brother.'

Calypso paused, then slipped her phone into the pocket of her close-fitting jogging pants. 'My boss will be back soon. We can talk for ten minutes, then you must leave.'

'Thank you,' Jessica replied.

'And I only speak to you,' Calypso said. 'Not to *syblu*. The blue-eyed man.'

Chapter Fifty-Nine

They sat in the empty restaurant surrounded by tables stacked with upside-down chairs. It felt like an interview for a new waitress conducted before service began. An interview that wasn't going especially well, Spike thought. Calypso had left the door open, ostensibly to listen out for her boss's car, in reality because she seemed comforted by a potential escape route. The oppressive roar of the river found its way into the space.

Calypso stared at the knots in the wooden table as she sipped her glass of water. The jug had been filled from a tap in the hillside; the taste was earthy, but the temperature – as Spike well knew, having only just recovered feeling in his feet – was searingly fresh.

It was always going to be a difficult conversation, and though Calypso had promised she would talk to them, she didn't seem to know how to begin. It was often like that, Spike thought, when something bad had happened. Jessica knew it too, so she started with an easy question. 'How long did you work at the bar in Kavos?'

The girl answered immediately. 'Six years. Just for the summer season.' She shrugged by way of explanation. 'There are no good jobs in Albania. Especially for women.' Her English was accented, but grammatically better than most of the native speakers she had worked with in Kavos. 'One night, two men came into the bar to watch cricket.' She looked again at Spike, still uneasy in his presence.

'What were their names?' Jessica asked.

'I don't know,' Calypso said, and Spike groaned inwardly. All this way for another dead end. But then she said something that made both Spike and Jessica sit up in their wooden chairs. 'One of them had dark skin. Like an Indian.'

'And the other one?'

'A white man. With red hair.' Spike and Jessica exchanged a glance, but the girl didn't seem to notice. She took another sip of water, and in the hush they heard the river give a sudden surge outside. It made Spike feel suddenly nostalgic for the gentle lap of the Mediterranean. 'Later, the Indian man came over,' Calypso said. 'He told me that his friend liked me. He asked if I would come to their house.' She rubbed her brow. The gash above her left eye should have been stitched, Spike thought. It would leave a scar. 'At first I said no, but then he showed me an envelope full of money. Hundreds of euro. It was more than I could make in two months.' She lowered her eyes. 'So I took it.' Her voice trailed off. Jessica reached over and touched her arm, and she started as though burnt. 'You've done nothing wrong, Calypso,' Jessica said, but neither of them looked convinced.

'The next day, I called the number the man had given me, and he sent a taxi. All the way to Kavos.' She looked as though she still couldn't quite believe the extravagance. 'When the car reached the house, the Indian came out and brought me in a back way.' Another pause. 'It was dark. He took me to a guest house by the sea. He gave me another envelope. Then the other man came. The man with red hair.'

Calypso's eyes gleamed with tears. Then her expression hardened, and she wiped them away with a brisk sweep of her hand. 'Later, when the man was finished, the Indian came back. Took me up to the gates and told me to wait for a taxi. I asked him for the rest of my money, but he just laughed.'

'Did the taxi come?' Spike asked.

Calypso shook her head. 'I waited for a long time. Then the Corfiot...Lakis. He came into the yard.' She smiled. 'He was kind. Offered to drive me home. I said no, but he told me he would be up on the road if I changed my mind. He liked to look at the stars, he said, and have a smoke. Like a teenager.' Her smile died. 'But the Indian had told me to wait, so I did.' She lapsed into silence again, and Spike reached for the packet of cigarettes he'd taken from the funeral, then remembered they were drenched, like everything else. 'Then I heard a noise on the path,' Calypso said. 'A noise that scared me. Like a groan. It was a man – very close. A security light came on. And the man stopped. Like a dog in the lights of a car.' She swallowed. 'He had blood on his clothes.'

'Then what happened?' Jessica pressed.

'The man ran down the side of the house. And the light went off.'

'Who was he?' Jessica said.

Calypso shook her head. 'I couldn't see his face.'

'Was it the Indian?'

'Maybe. Could be any man. Could be him.' She looked again at Spike, who for some reason shifted uncomfortably in his seat. 'I ran up to the road to find Lakis. He was lying on his car, listening to reggae songs on the radio.' She smiled again, as if thinking of what might have been. 'He drove me home. The next time I saw his face it was in the newspaper. And he was in prison.' She glanced up. 'But he did not hurt that boy in the cave.'

Jessica delivered her next question in a voice Spike knew well – anger tamped down just below the surface. 'So why didn't you go to the police, Calypso?'

The girl wrapped her arms around her slim frame, face set. 'These are powerful people, lady. Rich people.'

'And you saw an opportunity to make some money, right?' Jessica said, and by her tone Spike knew that she'd reached the end of her reserve of sympathy. 'You tried to blackmail them.'

Calypso nodded, without meeting her eye. 'I sent a text. I only asked for five thousand euros. Nothing to people like them.'

Spike gave a sharp nod. 'Not much for a young man's life either.' The girl coloured, and Jessica continued. 'Did you get a reply?'

'Yes.'

'Can I see it?'

'I deleted it.'

Jessica and Spike exchanged another look.

'What did it say?' Jessica asked.

'To meet him at Lefkimmi port and I would get my money.'

'Where's Lefkimmi?'

'Outside Kavos. The car ferry from the mainland stops there. But most of the time it's empty.'

Surely you weren't stupid enough to go there alone, Spike wanted to say. But then he realised that this slight girl with the wide eyes had probably not had anyone she could ask to go with her. So instead he just asked, 'What happened when you reached the port?'

'I got there early. Hid and waited for the Indian to arrive. I knew it would be him.' Another of the small, triumphant smiles that Spike had seen just before he plunged into the river. 'And it was. He drove up in a big car, and when he got out I saw he had a knife.' She looked again at Spike.

'So you waited for him to leave,' Jessica said. 'Then you ran?'

Calypso nodded. 'Back to my apartment. To get my things. But then the man came. He must have found out where I lived.'

'The Indian?'

'Maybe. I don't know.' She shrugged. 'I told you, he wore a mask. But his eyes were black. Like a child's doll.'

Spike turned to Jessica. The Hoffmann green eyes would have been hard to miss.

'He tried to drown me,' Calypso said.

'But you got away?'

'Yes.' She looked up. 'How did you find me?'

'Like I said, Spike's a lawyer,' Jessica replied. 'He was helping Lakis. We found your apartment. Then we found... Penny?'

'Penny told you where I was?' Calypso's face fell and she got to her feet. 'I have to leave. Go somewhere else. Somewhere the man won't find me.'

'We're not finished, Calypso,' Jessica said. 'Sit down.' And there was a coolness in her voice now that made the girl obey. 'Lakis Demollari is dead. He was shot by Arben's family.'

Calypso looked as though she was trying to take it in.

'They blamed him for Arben's death.'

She squeezed shut her eyes. '*Kanun*,' she whispered.

Jessica nodded. 'And now Lakis's brother, Spiros, has to live with a death sentence.'

Calypso stared into the middle distance.

'We need you to come back to Corfu. Give a statement to the Corfu police.'

Jessica hadn't phrased it as a question but Calypso was already shaking her head. 'I can never go back there. I am sorry for Lakis. And his brother.' She started to stand. 'But I have problems of my own.'

This time Jessica had no choice but to let her go. 'Listen,' Spike called over as she walked towards the door. 'Two men are dead and nothing will bring them back. But the boy... Will you at least talk to Arben's relatives? Tell them what you told us?'

Calypso turned to him with a smirk of disbelief. 'Go to *Lazarat*?'

'We'll come with you,' Spike said. 'We just need them to understand that Lakis didn't kill Arben. I'm a lawyer – I can help.'

Calypso shook her head. 'You understand nothing of my country.'

'I understand justice.'

'You talk of Lazarat like it is a place where that matters.' She held out her hand to the open door. 'Now please. Go.'

Spike walked over to the bar. 'I saw your brother's picture,' he said as he wrote Jessica's mobile number on the back of a beer mat. 'He was a good-looking boy.' He slipped the bevelled square into Calypso's hand and wrapped her fingers around it, feeling calluses on her soft skin. 'Take it. Just in case you change your mind.'

Chapter Sixty

Jessica slammed the car door, then turned to Spike, challenging him with her direct dark eyes. 'I don't think it's a good idea,' she said. He knew she was right, but didn't reply, so she just pursed her lips and twisted on the engine. Once they'd made it back over the ridge of the mountain, a larger, U-shaped valley appeared below, with a road and a river snaking along its base. Snow dusted the peaks of the mountains on either side, and Spike saw what looked like a golden eagle soaring in the distance. Augury, his father might have observed, and Spike hoped that on this occasion he would be right. On the slope below they saw a series of Gibraltar-style concrete pillboxes. Spike wondered for which war they'd been built. 'When's the last boat to Corfu?' he asked.

'Five p.m.,' Jessica said tersely, and he checked the clock on the dashboard. It was gone 2 p.m. With a shake of her head, she turned onto the road to Lazarat and, incrementally, Spike became aware of an aroma filling the car, a herbal fragrance that took him back to Gibraltar after he'd finished his A Levels, the glorious summer of interminable parties on the beach, impatiently waiting to start university in London, for life to begin. He remembered it as a honey-coloured haze of time, fractured only by the darkness of his mother's death. He'd avoided drugs since then, but the smell still tugged at his brain, like a shot of something sweet and strong.

Then the first fields of cannabis appeared. They'd only caught a glimpse of the shorn crop in the pickup truck earlier, but seeing the plants now, growing tightly together, straining for the mountain sun above, Spike was astonished by their size. Over twelve feet high, with huge green leaves and thick, sap-filled stems, glowing with an almost preternatural health.

At the edge of one field, a line of women in what Spike assumed was traditional Albanian clothing – woollen headdresses, ankle-length skirts – stooped as they scythed down the plants. They straightened up to stare as the Kia passed, faces weathered and lined, presumably half-stoned from the work.

'Up there.' Jessica nudged Spike and pointed at a white CCTV camera mounted at the top of one of the telegraph poles that lined the road. He looked up at the next pole and saw another camera pointing the opposite way. Access to and from the village was monitored.

'What if someone recognises us from Lakis's funeral?' Jessica's rising intonation reminded Spike of a teenaged stoner, so he leant over and pressed the button to close her window.

Another group of women, Romani this time, were working in the next field, overseen by a farmer who spoke rapidly into a walkie-talkie as he watched the car drive past. Buildings started to appear, old stone barns crammed floor to ceiling with freshly harvested cannabis plants, more pickup trucks waiting outside. Did they ship it out intact, Spike wondered, or process it somewhere else? The police believed that the man who'd killed Lakis had crossed the mountain border with Greece on horseback. Could these people do the same with the dope? Once they got it inside the EU, presumably they were home and dry.

Spike thought about the European flags flying from every other building. How could the government of Albania be serious about membership of the Union when they turned a blind eye to somewhere like Lazarat? But then he remembered Lakis's tales of the

Venetians planting Corfu with olive trees, turning a barren island green, exporting the oil for lamps. Maybe these people were just doing the same. Exploiting their natural resources for profit. Would any poor country behave differently?

Jessica touched his arm, and he refocused, following her gaze. Above the rickety farmhouses, with their ducks and hens and piebald dogs scrabbling in the dust, he saw newly built villas, outer walls topped with barbed wire, satellite dishes mushrooming on red-tiled roofs.

They pushed deeper into the village, passing a small domed church on one corner before entering a main street which ran parallel to the mountains. More concrete-shielded houses rose on either side. Within their walls, Spike made out neat rectangular nooks, like arrow slits. Wide enough to accommodate the muzzle of a Kalashnikov, he thought, increasingly aware of how quiet the village felt.

On the lower sections of the telegraph poles, they saw sheets of card staple-gunned to the wood. Jessica slowed, and Spike opened the window to find another photocopied photograph of Arben, with the words beneath, 'Familia Avdia, 14.00 ora ...'

'Restorant Skanderbeg,' he read aloud. 'Must be the venue for the wake.'

A vehicle was cruising along the street towards them, a Hummer in gunmetal-grey, more pimped-up than anything they'd seen in Saranda. It slowed as it passed their car, windows ominously dark, before revving aggressively away.

Then the road divided around some kind of municipal building, the old village hall by the look of it, constructed from the same slate-coloured rock that formed the mountains above. In front trickled a fountain, perhaps where the locals had gathered to draw water in more innocent days before they'd developed a taste for San Pellegrino. The front door was reinforced, the windows protected by metal shutters. On the slope above, Spike saw a group of even larger villas – sunlight reflecting from a swimming pool, what looked like a private putting green beneath. And all around, enveloping everything in a cloak of verdant lushness, spread the fields of cannabis.

'That must be it,' Jessica said, pointing at a building further down the street with tables outside, a few people sitting around them, glasses in hands. As the car drew closer, Spike saw that the drinkers were all male, and all staring at them. He glanced at the sign above the door: *Skënderbeu Restoran*.

Chapter Sixty-One

The Skanderbeg Restaurant looked like another relic pre-dating Lazarat's newfound wealth. It was little more than a converted cowshed with two low barred windows on either side of the large door. Yet the cars parked outside would not have looked out of place at a Premier League training ground – Baby Bentleys, BMW saloons – and it was from a keg of imported continental lager that the men drank, each liberally helping himself as though he belonged to a collective that rendered monetary payment unnecessary.

Jessica parked the Kia and, just for a moment, they paused, holding each other's eye. Spike waited for her curt nod of consent, then they got out and walked towards the restaurant, watched by six sets of unfriendly Lazarat eyes. The oldest man, heavy and moustachioed, got to his feet, furrowing his leathery forehead above thick black eyebrows. He took in the colour of Spike's irises, then ran his shrewd gaze over the smart trouser suit that Jessica had worn to Lakis's funeral, sucking hard on a cigarette that was burning down into his cupped brown hand. 'English?' he asked, and Spike nodded.

'We do not like strangers here,' he said, blocking their way. That much was obvious, thought Spike, eyes falling on the alarming bulge in the inside pocket of the man's leather jacket.

'We knew Arben,' Spike said, and the man's frown deepened. 'From Corfu,' he added, and was surprised to see the man relax as he turned to his companions and muttered, 'Kerkyra.' Then he stepped aside, and Spike took Jessica's hand and led her through the open door, feeling the men turn to watch her move.

Inside, the room was dark and smelled of stale smoke and charred meat. Most of the food seemed already to have been eaten: a tiny waitress in a traditional headdress was clearing plates, while in one corner an aged couple sat in silence, watching two overweight men stack cartons of cigarettes on a side table, sorting them into piles by their brand names and tar content.

The waitress stooped even lower as she saw them approach. 'Arben Avdia,' Spike said, as though it was some kind of pass-word. Faces turned, and the waitress gestured timidly at the couple in black.

The old woman's head was turned away, just the back of her shawl visible. Though her husband's face was gnarled with age and grief, something in its planes and angles, in the insolence of his gaze, told Spike this was Arben's father. 'Mr Avdia?' he said, and the old man slowly stood up. 'Lorik,' he snapped, and one of the stout helpers hurried over, a middle-aged man in a suit lined with emerald silk, whose choice of neckerchief marked him out as something of a dandy.

'English?' Lorik tried with a bashful smile, wiping his palms on the sides of his coat.

Spike nodded. 'We're friends from Corfu.'

'Kerkyra,' Lorik repeated to Arben's parents, and at last the mother turned her head to get a first glimpse of her dead son's friends from Greece. She might have been beautiful once, Spike thought, with her fine handsome features and intelligent dark eyes. But her sallow skin was as seamed as a fig, sagging around thin, chapped lips. She acknowledged Spike with a bow of the head, then fixed her reddened eyes on Jessica, touching one hand to her mouth and beckoning towards her with the other.

Jessica gave Spike a look of confusion, but approached all the same. The old woman reached out and took her hand, pressing it to her withered cheek, bathing it in tears, whispering softly in

Albanian. Then her husband muttered something harsh, and she reluctantly released Jessica's hand and lowered her head.

'It is difficult for the old woman,' Lorik said with a nonchalant shrug. 'To lose a son like that.' He took a swig of beer and suppressed a belch, hitting a fist into his sternum. The no-alcohol rule did not seem to apply to this wake. 'But still,' Lorik continued, 'the *Kanun* is patient.' A broad smile. 'We take our blood. In time.'

Arben's mother curled a finger at Lorik and he squatted at her knee, nodding as he listened to her stream of quiet, urgent words. Then he stood and scratched the top of his head, as though undecided how to begin. Finally he opened his arms, revealing dense patches of perspiration under each, and clasped his small hands together with a bow of the head. 'My aunt' – he was addressing Jessica now – 'wants me to say that you are very beautiful.' Another beaming shake of the head to imply that some things are so obvious that they need not be articulated. Jessica coloured. 'That she sees great kindness in your eyes.' He bowed again. 'And that she would have welcomed you as a daughter.'

Jessica stared back in bafflement.

'She says she is sorry for your sadness. The loss of a son is a terrible affliction.' He placed a hand on his heart. 'But for a woman to lose the man she would have married is a disaster, especially when she is no longer so very...' The briefest of hesitations, and even now Spike found himself close to smiling, '... young,' Lorik concluded with an apologetic grimace, and Spike sneaked a look at Jessica, seeing her nostrils flare. She tucked a hank of glossy dark hair behind one ear and lifted her chin. 'Please tell your aunt, ah...'

'Lorik,' Spike gallantly supplied, and her eyes flashed.

'... that I am grateful for her kind words, but that she is mistaken. Arben was not my... intended. Nor anyone else's, as far as we are aware.'

Lorik frowned, then turned back to the old woman, whose mouth tightened in anger as he relayed Jessica's words. She started to prise herself up from her chair, one elbow flat on the table for leverage. When Lorik tried to take her arm, she slapped him away, and he cowered as she hissed at him in Albanian. Then she moved towards Jessica, glowering, and Spike couldn't help but think that Arben's fiancée, whoever she was, had narrowly missed acquiring a terrifying mother-in-law. She spoke in a deep, guttural Albanian, firing out words and spittle into Jessica's horrified face, gesturing impatiently for her nephew to translate. When he did so, it was with a face as sullen as a chastened schoolboy. 'My aunt is asking where is this girl who Arben loved so much that we were willing to accept her into our family?' Lorik listened to more of his aunt's vitriol, then continued. 'She says her son is dead. That we have taken our blood. But still this girl does not come to pay her respects.'

Jessica pressed her hands together in wordless apology. The old woman responded by spitting on the ground by her feet and turning away.

Lorik moved towards Spike, thick lower lip jutting. 'You should go.' He shook his head. 'My aunt is old. She has misunderstood things. But you are not welcome here.'

Jessica threw Spike a glance that asked what on earth they should do now. He shrugged, still unclear as to what had gone on, but increasingly sure that now was not the moment to start talking to Arben's family about Lakis and vendettas.

Suddenly they heard shouting outside, then the splinter of breaking glass, and through the open door Spike saw a man putting out the passenger window of their hire car with the butt of a rifle. Job done, he turned with a thin smile of satisfaction, and Spike recognised him as Alex, the tall Albanian who had threatened them at Lakis's funeral. Locking eyes with Spike, Alex's smile faded as he picked up his weapon and strode towards them.

Once at the threshold, he raised the rifle to his shoulder and pointed it at Spike, shouting something that forced even Arben's elderly father to his feet.

Spike put an arm around Jessica and looked to their new friend Lorik to translate. But Lorik's genial manner had evaporated. 'You were at the funeral of the Demollari boy,' Lorik said coldly. 'He says you are with the family.'

Spike opened his mouth to explain, but Lorik was already pointing to the stable door at the back of the restaurant. 'Move.'

'Lakis Demollari didn't kill Arben,' Spike called back as he led Jessica into the walled courtyard outside.

But nobody seemed to be listening.

Chapter Sixty-Two

They stumbled out into the blinding afternoon sun. Above the courtyard wall, Spike could just make out the green tips of the cannabis plants trembling in the breeze. One fell, and he realised that the scythes must still be working, out of sight.

'Turn!' came Alex's voice, using the rudimentary English they'd first heard at Lakis's funeral.

Spike and Jessica obeyed, backs hard against the rough, hot concrete.

'Jesus,' Spike heard Jessica whisper under her breath. He hoped she wasn't crying, and picked up her hand, feeling oddly calm as he watched Alex level the rifle at him again. It was almost surreal, standing in this walled courtyard, dazzled by the sun, apparently about to face an Albanian firing squad. If the Foreign Legion had turned up, bayonets in hand, Spike wasn't sure he would have been surprised. He shook his head, wondering if the cannabis fumes were affecting him after all.

The upper panel of the stable door into the restaurant was open, and through it Spike could see Lorik and Arben's father watching them, sipping their drinks as though observing a horse race on which they didn't have much riding. Arben's mother was gone – presumably in Lazarat this kind of thing wasn't women's work.

'Your cell phones,' Alex called out. 'Slowly.'

They threw them to the dusty ground, Spike's white-screened from its unexpected swim, Jessica's ringing moments before the butt of Alex's rifle smashed both to pieces. Who had been trying to call her?

The lower panel opened, and Spike recognised Ismail, the other Albanian who'd ambushed them at the funeral, as he stepped into the courtyard. Alex passed him the rifle, then placed a hand on Jessica's shoulders and pushed her roughly round to face the wall. Once her palms were splayed against the concrete, he started to frisk her, like an airport security guard who took pride in his work, beginning at her ankles, then moving up her legs and hips, fingers lingering longer than was necessary. As his hands moved towards her chest, Spike tried to catch her eye, but she refused him, and his stomach lurched. Then Ismail called out something, laughing as Alex cupped Jessica's breasts. Spike closed his eyes; when he opened them, Alex was sweeping his palms along Jessica's arms before stepping away.

Spike assumed the same position, feeling the pressure start at his calves. He angled his head so he could see Jessica as she leant her cheek against the wall, her face pale, breaths uneven. As Alex's powerful fingers dug into the wound on his thigh, Spike flinched, then felt the man's hands patting down the damp pockets of his jacket.

There was a sudden cry of triumph as Alex held up the small kitchen knife Spike had forgotten he still possessed, the look of vindication clear in his eye. '*Ha mut*,' he swore, and then everything started to happen very fast, Ismail dragging Jessica away, the stable door slamming closed, Alex picking up the rifle and raising the stock tightly to his shoulder.

'I was right,' Alex said. 'You are here to take blood. For the Demollari boy.'

Spike might have laughed had not the rifle been pointing directly at his chest, so instead he tried the truth, knowing that it was unlikely to have any effect. 'Lakis was Arben's friend,' he said quietly. Alex smirked, but Spike kept going: 'He didn't kill Arben, he loved him like a brother...'

Alex refined his aim.

'You killed the wrong man,' Spike called out, seeing tears begin to slide down Jessica's cheeks.

'There's a witness.' He was shouting now as he saw Alex's long index finger arch around the trigger. 'A woman,' he kept going. 'She can tell you who killed Arben...'

'Albanian?' Alex said slowly, one eye still trained along the top of his rifle.

Spike nodded rapidly. 'At Blue Eye.'

Alex said something to his friend, then lowered the rifle. He circled Spike, staring into his blue eyes. 'If you are lying' – he raised the gun suddenly and Jessica flinched as he pointed it at her face – 'then she is dead.'

Chapter Sixty-Three

The reek of cut cannabis seeped through the broken window as Jessica struggled to start the Kia, her smooth forehead covered in a film of sweat. Finally the engine ignited and they pulled away from Lazarat, a gleaming Cherokee following tight against their rear bumper.

'I'm so sorry, Jess,' Spike said without looking at her. 'You were right.'

She didn't answer, but he went on anyway: 'It was reckless to have come. To have made you come.'

But Jessica just shook her head. 'You could never make me do anything I didn't want to, Spike Sanguinetti.'

He felt his heart catch as he realised that he had never met anyone like her. That the only reason he could have failed to notice her was because they'd known each other for so long. He was a fool, he thought. He hoped he wouldn't die a fool.

As they descended the mountain, he tried to visualise the layout of Blue Eye – the bridges, the paths, the road. But he knew the only thing that really mattered was that Calypso was still there. That they could make her tell these men what had really happened to Arben. That whoever had killed him, it wasn't Lakis.

As usual, Jessica had got there before him. He told himself it was because she was in the police, but suspected it was simply because she was brighter than him. 'If Calypso has run,' she said, 'we'll just have to play it by ear.' Her voice was steady now, but he could see the tension in her jaw, the fear in her eyes.

'I've got a plan,' Spike said, but he didn't sound that convincing, even to himself.

Then she did turn, giving a flash of the smile that had knocked him off balance years ago, and still had the same effect now. 'I never had a moment's doubt,' she replied, swinging the wheel and turning onto the leafy path that led towards the Blue Eye Hotel.

*

Calypso glances into the restaurant as she passes, seeing the chairs still down, their dirty glasses on the table. She checks her watch. She has to go. It could be evening before Petra and Samir return – if vets are like doctors they will string things out, charge by the hour. But she can't leave the place in this state, so she puts down her packed bag and hurries inside. She will give them until 3 p.m., she decides, then walk up to the main road and wait for the bus.

In the kitchen, she works quickly, closing drawers, replacing the fallen cooking pot on its hook. Her hands are still shaking. Who were they, these people? The pretty policewoman with her calm smile and icy voice. The tall, lean man with his bright blue eyes, who looked more like a sportsman than a lawyer – an injured sportsman, she thinks, smiling despite herself as she remembers the shock on his handsome face as he hit the water. Then she thinks of the man in the mask, and her smile fades.

How could she imagine she could just walk away from what happened in Corfu? Leave it all behind? Not even Blue Eye is far enough. Perhaps she should head north. No one would find her in the capital. But how will she live? The bars that might give her work in Tirana make those in Kavos look tame. She thinks again of her brother's photograph, the image she will never see again. It was Vladimir who brought the blue-eyed man here – her Vlad, influencing events from his grave. How she misses his impish grin, his hunger for life. Perhaps she could find a job at a school, she thinks suddenly, then chides herself for her stupidity. What school would employ a girl on the run with a scar on her face?

Checking the time again, she tears a sheet of paper from the kitchen pad. Then she looks up, hearing a distant noise. The sound of a vehicle coming down the track. She sighs in relief. At least she will be able to talk to Petra face to face. To explain.

She runs outside, hoping that the fact they are back early is a good sign, that Laika is all right. Shielding her eyes, she waits for the white van to come into view. But the vehicle that pulls up is not one she knows, and as the driver's door opens her heart begins to pound, so violently that she hopes it will be the fear that kills her first.

Chapter Sixty-Four

Ismail gripped Jessica's shoulder and shoved her roughly forward along the path, twisting the muzzle of his black revolver into her spine with a force that made her gasp. Then Alex gave a lazy jerk of his gun, and Spike obediently stumbled after them.

The bullfrogs fell silent as they passed. As they neared the spring, Spike heard the deep animal groan rising from the bowels of the earth. Seeing the rotten bridge, he felt his leg ache, as though the muscles themselves remembered his fall. He heard voices in the distance, a shout above the roar of the river, and Alex stopped and put a finger to his lips. He whispered something to Ismail, and a moment later they resumed their silent convoy. Was that a male voice, Spike thought? Speaking in English? Then he saw Calypso at the edge of the path, backing away, hands raised as a dark-skinned man walked towards her.

'I didn't say anything!' Calypso screamed, and Spike could hear the terror in her voice. 'I swear!'

Standing opposite her was a handsome Sri Lankan man Spike had last seen playing table tennis by the Hoffmann pool. Now he wore grey tracksuit trousers and a blue T-shirt, as though heading out for a jog. But in his right hand he held a large serrated hunting knife.

'Calypso,' Spike shouted, and Rajesh's head snapped around, his black, almond-shaped eyes calmly taking in the curious group walking towards him, sizing up the Albanians and their weapons.

Ismail threw Jessica to the ground as Alex turned to Spike, jaw tense between his sideburns. 'Is this the woman?' he asked, flicking his gun towards Calypso.

Spike nodded, then Alex turned his attention to Rajesh, eyes scrutinising his open face, so much at odds with the jagged knife in his hand. 'And him?'

The question was aimed at Spike, but it was Jessica who answered, calling up from the mud-packed ground. 'That's the man who killed Arben.'

No one spoke, but then Rajesh stepped forward, arms wide in conciliation, offering rapid, fluent denials in a language Spike was surprised to note was probably Albanian. Whatever it was, Alex was so busy listening that he only seemed to remember the hunting knife when he looked down and saw it protruding from his ribs.

'*Te qifsha*,' he swore quietly as he slumped into a sitting position, staring down with baffled eyes at the handle of the knife. Then Rajesh was gone, sprinting past him down the path towards the car park.

Nobody moved, just watched as the red stain on Alex's white shirt blossomed with a speed that could only mean the wound was catastrophic.

Suddenly Ismail shook himself into action and raised his revolver. The first shot was deafening, echoing through the wooded valley. A flock of rooks burst from the branches of the tall trees, cawing in panic. Rajesh glanced round then picked up his pace, weaving from side to side, relying on some deep-drilled training. Ismail fired again, and on the fourth shot they heard a distant cry of pain, and saw Rajesh tumble to the ground, clutching the back of his leg.

Spike looked down and saw Jessica kneeling by Alex, pressing her jacket around his wound. He clawed at the knife, desperate to pull it out, so she took his hands and held them in hers, shaking her head sadly. His face was a greenish-white now, his lips pale. He suddenly looked very young. Ismail crouched down beside him and laid a tender hand on his dying friend's cheek, pushing a mobile phone between his fingers. Then he reloaded the pistol and started walking slowly towards Rajesh.

Rajesh was on all fours now, crawling forward on the path. Ismail caught him up, kicked him onto his back and stood astride him. Spike saw a heavy foot pressing down on Rajesh's injured leg, then made out a few words exchanged in Albanian. Some time later they heard two more cracks of gunfire, and a last resilient flock of woodpigeons took off and made in desperation for the clefts of blue sky between the trees. Then, the only sounds left were the relentless roar of the river and Alex's final, laboured breaths.

PART FOUR

Corfu

Chapter Sixty-Five

The sun was starting to set when they finally stepped onto the ferry, instinctively drawn to the same seats they'd taken on the outward journey. The only other passengers were hungover backpackers, gearing up for the next leg of their Balkan adventure.

Jessica had said little on the long, slow drive back to Saranda, and now she looked exhausted, so Spike put an arm around her and let her close her eyes. By the time she woke, he could make out the twin Venetian forts of Corfu Town rising in the distance. Jessica stretched like a pampered cat and smiled up at him. Then she remembered where they were, and what had happened, and her face changed. 'It's not over, you know.'

Spike nodded.

'But at least Spiros will be safe.'

Spike hoped she was right, that they'd at least managed to clear Lakis's name in the eyes of Arben's family. At any rate, they had been allowed to leave Blue Eye unpursued by armoured supercars with smoked-glass windows. What Calypso was going to do now Spike couldn't say, but he'd seen her smile as she'd stared down at Rajesh's corpse and had known what it meant. The man had tried to kill her and he'd got what he deserved. Arben's relatives had taken their rightful blood.

But something was niggling at the edge of Spike's brain, something that still didn't make sense. He turned to Jessica, and when she saw his expression she sat up, rubbing her eyes. 'When do you think Rajesh planted the murder weapon in Lakis's room?' he asked.

He could see the almost physical effort required for her to look back. 'It would have taken Lakis a couple of hours to drop Calypso in Kavos then drive back,' she said. 'Plenty of time for Rajesh to break into the staff quarters at the Olive Press and hide the weapon.'

'He wouldn't have needed to break in – Katerina always leaves it unlocked. But that doesn't explain the fingerprint.'

Jessica thought for a while. 'Maybe Rajesh hid inside, waited until Lakis came home, then pressed it into his hand while he was asleep. Lakis liked a smoke before bed. He was probably spark-out.' She paused. 'It was a risk but...'

'Rajesh was a professional,' Spike offered. He was about to add that the Greek police might have come up with the finger-print themselves to make their job a little easier, but thought better of it. 'So Lakis gets arrested for Arben's murder. Job done. Especially when he ends up being killed by the Albanian Mafia.' Spike shook his head. 'Bet Rajesh couldn't believe his luck.'

'Until Calypso gets in touch and tries to blackmail him. Silly girl,' she murmured to herself. 'So Rajesh attacked her in Kavos, but she fought back, so he was forced to follow her to Albania. Tie up the last loose end.'

'How did he find her?'

'Penny?' Jessica said. 'Or maybe he just followed our tracks. It's not like there are many places to rent a car in Saranda.'

Spike nodded, then turned back to the window. They'd dumped the half-wrecked Kia near the port. The pain that would soon be hitting his credit card would have to be dealt with back in Gibraltar. He stared out at the heft of Pantokrator – the Almighty Mountain – silhouetted against the pale blue sky, seeing the Hoffmanns' pristine promontory beneath. But the niggle remained. 'Except...' he said, and Jessica turned again, impatient eyes searching his face. 'What, Spike?'

'Most of it makes sense. Framing Lakis, the need to silence Calypso. But I still don't see how Rajesh could have murdered Arben.'

Jessica's mind was waking up now. 'Because he was with the family at the time of the murder,' she said slowly.

Spike nodded. 'Watching a film. With everyone except...'

'Zach and Alfie.' Jessica paused. 'But Calypso said she saw Rajesh running from the scene of the crime.'

Spike shook his head. 'She just said she'd seen a man covered in blood. That she didn't see his face, but knew it couldn't have been Lakis.'

'So we just assumed it was Rajesh because he was the man who came after her.'

The boat started its approach to Corfu Harbour.

'So what you're suggesting,' Jessica said, 'is that someone else killed Arben, and Rajesh helped to cover it up?'

Spike nodded. They both knew there were only two or three people who could have persuaded Rajesh to do their dirty work. The question was which one – and why.

Chapter Sixty-Six

'Hello?' Spike called out, swapping a concerned glance with Jessica. 'Anyone there?' His voice echoed across the landing. The Olive Press was deserted. Even Peter's canes were missing. With a sense of foreboding, Spike reached for his phone, then swore as he remembered. It was gone – splintered to pieces by the butt of a Kalashnikov. *And what should I do in Illyria?* he asked himself, and almost laughed. Then he turned sharply, hearing a noise behind him. But it was only Katerina, one hand pressed to her chest. When she saw who it was, she gave a faint smile. 'You scared me.'

She'd lost even more of her bulk now, body swamped by her black dress, but at least she had a better colour to her face. 'Your father will be pleased you're back,' she said.

'Where is he?'

She looked a little taken aback by Spike's tone. 'With Peter,' she replied. 'At the party.' She dropped her eyes, mouth tightening. 'At the Hoffmanns'.'

Of course, Spike thought: the completion of the interminable Phaeacian Games. He looked up suspiciously. 'How did they get there?'

'Your father drove.' Her lip curled in amusement when she saw the look of horror on Spike's face. His father hadn't driven in this century, with good reason.

'Why don't you let me call you a taxi?' Katerina asked, picking up the landline. But Spike had already taken Jessica's hand and was leading her towards the door.

'Don't worry,' Jessica called back, 'we can walk.' Katerina gave a distracted wave, and they set off towards the coast road.

Chapter Sixty-Seven

Mike eyed them through the iron bars of the Hoffmann gate, then reluctantly pressed the button. 'I didn't know Sir Leo was expecting you,' he said in his disdainful West Country burr.

'We wouldn't miss the end of the Phaeacian Games, Mike,' Jessica replied, and the man's froideur melted in the warmth of her smile. 'The main house is locked, Miss,' he called over, blushing beneath his beard. 'You'll have to go down the side way.'

So once again they walked down the path past the flank of the mighty house to the distant strains of classical music. When they reached the edge of the terrace, they both stopped, disconcerted by the familiarity of the scene. There were the Mayor and the Chief of Police, Lady Lucinda in her flowing robes, Alfie sunning his face in a rattan chair by the balustrade. Spike half-expected to see Rajesh steadying a champagne flute on the wall.

Though the players remained the same, the ornamentation had changed. One of the massive statues from the site had been winched up onto the terrace, stretched on its side like a felled mythological beast. The canine features were clearly recognisable now, though a great deal of restoration would still need to be done. Spike watched Rufus chuckling as he examined its huge jaws, his enthusiasm observed with affection by Sir Leo. Then Peter saw them approaching and lifted his cane in greeting, pulling himself up from his seat. But Spike ignored him, leading Jessica instead through the crowd to the other side of the terrace. Towards Zachary Hoffmann.

'Where's Rajesh?' Spike called out as India stepped forward to kiss Jessica hello.

'Couldn't say,' Zach replied, green eyes scrutinising Spike's face. 'I'm afraid I had to let him go.'

'Odd,' Spike said, holding his gaze, 'I always had Raj down as a diehard Hoffmann employee.'

Zach frowned, and for the first time since they'd met, Spike saw him look uneasy, his pink, freckled forehead perspiring in the late sun. He slipped a pair of sunglasses over his twisted nose. 'How's the leg?'

'Healing nicely.'

'It was good of you to come,' India interrupted, eyes flitting anxiously between Spike and her father, trying to interpret the strained dynamic. Over the girl's shoulder, Spike watched her stepmother approach – Hélène de Savois, yellow summer dress split at the thigh to show a flash of over-toned brown leg. This was the woman Zach had betrayed for a night with Calypso, Spike realised. Judging by the way she was looking at her husband – with all the contempt of an impoverished aristocrat who knew she'd sold herself to a parvenu – Spike wasn't entirely sure he blamed him. Perhaps she knew about her husband's indiscretions and didn't care: Hélène had always been a pragmatist. She laid a manicured hand firmly on Zach's arm, and he turned away from Spike, stooping to allow her to whisper something sharp into his ear.

India was watching her stepmother, twisting a strand of blonde hair between her slim fingers, looking for a moment like Rapunzel on day-release from her tower. Spike suddenly felt very sorry for this privileged young woman, blessed with intelligence, beauty and wealth – yet cursed with a broken family. Looking over at Rufus, who was lowering his creaking frame to get a better look at one of the statue's paws through his half-moons, then at Jessica, listening patiently as an elderly Greek matriarch finished her story, Spike realised that he was lucky. It was an unfamiliar sensation, but one that Kitty Gonzalez might consider progress.

'Can you spare one?' he asked, seeing India step aside to light a cigarette. She nodded, then offered him the pack. He remembered the last time they'd smoked together, when she'd spoken to him about love. At least she'd found someone, he thought as he screwed the cigarette between his lips and leant into her light. 'Is your boyfriend coming today?' he asked as he exhaled.

His smile faded as he saw India's face, heard the tinkle of smashed crystal as her champagne glass hit the flagstones. All around, conversations stopped, people watching with concern and curiosity as she swung away from Spike and pushed blindly through the crowd. It was then that the realisation struck him, and everything finally made sense. He edged back to allow a waiter to sweep up the broken glass at his feet, shaking his head at his stupidity. Of course India's boyfriend wasn't coming. He wasn't coming because he would never have been welcome as a guest at the Hoffmann house. But more accurately, he wasn't coming because he was dead. India Hoffmann was the woman that Arben had told his mother about. It was India he had naively hoped to marry. What a waste, Spike thought bitterly.

On the other side of the terrace, Spike saw Alfie sitting with his pretty face tilted towards the dying rays of the sun, the panoramic view stretched out before him, Albania darkening beneath the shade of its mountains on the other side of the glittering Corfu Channel.

'Still here?' Alfie asked in his deep, insinuating drawl as Spike approached. He wore tortoiseshell Wayfarers, the stem of a champagne flute laced between his slim fingers on the wooden arm of his chair.

'I wondered if you fancied a round of backgammon,' Spike said, pulling up a chair.

'Can't stand the game, mate.'

'Then I suppose you must have been doing something else the night that Arben died.'

Behind his shades, Spike saw the young man's green eyes flick open. But there was obviously some of his father's steel in him, as he just picked up his glass and lifted it calmly to his mouth.

Spike moved closer. 'When did you find out that Arben was sleeping with your sister?' he asked. 'Did you see them together? Your twin sister, a *Hoffmann*, screwing the help?'

Alfie didn't reply, but Spike watched an ugly dull red flush seep over his cheeks, a vein rise in his temple.

'Did you plan to kill him?' Spike asked more loudly, 'or was it an accident?' He plucked a glass of champagne from a passing tray and took a thoughtful sip. 'Or maybe you just wanted to confront Arben. To remind him of his place. Must have been hard to watch your grandfather fawning over the man.' Spike took a risk: 'Especially when he'd always found his own grandson so...' He selected his word with a little of Aristotelis's precision, '... disappointing.'

The bluff seemed to work, as the young man swivelled round, hands clenching his knees, face just inches from Spike's. From the sweet-sourness of his breath, he must have been drinking since midday. He pulled off his glasses, revealing small eyes glassy with booze and fury. Behind him, Spike saw India and Zach approach, just entering earshot.

'Arben was a nobody,' Alfie said, too drunk now to bother lowering his voice. 'An Albanian freeloader. An *immigrant*' – he spat out the word – 'who knew he'd got lucky. My sister was just too thick to realise he was using her.'

India was right behind Alfie now, registering his words. 'Just leave him, Spider,' Spike heard Zach say as he put an arm around his daughter's shoulder, trying to steer her away. But she just shrugged him off, her beautiful face frozen with shock. Other people were beginning to pay attention now, edging closer, and

Spike saw his father whisper something to Sir Leo, who turned, the easy congeniality draining from his face.

Spike raised his voice again but Alfie didn't seem to notice. 'You must have been scared when you realised Arben was dead. That you'd actually killed him.'

Alfie nodded, face defiant, as Spike leant back in: 'But at least Rajesh was there to help. To sort things out. Like he always did.'

Another slow nod as Spike picked up a bottle of champagne from the terrace wall and refilled both their glasses.

'Raj said he would take care of it,' Alfie replied, draining his glass and holding it out for more.

'Above and beyond, really,' Spike said as he poured the champagne. 'Raj was taking a real risk for you. I mean, imagine – what would your father have done if he'd found out?'

Alfie laughed. 'It was my father who told Raj to handle it, you fucking half-wit.'

A slap rang out above the hum of the crowd, and Alfie turned and saw his sister flailing at Zach, nails clawing at his hair, his eyes. Jessica managed to pull her back, whispering into her ear, trying to calm her.

The whole party was watching now. 'Shut up, Alfie,' Zach said, straightening up. 'Just shut the fuck up.'

Alfie swayed to his feet, dangerously drunk.

'Why?' India screamed to Alfie. 'Just tell me why!'

But her brother just laughed. 'I did you a favour, you stupid bitch.' Then he shook his head. 'You never did have any taste in men.'

Spike realised that the music had stopped, performers aghast at the scene. The silence was so intense that Spike could hear the distant sound of a speedboat down on the sea.

'Party's over,' Zach Hoffmann said, placing a strong hand on Alfie's shoulder. 'I'm afraid my son has had a little too much to drink.' But Alfie shoved him away. 'What are you worrying about, Dad? We're Hoffmanns, aren't we? And this' – he swept a hand across the terrace – 'is Corfu. We *made* this place. Isn't that right, Spiros?' He leant over and chucked the Mayor of Corfu Town fondly under the chin. The fat man coloured and slapped his hand away, but Alfie just laughed. 'We're untouchable.'

Just as Spike saw Sir Leo's face contorting with fury and shame, he heard a sharp, hollow bang from below, and watched Alfie Hoffmann drop to his knees as if urgently called to prayer, triumphant smile still on his face.

'Get down!' Jessica yelled, and suddenly everyone was flat on the ground, cheeks pressed to the warm stone, women screaming. A second shot rang out. It struck Alfie in the side of the face and spun him round, revealing the jagged bloody roots of his teeth and jaw.

'Alfie!' India shrieked, crawling towards her brother. From the sea below, Spike heard the boat engine rev again.

'Ambulance!' Sir Leo's voice called out. 'Someone get an ambulance!'

Crouching low, Spike moved to the edge of the terrace. Down in the water he could see a black inflatable dinghy motoring away with three figures hunched inside. Instinctively, he expected it to be roaring towards Saranda, but instead it hugged the shoreline. The Albanians must be planning to cut across the channel at a safer point, Spike told himself, but then he saw the boat turn towards the concrete slope of the Olive Press. A moment later, a small lithe figure jumped out, scrambling up the rocks without looking back as the RIB sped away towards Albania.

Spike turned back to the terrace and saw India on her knees, kissing the bloodied, mutilated face of the twin who had killed her lover. The law of the *Kanun* was pitiless, he thought. But both Arben and Lakis had been avenged.

Chapter Sixty-Eight

Spike sat next to Aristotelis Theofilatos on the esplanade, staring out at the Old Venetian Fortress, a beautifully ribboned box of glazed fruit and Greek pastries positioned between them.

'So you are going home tomorrow?' Aristotelis asked. 'Not tempted to extend your relaxing holiday?'

Spike smiled. 'We've already printed out our boarding passes.'

Aristotelis reached into the box and offered Spike a candied kumquat. Even perched on a park bench the man looked immaculate. 'Then perhaps you will permit an old lawyer to give you one last piece of advice,' he said, delicately wiping the corners of his mouth with a silk handkerchief.

Spike gave an apprehensive nod.

'Do not be disappointed if the story you read in the newspaper or' – a flicker of the lips – 'on the internet is not quite as you remember.'

Spike waited: he had an inkling of what was coming.

'If the story that the world hears is one in which the Hoffmann boy was the innocent victim of an Albanian attempt to assassinate…' Aristotelis paused. 'Shall we say – the Chief of the Corfu Police?'

Spike gave a quiet groan.

'It would be a neat solution, would it not?' Aristotelis said. 'Providing us Greeks with enough leverage to make the Albanian government finally do something about Lazarat, the great drugs Mecca of the Mediterranean, while…'

'Protecting the Hoffmann family name?' Spike said, wondering, not for the first time, just how much the Hoffmanns had contributed to the Corfu economy. Enough, he was beginning to suspect.

'Was it not ever thus?' Aristotelis murmured, helping himself to another sweetmeat.

Spike knew he should probably nod, but couldn't bring himself to do it. Seeing his friend's discomfort, Aristotelis reached over and patted him on the arm. 'You did everything you could for Lakis. More than most lawyers would. You cleared his name ...'

'So Rajesh takes the blame for Arben's death, and Zachary Hoffmann just gets away with it,' Spike said, feeling his fury rise again as he remembered the man's amused, appraising eyes, the unshakable sense of entitlement he had passed on to his son. 'Zach covered up the fact that his son was a murderer by arranging for an innocent man to be framed. It was because of him that Lakis was killed.'

Aristotelis examined his neat nails. 'Justice is an unreliable mistress, Spike. Often she misses her mark. But time has taught me that she is also patient and merciless, and sometimes uses instruments other than the law and the police to achieve her ends.'

Spike stared at him, unconvinced.

'There are many prisons in this life,' Aristotelis went on in his quiet voice, 'and not all are made of concrete and iron. Zachary Hoffmann watched his son die before his eyes. He is shunned by his parents and his surviving child considers him a monster.' He brushed the sparkling sugar crystals from his flannel-covered knees. 'For a man who values his family, that is a cruel punishment indeed. And one with no respite.'

Spike turned to watch another group of tourists arrive at the top of the fort, perhaps wondering – as he had – which country lay across the water. 'I think I saw Spiros on the boat,' he said before he could reconsider. 'It looked like he was with the Albanians when they shot Alfie Hoffmann.'

Aristotelis turned in amazement. 'Spiros?'

'Lakis's brother.'

Aristotelis frowned, and once again Spike found himself wondering how old he really was. Seventy? Ninety? 'Are you sure?' he asked.

'No,' Spike replied truthfully.

The Greek lawyer turned back to the view of the fort. 'In that case, perhaps it would be wiser to…how do you say?' Spike suspected he knew perfectly well, but let him finish anyway. 'Let sleeping dogs lie?'

They sat for a moment in silence, then Spike helped Aristotelis up from the bench. 'How's your wife?' he asked.

The old man straightened his shoulders and smiled his sad smile. 'We forge on, Mr Sanguinetti. We forge on.'

*

Calypso feels the fear returning as they drive through the concrete streets of Saranda. Then she remembers the Indian's bloodied face. How she watched the man from Lazarat shoot him like a dog once he'd extracted the information he wanted. Her attacker was gone for ever. It was over.

'Down here,' Petra says, and Samir obediently turns past the Roman ruins and onto Saranda's main avenue. There is a bustle to the air this morning, Calypso sees. Watching the locals buying and selling, chatting and laughing, she feels a sudden wave of hope. They've been through a lot, her countrymen. But today she thinks they will survive. Maybe even prosper.

As they pass the entrance to her parents' street, she notices that the pile of rubble has been cleared from outside their apartment block. Her father perhaps, finally giving in to his wife's gentle demands.

'Just here,' Petra says.

Samir stops the van, and Calypso leans over and kisses his sandpaper cheek. He almost smiles. In the back, Laika slowly wags her tail. Calypso gives her a stroke, then follows Petra down onto the street. 'Her name is Ana,' Petra whispers, pulling Calypso close. 'She's expecting you.'

They hold their embrace, then Petra climbs back into the van and Calypso watches them drive away. From around the corner, she hears the children's shouts filtering through the gates of the playground. She waits outside, watching as a young woman in a blue overall bends down to answer a question from an eager little boy. The woman looks a bit like Calypso – there's even a hint of henna in her hair. When Calypso catches her eye, she raises a hand and makes her way over.

One of the children looks up and smiles. Calypso opens the gate, then smiles back.

PART FIVE

Gibraltar

Chapter Sixty-Nine

Against the odds, the law office of Galliano & Sanguinetti was back in business. These days, Spike liked to leave his door open. After so long working alone, keeping the clients and creditors at bay, it was good to hear Peter barking down the phone at opposing counsel, or laughing at one of his own bad jokes, or swearing as he skimmed through his case-notes. Though Peter's walking had improved, he still relied heavily on his cane, and the daily climb to and from his house on Trafalgar Road exhausted him. So Spike was called upon to assist with the necessities, like adjusting his footstool, or taking down a copy of *Chitty on Contracts*, or opening a good bottle of Rioja at 5 p.m. Spike knew his forbearance of Peter's demands would not last for ever, but strangely, he didn't seem to mind too much at the moment.

'Sanguinetti?' Hearing the plaintive summons from next door, Spike rose gingerly from his desk. His own war wound still hurt, especially when the autumn humidity soared, as it had today, but he was determined not to let himself acquire a limp. 'Yes,' he sighed from the doorway.

'Guess who just emailed?' Peter called from his desk. 'Katerina Demollari.'

Spike stepped inside.

'She's finally agreed to look after my summer tenants,' Peter said, rubbing his hands in glee. His dismay at the withdrawal of Sir Leo Hoffmann's offer to buy the Olive Press had been swiftly offset by Corfu Villas' enthusiastic interest in renting it out. 'We'll need to do some basic renovations,' he added, 'but Katerina will oversee everything.' He looked up. 'We should be ready to go by April.'

Spike could almost see the euro signs in his eyes. 'No digging around the rocks,' he warned, and Peter pulled a face. After the death of his grandson, Sir Leo had closed up the archaeological site, resealing the dog statues within and using his influence to hush up its existence altogether. In this, as in most things, Aristotelis's predictions had proven depressingly accurate.

'Does she mention Spiros in her email?' Spike asked carefully.

Peter shot him a glance. Against his better judgment, Spike had told him of his suspicions about the boy. Peter hadn't wanted to discuss it since, but now seemed as good a time as any, Spike supposed.

Peter reached down and lifted each heavy calf onto his cushioned stool. 'The young man wants to leave, she tells me.' He rubbed his beard, and Spike could see from the hang of his cheeks that he was starting to regain the weight he'd lost after the accident. 'He's asked if he can stay with his uncle Idriz.'

'In Albania?'

Peter nodded, and Spike moved towards the wooden case in the corner of the room and uncorked a bottle of wine. They drank together for a while, then Spike broke the silence, his voice low and angry. 'I made her go to Lazarat,' he said, remembering Jessica's eyes as a man with a gun had run his hands over her body in a sun-flooded courtyard. Then the drive back to Blue Eye when he'd been sure they were going to die. 'I made her go there to plead for Spiros.' He wasn't expecting an answer, and Peter didn't offer one. When he looked back up, Peter was already angling for a refill.

'The whole thing's been a strange business,' Peter said, leaning back with a sigh and contemplating the chandelier on the ceiling. 'Murder, revenge, star-crossed lovers...'

'Money, corruption,' Spike went on. 'Shame.'

'All the elements of a Shakespearean tragedy.'

'Or a Greek one,' Spike said, brooding again on Spiros's fate; whether Lakis would have expected better of his Gibraltarian lawyer. 'Who'd have a family?' he asked.

Peter puffed out an impressive ring of water vapour. In the darkening room, at that moment, with his sagging neck and tired eyes, he suddenly looked like a vulnerable old man. Then he smiled, and one version of the future was gone. 'You've always been a fool about some things, Sanguinetti,' he said, reaching forward and slapping Spike's good leg. 'But I still cling to the hope that you might grow out of it. *Vale...*' He set down his empty glass and picked up a file. 'I had a call this morning. From Eloise Capurro.'

'John Capurro's widow?'

Peter nodded. 'She wants to take out a restraining order.'

'Against?'

Peter smiled, and Spike realised that he'd just landed himself with the case. Was he really that easy to manipulate? 'Send through the details,' he said, finishing his glass and walking back to the door.

'You know, Spike,' Peter called after him, 'a man can tolerate being alone for a while – maybe even enjoy it. Just as long as he realises that a while sometimes turns into for ever.'

Spike waited for his friend to elaborate, but he'd already turned back to his computer.

Chapter Seventy

Spike left Rufus putting the finishing touches to a watercolour in the kitchen, humming along to a dusty copy of *Nausicaa* that Spike had dug out of one of his mother's tea chests. Outside, the gentle autumnal light gilded the Old Town, softening the crumbling buildings that clung to the side of the Rock, the narrow North African alleys that descended into streets lined with Georgian townhouses, originally designed as officers' lodgings.

As Spike came into Casemates Square, he heard an explosion up on the Rock, and felt the old panic surge again in his chest. He shielded his eyes, staring up at the mountain's sheer limestone flank – his own personal Pantokrator – seeing a plume of smoke rising into the sky, gulls circling, hearing dogs barking in the streets below. A second explosion followed, and Spike realised they were coming from the Grand Battery. There'd be nineteen more, he calculated as he came onto Main Street – 14 November, Prince Charles's birthday. Every year, both he and HRH his mother were treated to a twenty-one-gun salute that neither would ever come to Gibraltar to hear.

A celebration for Charlie, Spike thought – appropriate, really. He nodded at half the people he passed – distant cousins, family friends, former colleagues – as the cannon continued to fire behind him. To his right, rising on the reclaimed land, he made out the tower block where Dr Kitty Gonzalez rented her office. He stood motionless for a moment, catching the acrid scent of gunpowder on the levanter breeze. He didn't intend to see Kitty again, but he still felt grateful for one thing. Take a break, she'd advised him, and while his week in Corfu hadn't been much of a holiday – more of an odyssey – he'd somehow survived it. The panic attacks had gone and most nights he could sleep. Things weren't too bad, he thought, smiling as he saw Jessica Navarro waiting for him on the corner of Horse Barrack Lane.

Jessica laughed when she spotted the badly wrapped present in his hands. 'I got him something as well,' she said, holding up a soft-toy Barbary ape as she leant in for a kiss.

They heard the cannon fire its last salute as they walked on together towards Charlie's grandparents' flat.

'Are you sure you want to do this?' Jessica said with an anxious smile. 'If you take Charlie on, there's no going back.'

Spike stopped and turned. 'A child *is* a big commitment,' he agreed.

She frowned, trying to work out if he was serious.

'So I might need some help.' Then he reached into his pocket and took out the small green leather box that contained his mother's engagement ring.

ACKNOWLEDGEMENTS

In France, someone once asked my father what I did for a living. Perhaps thinking of his lunch, he answered 'écrevisse' (crayfish) rather than 'écrivain' (writer). I remember thinking at the time that neither was particularly accurate, so, a few years on, I'd like to thank the following for helping at least to shift things in the right direction:

In Corfu – Cinty Jacks, Marios Paipeitis, Nikoleta Koutsouri, Natalie McIlwraith, Paula Lamb, Karen Bacon, Tim and Nicky Britton; in Albania – Viktor Avdia, Ida Milby-Low and Sonya Buds; in Gibraltar – Peter Canessa, Dion Darham, John Restano QC and Lewis Baglietto QC; at Bloomsbury – Michael Fishwick, Anna Simpson, Oliver Holden-Rea, George Gibson, Madeleine Feeny and Isabel Blake; copyeditors Kathy Fry and Steve Cox, and proofreaders Zoë Carroll, Catherine Best and Dick Clayton; and at Greene & Heaton – Nicola Barr.

For this, previous books, and much more besides – my parents, Sophie, Jack and Molly, Susan and Will, Des and Maeve, Lewis and Imke Crofts, Felix Zimmermann, Ali Warshaw, Peter Buckman, Emily Hayward Whitlock, Walter Donohue, Judith Murray, Donald Rice, Will and Jemma Fenton, Neil and Taron Unmack, Eva Rice, Nick and Fiona Craig, Charlie Campbell, Jenny Rea, Alexander Van der Bijl, Susie and David McDowell, Luke Stellini, Catherine and Charles Lyon, Mats Ruontti, Rob Watson, Matthew Kimberley, Susan Hill, Stewart and Julia Chirnside, Simon Conway, Ed Attenborough, Geoff Conlin, Toby

Stephens, Dan Pirrie, Olly Fetiveau, Rhian Davies, Kate Bland, Serena Gosling, Priscilla Parish, Stuart Woollford, Al Lewis and 'Raven Crime'.

And above all to Ali, my partner in crime. Having my name alone on these books often feels like a breach of the Trade Descriptions Act. You never ask for thanks, yet all the best things in my life come from you. I love you.